Where Everything Begins

K.R. Brendlinger

Interior Artwork by EUREPHORA

Cover Design by K.R. Brendlinger

First Edition 2023, Second Edition 2025

ISBN 979-8-9907394-3-7

Note From Author:

This book was written from both the first <u>and</u> second points of view. Some *italics* emphasize a word, but for the most part, it signifies Bennett connecting with his audience through the book he's writing. **He's talking to you, the reader. Following book one—When Everything Ends—**the reader is now introduced to the written thoughts of Cherry in Where Everything Begins. *It's her turn to talk to you.* **This is the second book in the Fluke series.**

Your mental health matters.

The following is a <u>content warning</u>.

This book contains, explicit language, violence, criminal activity, explicit sexual scenes, and dark themes including suicidal intent. It also includes *mentions of traumatic experiences,* including rape, drug use, suicide, and abuse. This book is intended for mature audiences of adult age. This book is not intended to be a guide, a reference, glamourize any specific act or trait, or idealize relationships.

It is a work of fiction.

United States: <u>National Mental Health Hotline</u> 866-903-3787

<u>Suicide Prevention</u> Call 988, 998lifeline.org

<u>Crisis Text Line</u> Text HOME to 741741

United Kingdom: <u>Suicide Prevention</u> Call 116 123, samaritans.org

<u>Crisis Text Line</u> Text SHOUT to 85258

Canada: <u>Suicide Prevention</u> Call 1-833-456-4566, talksuicide.ca

International: <u>Visit</u> befrienders.org

Dedication

To a wallflower in a crowded room;
your thoughts are the loudest.

Contents

PLAYLIST

Cursed – Ari Abdul

Nowhere Generation – Rise Against

Past The End – Siamese

Consume – Chase Atlantic, Goon Des Garcons

don't sleep, repeat – 44phantom, mgk

Set You Free – Crobot

deathwish – Stand Atlantic, nothing,nowhere.

Holy – Siamese

Pray – Jessie Murph

Wait – NF

Tell Me All Your Secrets – Mod Sun

Paradise – Sixlight

0-0-1
Bennett Larson
"The Zombie"

0-0-2
Charlie Houser
"2002"

0-0-3
Seth Willas
"Six-Foot-Wonder"

0-0-4
Cherry Kaas
"Cherry Bomb"

0-0-5
Veronica Brili
"Rowdy Ronnie"

0-0-6
David Mondroe
"Shifter"

0-0-7
Wesley Baker
"Sourthern Whiskey"

0-0-8
Solomon Rice
"Slow"

Six Days Ago, Cherry Wrote In Red

This is where I dislocate—within Bennett's touch, his taste, his air-filled moans. They escape his mouth like a string quartet—music to my ears and liberation to my tangled mind—cloaking the mental breakdown that consumes me.

Deep breaths. One. Two. Three.

I don't know how I got it wrong. I was sure none of the lab rats survived, but then again...that night has as many blurry pieces as it does clear. Everything has been happening so quickly since I confronted Bennett at knifepoint in his house. It's hard to separate what was in the past, what's a dream, and where I am now. I don't feel like that same woman anymore. I lost her confidence and certainty after I spent years becoming unbreakable.

And worse...

I did something bad.

Worse than attacking Ronnie. Worse than the fate I gave Cassie.

How could there be a more heinous act than killing a human being?

Six days ago, I made one rash decision—less than a week after Christmas. What kind of person does that? My mind refuses to quiet. It replays that day over and over—the same nightmare. This is how I remember it.

<u>Six Days Ago</u>
"Cherry! Fuck!"
I want to scream at Bennett—I can't let go.
"She's not going to stop until he's paid the price." Shifter is right.
For the first time, I couldn't say B was the calmest person in the room. He fears my unruly, foolish decisions will ruin our plan. I'll derail it and destroy us all.
My arm is twenty-five pounds—a heavy weight that drives forward over and over as the angled blade clenched painfully tight in my fist slices the man pressed into the cheap commercial-grade carpet below me. His round cheek spews a crimson river.
"Take back your control, Cherry." I abruptly snap back to Bennett. He looks down at me, a foot away, knowing better than to come between me and my mission.
"I am in control!"
I'm lying. I'm doing what I should have done years ago.

That roar—*I am in control!*—echoes in my head.

It won't shut up. Every time the world becomes too quiet, the savage beast haunts me. I'm a monster. I can't look in a mirror without seeing the reflection from that disgusting bathroom. I see the crimson splattered over the bridge of my nose and smudges on my jaw—the little flecks covering my face like freckles in the heat of a July afternoon. I'm the only heatwave to cross California this month and if I can't be the hero I want to be, I'd rather be dead.

"I don't want to do this anymore." The words come out of my mouth, but I keep riding his thighs. My pubic bone uncomfortably rubs his stubbled hair, making me wish he hadn't decided to shave. He feels so good in flashes, and then my distractions steal me away. I push back tears, desperate to shut it all off.

I will not cry right now. *I will not.*

I dig my fingers into the leather headrest. "We can get in the backseat," Bennett says as he continues to kiss my neck.

The drive to Florida was a blur after my—what I did. It wasn't until we found Dr. Romberg's apartment that I began to process what was at stake. A glass-framed entrance illuminates the lavish complex, and the parking lot primarily consists of empty parked cars. We had to park the Range Rover close to keep an open eye for Shifter's signal.

The twinkling lights in the sky only faintly exist in the city. They don't have any spotlights in this section either—the darker the better. The only way someone would know what's going on in this car is if they were studying the windshield.

My stability transformed into uncertainty the night I spared Bennett's life. Since then, I've been going down a slope. Is any of this worth it anymore?

Ugh, he doesn't understand. "Not this." I swing my hands down, gesturing to where we are joined. My eyes find his, and I fight to suffocate the tears.

No! I will not cry. I'm not that girl. *Nobody* gets to see me break down.

I swallow the panic, and beneath shaky inhales, I mutter. "I want to see my final stars." Cut me up and watch me burn to ash. Nobody will be able to bring me back.

"You meant quick when you said *a quickie.*" His laugh is cutting. It slices me in a way it hadn't before. The weight of his fingers presses to my forehead, and he brushes the hair from my face. It's supposed to be reassuring *as if* he could calm me. He has no idea how close to the ledge I am. There is nothing that could alleviate the building snowball that is rolling around my head, packing more and more snow on with every breath I take.

I want it to stop. Just stop. Stop!

I smack my hands off the seat bordering his shoulders. "Not like that," I huff. I close my eyes as tight as I can until the red turns black. With the shake of my head come words I shouldn't speak out loud. "I want you to keep squeezing—" I find him through a bloodshot fog. "Until I don't come back."

His white pupils settle on my face, and he stills my involuntarily slow-moving hips. I bandage my hands around the headrest, purposely circling into him once more as I veer forward, and the pressure of his body deepens against my clit.

"Cherry." A gap hangs between his teeth before he finally licks his lips and continues his thought. "I don't know what waits for me when I die, but do you honestly think I'd gamble with your heart? Am I to let you go and bring you back to see if the grass is greener on the other side? Fuck no. It's not happening. You're mine." He tilts his hips, pushing deeper into me. My hands fall to the sides of the headrest, and I arch my back away from the steering wheel. His lips hover over my shoulder. "She can run," he whispers. "But she can't hide. We'll find her again and I'll drain the fucking life from her body ten times over until she finds a cure. No—" He puts a stop to anything I could say. "I know already—don't kill anyone. *It's a deal breaker.* I think we're past deal breakers, darling." I don't need the reminder of my weak choices. "When this is over, I'm taking you far away from here. Just you and me and miles of sand."

The pad of his thumb dredges across the supple flesh of my lower lip, and the thick of his fingers drag across my jaw. I empty my lungs, holding onto the pieces of hope he dangles in front of me. "Do you see the house tucked away up on the hill? I see it." His mouth pulls at the corner, tempting a smile. "It's wrapped in glass with a huge patio lined with bushes and flowers, and embers flicker from the fire pit as you take in a spectacular view of the ocean below. I know you see it—a life far away from here where we don't have to think. We'll just feel." I'll need a miracle to allow me to forget where I've been and what I've done. I pull away from his eyes. "If that's what you want, I'll make it happen. For now, I insist you behave." His gentle lips meet my jaw, and his dick pulses within me, earning a glare he could only interpret as a challenge. "Put all of *your* stars in *my* eyes. Allow me to carry your pain, only for tonight."

I'm powerless, trapped on a never-ending carousel.

And Bennett. I look over his exposed chest. *He's sexy, tempting, and relieving.*

Returning to his devilish irises, he sees through my concrete mask to the damaged soul that he loves with every fault.

He'd never let me go. I could break his heart repeatedly, stab him in the back, and starve him for days, and he would offer me the first bite at the dinner table. Nobody would do that for me. It's disgusting how much he would give and more how I continuously succumb to a spell of sexual desire. I question if I care for him half as much as he does for me.

I'm in a spiral, going down the rabbit hole of depression. I've dug myself out of it enough times. This time is different, and Bennett wants me to picture this paradise he's chasing for us. I don't need to see it to know Cloud Nine will be in his eyes until our dying breaths. No matter how much I want to surrender; I can't because I'm addicted to him in the most pathetic and endearing way. Love or lust, the agony will return—but for the time being, he'll harness it for me.

A smirk tugs at my mouth as I grip his throat, sinking around his Adam's apple. The hard gulp that beats against my palm only pushes me to keep going—to embrace his need to please me. As I lean in, I steal every breath he has with my hands, ripping any lasting trace of oxygen from his lips. He sucks my tender flesh in between his teeth, and with each little tug, he desperately reaches for air, sucking in through his nose. I tighten my grip and draw circles across his lap, riding what's mine and refusing to let him feel anything else.

I give him everything—all of my pain and despair—and he accepts it, desperate to feel what I'm willing to give. Bennett Larson only has one weakness—me.

"It won't hurt much longer, B," I mutter against his stubble. This devilish man lets me do this to him because it's my poison—he knows what the apple is tainted with and always wants more.

He tries to smile, but it quickly falls with his eyelids. I let go, continuing to grind against his dark-haired thighs while I wait for him to snap back.

I'm a lunatic who loves to watch my boyfriend nearly die while his dick is buried deep inside of me. It's nearly my favorite thing in the entire world these days. I'm the muse of "the Bennett Larson," renowned film director, and writer. I'm the "it" actress who fought with every ounce of my being. Those are good things—sure, but they don't compare to feeling desired beyond measure by a man who would paint the world red at any cost for my happiness.

It's terrible, but we're terrible people living in a terrible world. I've never felt this type of fatal love. I mean—my mom loved me. It was unconditional and even. The way I feel with B is different—a monumental high. When the avalanche engulfs me, he draws me back. Will it be eternally enough?

Flattening my palm to his chest, I hunt for the oscillation. It's slow and muffled like it always is when he does this. He gasps, swinging a handout. His palm wraps around my throat, his fingers deepening along my jaw, and he pulls me back into his lips.

He tastes like coffee. The darkest roast—bitter, and every bit satisfying, like him.

"My fucking angel," A harshness scuffs his reborn vocals. The word fucking shouldn't be used in conjunction with the word angel, although it's more accurate. "Take me. Take every fucking inch like the stars are closing in for the last time." His thumb plays at my jaw, the heat of his sweaty palm floating inches from my skin.

"No." As close together as we are, I glance up at him the best I can. "I'm dragging you to hell with me. It will never be the last time. The devil himself couldn't pry us apart. I'll cum around your dick until they find a way to burn our souls from existence." I'm lying, and the guilt is eating at me. I'd leave this Earth without him. He's better off. All of the rats are better off. I'm a liability.

"*Fuck,*" he moans. With each sultry noise that evades his lips, I ride the edge of ecstasy—the space that feels intensely good, teetering on another dimension. I never imagined that the sound of a man's voice could be my undoing. Then again, I never thought I would be here with him. "I'm right here, darling. I got you."

I was supposed to kill him, and if I did, I would have been next. All of the monsters would be gone. My soul mirrors his.

"Fuck, baby...you feel so good," his airy words surround me. "I bet you want to tie me up right now," he chuckles. "Tie my arms behind my head to the back of the headrest, huh?" He leans his head back, and his narrowed eyes ravage me. "Take your top off."

"No," I sass. "Not here. And I'd tape your mouth shut first."

He stretches his arms behind his head and flexes his hips, deepening into the spot that sets me off every time. It would feel better if I turned around until his little barbell would press to that same spot. I follow the veins shaping over his lean muscles, not wanting him to notice.

"Eyes up here, Cherry bomb," he demands. "Take it off for me." I pinch my lips together and try to climb off of him. "Where do you think you're going?" He un-pretzels one arm, trapping my lips between his pointer and thumb, forcing my cheeks to sink in. "You're not done. You're not going anywhere until you get what you want and I get what I crave." It's as if I should be thanking him right now. I need this.

His hands take my shoulders, pushing my back into the steering wheel hard enough to make the horn squeal for a second. "Whatever you want, it's yours, but if you piss me off, I'll dump you off of my lap, out of this car, and leave your bare ass in this parking lot."

"You're such a fucking liar." I laugh, not bothering to make sure the honking went unnoticed. "It's in the seventies in the Sunshine State. I'll be fine." East Grenton wasn't too bad, but the set in Nevada sucked going into February. Anything under sixty is unacceptable. I don't think I could take a job that required me to stay in a snow-covered location. I'm lucky the job I was supposed to start after Bennett's film had delayed production.

Who am I kidding? I talk people into doing what I want without being aware of it. B wasn't wrong. It's the only logical explanation as to why I can see the glacier that takes over both his and Shifter's eyes when they become fueled. I've somehow tapped into the same ability that they own. I've spent years honing my other abilities—creating illusions and melting to the point where I can make a rainbow appear in the desert. Yet, I never considered the fact that I may share an ability with Shifter or one with Bennett. He was the devil reincarnated mere months ago.

Maybe this is who I am and has nothing to do with being a lab experiment. Maybe it's who I've always been—desperate enough to do anything it takes. Ugh. I don't know anymore.

He tilts his chin as his brows draw together. "That mouth is getting rated R."

"It's from your terrible influence." Being stuck with B, Shifter, and Wes in a vehicle for days, I wouldn't be surprised if I felt the urge to put my hand down my pants with the excuse of *"I'm adjusting."*

He slaps his hands against my thighs and leans forward, teasing his lips in front of mine. "Who's the liar now?"

I am. I'm not *just a liar*. I'm the best.

Admitting I'm not the hero pushed me overboard. Looking back, I always knew. I went after B for revenge. Satisfying revenge. Blaming everything on him was easier than admitting he wasn't the reason my life was a mess.

Then, there's Jack. I want to stay angry with him. I'm not ready to move on from that, but I have no choice. I feel so stupid. How did I not see it? He had that perfect mask, and I fell deeply for it while he was getting his thrills on the side. I don't want to keep replaying that part of my life.

His laugh remains over everything. It was nothing like Bennett's. It wasn't deep. It was soothing.

The night he first showed me how to properly throw darts, it was around nine, and I was bored. There weren't a ton of activities to do at the lab, yet everyone else seemed to find something to do that night. I found myself alone in the recreational room.

It had a giant Connect Four game. The night before, Charlie played Slow. I don't know how they haven't offed each other yet. I spent some time fiddling with it and then decided to take a stab at the dartboard. The first dart I threw nosedived to the carpet. I shrugged it off and chucked another. The dart bounced off the wall and into the aquaterrarium. Whoever thought it would be a good idea to place a small turtle tank in a game room was clearly mistaken. Jack walked in while I was elbow-deep, trying to fish it out of Sparky's playground.

I don't want these memories. I don't want to think about him ever again. I don't want to be angry or upset or confused. Running away with B and starting a new life sounds better every second. I'm tired of everything.

I return from my momentary daze, connecting with his perfect almond-shaped eyes. "Where did you go?"

"Don't worry about it." I smile softly before spotting the bright red stream rolling from his nostril. "Your nose is bleeding." It can't be a good sign, and to some extent, I'm glad for the distraction. At least I won't have to tell him I was thinking about another man while his cock takes my pussy.

He catches the liquid with the side of his hand and looks around for something to clean it with. I lean over the center console, opening the glove compartment. I find the napkins I saved a few days ago from the dive that Wes declared we stopped at. I hand Bennett one, and he wipes the blood from his hand, and then his nose. He holds the napkin in front of him, reading the logo before dabbing it above his lip once more and gently tugging at the skin that makes up his soft lips.

How is he in slow motion? It's turning me on all over again. I have the urge to clean him up and then blow him until he paints his signature across my tits in cum. I'm sick. I wish he could heal this brain of mine.

"Look what you do to me." His gaze sails down my body, mind-fucking me ten times rougher than he currently is. If that look didn't give it away, the jump of his cock did.

"Can't hang, B?" I taunt him because I wouldn't dare give him the satisfaction of knowing that I'm just as affected as him. We like to hurt together...and heal together.

"Oh, darling." He cocks his head to the side. "You already know the answer to that question." And there it is—his deep chuckle that rumbles from the back of his throat through his lips and burrows into every vessel in my body. "Swing your leg over my lap and turn the fuck around." It's what I want, and I challenge him anyway. "Ay! No. *Cherry.* Don't give me that look. Don't do that shit. Not again tonight."

I sigh, rolling my eyes. Then, I swing my leg over his thighs. He's lucky I don't purposely kick him in the face. Or unlucky—he might prefer a foot to the jaw. The balance between letting him hold the control and being the ringleader doesn't get easier for me.

I wrap my fingers around the grooves of the steering wheel and reposition my legs tighter to his thighs. His hands robe my hips. The pressure of his fingertips deepens as he lifts me and slams my body back down. I desperately hold my breath in, refusing to give him the satisfaction of a gasp or whimper.

Bennett's chest presses against my back and he pulls my hair to one side, letting it fall over my shoulder. Heat hits my neck with his whisper. "Am I still good enough?"

His stubble-covered jaw catches my eye as his warm breath caresses my skin. "You're the only one I love, dummy." If this is love, I mean it. He makes everything complicated seem simple, and I want to be happy with him.

"*Fuck*, I love it when you call me names," he groans sarcastically, sitting back and lifting my hips again. He slams me back down, slapping the sides of my legs. "You better hold on tight," he whispers against my neck.

I can't hold my gasp this time as he drives into me, pulling my hips to his solid legs.

Oh, God. And again. *Yes.* And again.

His long, slow thrusts feel so damn right. I wrap my arms around the steering wheel, leaning my face against it. His fingers thread into my hair, shoving my face harder into the leather. "Keep quiet, darling."

I tug at his wrist, turning my head enough to bite him in the forearm. "I don't take orders."

"You don't have any cute pink knives hidden in here either, now do you?" His brows raise when I don't answer, continuing to stare over my shoulder at him. "I can handle the teeth, not the knife—not today."

"No knives, check. What *can* you handle today?"

You can live with someone for years and never fully know them. I've known B less time and yet I know how much he can tolerate and how much he's willing to give.

"More than you can."

A short laugh escapes me. "What would be so horrific that I couldn't handle?"

"Marriage." He deadpans.

He's messing with me the same way I was when I told him my drama-filled plan to marry him and have his baby, who *wasn't really* his baby.

"Oh, so now you're offering to give me ownership of that last name? I can handle that if you can handle Shifter as your best man." I tighten my jaw until my lips begin to purse. I can disguise the smile pulling at my mouth all I want, but I can't bury the pollution in my eyes as I greedily look him over.

"Uhhh," he groans. "I fucking hate you…stripper." A dark chuckle vibrates through his chest, straight into my body. He pushes my face back to the steering wheel and just as quickly slaps my ass. He wraps his hands over my hips and lifts, dragging me back down his length. I smack him back, shoving his hands off of me. As I tire every muscle in my legs, the burn from hell races through my thighs, and I ride his dick, trying to savor every minute of escalating heat. His body is my unhealthy escape. My mind is an empty canvas. It's wishful thinking.

I need to get out of my head. I need it to be *quiet*.

I'm so lost in thought, I barely notice where his hands are—tracing my clit as his forearm rests against my thigh.

"Baby, I…fuck, you feel so fucking good."

He's going to freaking cum. We've been at this for a while. I get it and still…I can't help to feel salty that I've been unable to reach his level.

He pulls me tight until my back is against his chest, hooking his arms under my knees and suspending my spread legs in the air. As he lifts his ass from the seat, he digs his heels into the floor mat and uses me to stroke his cock until his heart heavily pounds against my lungs, playing the cadence I've become accustomed to. He keeps his moans hushed, pulsing and twitching inside me as I squeeze around him.

"Fuck," he exhales, leans back, and lets my legs free.

I sit forward, hold onto the steering wheel, and look into the darkness through the windshield, breathing through the remaining shudders.

"Turn around."

"Why?" I roll my eyes as if he could see.

"You're not done."

"You're not done with me?" I ask, dryly.

"That's not what I said. *You* are not done." He tilts his head to the side, giving me that look. The look he always gives me when I test him, when I argue with him, and when I tell him the truth when nobody else will. Lately, I've found myself arguing with him to occupy my mind. It's unlike me. I challenge him. I don't start pointless word wars.

"I'm just not that into it tonight. It's fine." Partial lie.

"Liar." *Stop reading my mind.* "Turn the fuck around, Cherry." He grabs my forearm and pulls me, practically spinning halfway on his dick until I have to swing my leg over, which is another protest.

"That better not leave a mark," I snap.

"What if it does? It wouldn't be worse than the marks on your neck or the bruises from my mouth across your chest. How about the fucking welts I left on your ass four nights ago?"

"That's not funny. It took two days for those marks to stop hurting. The marks make you look like a woman beater. You don't want to ruin your reputation, do you Mr. Big Time Director?" He tucks his chin, giving me that look *again*.

"I said turn around. Don't argue with me." He weaves his fingers through his hair, pressing his palm to his forehead, and brushes dark, loose pieces from his face. His concave cheeks cut to his beautiful gaped lips that he refuses to smile with.

I don't *like* his demands. I *love* them. He's the only person I'd let have any control over me—the only one I've given that opportunity.

He shifts forward, cuffing his hands around my ankles, and tucks them behind him. Grabbing my chin, he runs his thumb across my lower lip, dragging it down. I clench my teeth together for a moment, but I don't want to fight. I dip forward, sandwiching two of his fingers with my mouth and coating them with my saliva. He draws back, taking the same two fingers I sucked on, into his mouth.

He turns me on, twisting his wrist as he rolls a warm finger over my clit. Sensation overwhelms me, desperate for what he's teasing. He drops his finger lower, pressing into my dick-filled pussy. I nearly choke on my spit as he sticks his finger in.

Oh, my g—I drop my head back, grinding into the friction of his bent finger that fills and stretches me.

"B." I gasp, and moans hum through me.

"It feels good, doesn't it?"

I barely move, giving him a slight nod.

"Cherry," he growls. A sigh takes his voice—a tell-tale sign that he wants my eyes on him. "It doesn't. It's not enough. You want more." The smug asshole demands my obedience the only way he knows how.

"What?" I pant, blinking rapidly and refusing to stop rolling my hips. He feels so damn good. I swear he better not stop. He doesn't. He slips the second finger in as deep as he can go. Then he pulls out, only to repeat it several more times. As he dives back into me, he curls at the knuckle and stares into my eyes. I combat keeping them open as my body continues to take over, riding him uncontrollably. A mixture of his cum and my wetness coats my inner thigh. I dig my nails into his shoulders, ignoring how soaked I am.

"Talk to me. Tell me how close you are."

He needs to hear what he's doing to me and how good he's making me feel. That's what gets him off the most—the praise of my moans and exhausted words.

"B..."

"Shhh," he hushes, covering my mouth with his palm. "I change my mind. Nobody else gets to hear your spent sounds."

I glance up, looking through the tinted windows surrounding us. A shadow hangs just past the rear driver's window. I can't stop it, and I swear the adrenaline of the approaching figure is fueling the fire that burns and tenses my core. *Oh my God.*

"That's right baby." I lean into his hand, not holding back as he tries to cover my sounds. His palm takes the warmth from my throat. "Oh, darling. You come undone beautifully on my cock. Breathe through it," he whispers against my hair, cupping the back of my head with his free hand. His skin hardly muffles my moans as much as he tries, and he doesn't care. It's in his eyes. They never leave me. I'm all his.

Three taps on the window pull both of us out of the perfect trance. "Police!" The masculine voice scolds, shadowing the glass with his chest. "Having your dick out in public is punishable by law, sir."

Bennett lowers the window halfway. "Unwanted voyeurs are punishable by death."

"While Sid and Nancy are fucking on the job, I've been working." Shifter dangles a ring of keys from his middle finger and a cunning grin from his mouth. "You two were a nice distraction. I wasn't the only peeping pervert." He looks back at the hotel, nudging toward the building, and tugs at the neck of his charcoal hoodie. "You'll draw too much attention if you walk around with your dick out. Not because of the size. Not that I paid attention to the size—or girth."

Bennett smirks as his eyes rise to Shifter's face. Add to his ego, why don't you. "Give us a minute." He hits the button to the window, and I stretch to the passenger seat, grabbing my black athletic leggings with the pockets and untangling my panties from them.

"Give me your shirt."

"Use your own," he counters. "Don't look at me like that." He captures my chin in his hand. "Why do you always get what you want?"

"Not everything."

He leans forward, yanking off his two-tone vintage band tee and stiffly handing it to me. What's his deal with these ratty t-shirts? I can hardly make out the name anymore; he's worn this one so many times.

"You know I love you, right?" I ask, not sure if I'm questioning him or myself.

"Enough to leave Shifter out of our wedding?" *Our mythological wedding?*

"Afraid he'll look better in a suit than you?" I push off of him, climbing over the console to the passenger seat. As I drop my pants to the floor, I use his shirt to dry off. His narrowed glare remains fixed on me. I can feel it without trading grimaces.

"I'm not insecure, Cherry."

I glance up, challenging him with the same tensed jaw and dead eyes. "I am."

"You do a damn good job playing the role, but I know it's bothering you."

No. We are not talking about it. "I have to pee."

He softens and shakes his head. "I'll take my shirt back."

I fold it, handing him the driest part of the fabric. He reaches for it, and instead of taking it, he clasps around my wrist. "I'm sorry. You can't blame me for not liking him." My lip twitches at the corner, and he stops me. "*Don't smile. Put your pants or leggings, whatever the fuck they are, back on and go pee. I'll meet you by the door with Southern Comfort and *Shifter*."

He lets go of my wrist, and I pull on my leggings and open the door. I look around that dark, full parking lot, spotting the camera locations and bushes that line the far end.

I'm not going to wait until we get inside. If Dr. Romberg is in there, I'll never make it to the bathroom between two alpha men who can't get along and Wes, who would sit back and watch them battle for superiority. It's funny because Shifter never seemed like the go-getter before. He was fine offering his opinion and then walking away.

A lot has happened in the past few weeks besides making decisions that I can't take back. Everything I thought I knew—the reason I even met Bennett—turned out to be meaningless. Jack and Ronnie. How stupid could I be? *Greg.* What I did to Shifter—I wish, so desperately, that I could forget. I want to erase everything—not just the last few months or years, but *everything*. I'm supposed to create my happiness. That's easier said than done when all that I know is burning buildings and bleeding hearts.

As I approach the building, I don't see the peeping security guard. How did he see us? Security cameras?

I suppress my laughter, biting at the skin beyond my teeth.

I can tell B that I finally own his sex tape. That's if I can manage to slip away long enough to steal the footage—if it exists.

Bennett hasn't let me out of his sight much. I can't blame him. After the first impulsive fuck-up, I thought he'd stop me from making more rash decisions. He didn't. Maybe he couldn't. It's unlikely that he foresaw the amount of destruction I'd cause in less than a week, either. God, this is unlike me. Why am I doing this?

"Hey sweets, you okay?" Shifter bows forward at my side, dipping his mouth next to my ear.

I continue looking straight ahead at Bennett's hands as he swings them out to his sides. He must be going over his plan with Wes. His dark red t-shirt fits over his defined arms snugly while the hem ripples loosely in the evening breeze as he nods in understanding.

Wes is a teddy bear of a lab rat. No matter how precise he appears with his tapered, short beard and matching light brown hair, he's not that stern. The gentleness in his warm brown eyes is the first giveaway. We got along since the first day of the trial.

I got along with everyone, so is that saying much?

"I'm fine," I answer before I look up at him and cross my arms over my chest. "Do we know if she's inside?"

His forehead creases with lines. "We're about to find out."

"Ready?" Bennett looks between me and Shifter, grabbing my hand and weaving his fingers between mine. "Everyone plays cool. We're visiting our friend. We've been here before and know where we're going." Shifter spins the key ring around his finger once more, tucking his hand into his pocket.

I keep silent, glancing between the men, and settle on staring into the lobby of the four-story complex.

"Good evening," the peeping guard greets us, shoving his phone in his pocket. He makes eye contact with Bennett first with a stupid grin on his face and then looks at me before quickly glancing away.

B nods, giving a quick reply as he heads toward the elevator. Instead of following him, I stop and face the security guy. He's not at all intimidating—nor much taller than I am, with broad shoulders and a husky build, clean-shaven, and slightly shaggy brown hair tucked under his navy cap. "Did you enjoy the show?"

He freezes, searching over his words.

"The game," Shifter points to the man's pants pocket with his phone. "She's talking about the game. Ignore her dry humor. I know how much it sucks to have to check the score while working."

"You caught me. It's still tied. Might go into overtime," he replies, almost with a sense of relief.

"Sorry," I softly smile. "My friend's boyfriend just broke up with her, and she's having a hard time. I guess I'm bitter that I'm missing the game too, but if you hear screaming, it's only her drunkenly leaving awful voice messages on his phone." I bat my lightly mascara-coated lashes.

"They put high-quality insulation in the walls of this building. She can cry her poor heart out. Good luck." His eyes drift to the side with the tightening of his lips. He must have teenage daughters, or at least one.

"Thank you." My big, movie-star smile takes over my face as I thank him and step into the elevator B has been holding. As soon as the door closes, he turns to look at me.

"What the fuck was that, Cherry?" He deadpans. "I know you're not trying to make friends."

"Cut her a break. This isn't easy on any of us."

Bennett veers his stoned-over glare to Shifter. I'm going to lose my mind if these two start fighting again.

"Can we go over the plan?" I interrupt.

He slowly centers back on me. "The plan is there isn't a plan. We go in and if anything—and I mean *anything*, Cherry," his voice deepens, defining his point. "If anything is off, we get the fuck out. Otherwise, the goal remains. Attain her without harm."

I step back, lean my elbows against the banister, and watch the numbers climb above the door in silence.

The doctor already ran from us once. She's bound to try to take off again. I don't want to think about it. Hurry up. Get to the third floor already.

I eagerly wait for the unknown, drifting my sight amidst the three men towering around me. The elevator pings, jolting as it comes to a stop, and the door opens. Bennett grabs my hand, pulling me into his chest.

"When this is over, I want to dance on a rooftop with you and forget the world." His fingers take the side of my neck, and his thumb drifts over my jaw before gently swiping over my lower lip.

"With perfect posture," I smirk and kiss the pad of his thumb.

"Fuck the posture. As long as you're in my arms, anything goes."

THE PLOT THICKENS UNDER BENNETT'S FOOT

"Ah, fuck. Here we go again."

You can do everything in your power to manipulate time, but you're never really in charge. When I died, I didn't have that flash of memories the movies portray. What I got was a million times better—another chance. I don't know if this is where everything begins or if I shouldn't have come back.

You should know me by now. I'm not exactly a zombie or a vampire, and I'm certainly not talented enough to be from a comic book. I'm a fucking lab rat, I guess. At least I'm kind of a big deal. And as for Cherry, her face shows up in new places daily. She's pop-icon famous.

Recap: Cherry kidnapped me. I was a helpless victim—for a whole two hours. Then I awoke, managed to escape, and we fought to our horny little deaths—psychotic sex. Then I told her I loved her, and she sort of admitted she felt similarly and talked me into a flight to the town where I got shot. It's a place of fantastic memories for both of us. Once we got to the laboratory, which turned me into a *zombie, I was unpleasantly surprised with the surviving and thriving self-titled Lab Rats that miraculously remained. The place got raided by mystery men that Shifter knows something about, and we've just set out on a road trip to Florida, where Dr. Feather Romberg—the last living lab rat scientist—resides. I swapped my SUV out for a rental last night—same model, different shade. The blue isn't as discreet as the black. It's not as flashy as the red, though.*

Someone out there knows what we are and not just Dr. Romberg. It's the only reason I agreed to both Shifter—the rat who nobody knows is also a zombie—and Wes—the bodybuilder cowboy—coming with us. What Cherry wants, Cherry gets. I never thought I would utter such selfless words. Did you? Wait—that's the one part of the story you "called." I'd fall for the girl. Get off your high horse and keep your lips sealed.

The sunshine evaporated from Cherry's smile the minute my tires took the asphalt past that East Grenton sign. It hasn't returned since. I miss that brightness, and unfortunately, I get it. We have this scourge. It's sunken into our bones, marinating and growing stronger. It doesn't transmit to someone else. Instead, it reinfects the host repeatedly until we let it take over or go mad trying to stop it. Even rats deserve a fair trade. I can own that title—a rat—although the only beast to label another human to be as expendable as a rat is a pig. A pig scarfing down everything thrown in front of it out of pure gluttony.

I know, who the fuck are you to talk about gluttony, Bennett? Yeah, maybe I shouldn't get ahead of myself. I'd dig a thousand graves in the name of love. It's contradictory if you think about it. Love is not self-seeking. Doing terrible things for Cherry is not self-seeking. I don't help her for my benefit, so why isn't it acceptable? It's the fucking moral thing, isn't it? Whoever said love conquers all didn't count on the bad guy winning her heart.

Try to keep up because I have a feeling this is only the beginning of a long week.

"Are you hungry? I'll stop at the next gas station." It's been ten minutes since we left and I'm dying to put several more miles between us and this town.

"The one on Oak?" Southern Whiskey pokes his head between me and Cherry. "They have those soft pretzel wraps with the ham and cheese in them." This guy consumes more calories than all four of us combined in one sitting. Lucky me, I get to fund this entire trip, including his fucking buffets.

I have no doubt he spent the last several years working on gains and telling society to fuck off while he lived free in the rat hotel dodging the traps and grenades. *I don't care about the money.* It's the fact that I figured out how to turn this curse into a reward while they simply existed. How long would they have lasted if I didn't return? Oh, that's right, they had *Shifter* protecting them. Fucking chivalrous.

"You would fucking know that, wouldn't you?"

"B." Cherry's eyes half-circle and harshly land back on me. Let me guess, *language?*

She stares out the passenger window at the gloomy overcast sky as I check my mirror instead of apologizing for being utterly asshole-like to her friend. Likewise, Shifter is doing the same—living in a cloud city while I'm forced to abide by the laws of gravity. Wes smirks when he catches me grimacing at Shifter.

We're asking for trouble dressed in dark hoodies and jeans like a bunch of punks. And unfortunately, it's our entire wardrobe for the week. I'm kind of missing those cropped shirts Cherry usually wears. It doesn't make a difference, though. Men will lock onto her beauty beneath oversized attire, and women will continue to gawk in judgment until she talks to them. Once she opens her mouth, everyone falls in love with the girl next door—except the bitter. I wonder if Cherry can see the future, and she's awaiting one of us to rob this little gas station for a whole three hundred dollars in their register and a box of Twinkies for the fun of it. My money's on Southern for the Twinkies.

I cut the engine at the pump, and Cherry jumps out before I remove the key from the ignition. She waits with her pretty blue eyes stuck on me as I get out, and she rounds the front of the vehicle. Her hair disappears from her shoulder, taken by the wind. I pull several folded bills from my pocket and grab her wrist, sliding the cash into her palm.

"Pay for gas and get anything else you want." With a heavy exhale, I press my tongue to my cheek. "And whatever Southern is having." Despite her straight lips, the dancing lights in her eyes tell me all I need to know.

To my left, Shifter leans against the rear quarter panel. His brown eyes skim over her ass as she walks away.

"I remember her…your sister," he says, pulling a pack of gum from his pocket and sliding a stick out.

What? *My sister.* Why the fuck is he bringing her up now? He didn't seem like he recalled much about her the last time I mentioned her. "Annie?"

His glance reaches me for a second before his focus returns to the chewing gum he's unwrapping. "Yeah. Anna Banana."

Fuck, that's right. He used to tease her with that nickname when she would piss him off.

I remove the cap from the gas tank, placing the nozzle inside before he starts chomping obnoxiously. He tosses the paper in the brown plastic trash bin beside the pump as I press the premium-grade button.

"You used to smoke?"

"Yeah," he admits. "Does the gum give it away?"

"It's either that or an unhealthy obsession with blowing bubbles."

Healthy obsessions don't exist, at least not for us. He steps back, slouching against the steel body again. This time I join him on the opposite side of the house, leaning back and crossing my arms.

"It fucking sucks."

"Let me guess, you quit because of her." An inverted nod raises his chin toward the building. We both stare through the large glass windows. Cherry tilts her head back slightly with a huge smile plastered on her beautiful face, showcasing the rounded apples of her cheeks. She put that baby pink blush over her fair skin this morning and a little something on her eyes. For her, it was a simple, one-and-done fix-up. To me, she fought with the thought of *why try* and won.

The distance silences her laugh as it continues to echo in my head. "What's the story on him?"

"Wes?" The amusement coats his voice. "He's harmless, but I get it. You want to keep her safe and protect her at all costs. The thing is, you already know Cherry doesn't need anyone to save her." As he talks, he doesn't look away from her. "Sweets is a big girl. As for Wes, he's been on his own since he was sixteen." He glances over at me. "Emancipated after his grams died. He lived with her for nine or ten years after his mom was killed by a drunk driver."

"He doesn't have any other family?"

"We're his family." The pump clicks, and I straighten. Shifter steps forward, meeting me before I grab the nozzle. "We've all been in fucked situations that I'm not sure you genuinely care about. Why did we all stay at the lab? That's what you want to know. You don't have to dig too deep for the answer. It's pretty straightforward, chief. It's because we are all each other has." His eyes widen, and his lips pull into a tight line. "Charlie talks to his dad on the occasion, Seth hasn't seen eye-to-eye with his folks...ever, Slow was in and out of foster care his whole childhood and Ronnie...Ronnie's a bitch, but she was raised by assholes that disowned her for not wanting to continue the family business."

I hang the pump up and tighten the cap back on, flipping the lid closed.

"What about you? Daddy spank you too many times?" His look solidifies and I hope I hit a nerve.

The bell on the storefront chimes as Wes opens it, leaning his back against the frame while shoveling food into his mouth. Cherry walks past him with a bag full of snacks in one hand and what looks like a bag of beverages in the other. We're going to stop twenty more times today so she can piss. At least she's in a better mood. More...cheery and bouncy.

"What's going on?" She asks as she approaches.

"Just learning about your..." I side-eye Shifter. "*Family.*"

She glances at him, and he shrugs his shoulders. "Yeah, yeah, yeah. We're good, sweets."

Come on, did you really think I would become best buds with David "Shifter" Mondroe? In a past life, I knew the guy. He played a video game or two. Sharing a brief history with him doesn't signify a brotherly bond.

"Here's the key. I want a coffee." I glance back at Wes stuffing his face. His mom is lucky she died before she had to witness the slob he became. Mine's lucky I disappeared before she could witness the monster I grew into.

"The clerk is a flirt. Watch yourself," she warns, opening her door with a giggle.

The bell chimes as I swing the door open and make my way to the self-serve coffee. I set the brown and white paper cup under the dispenser and press the button. Although it appears fresh, there's nothing quite like living on the edge.

Shifter walks up behind me, setting his yellow and black striped aluminum can on the coffee bar. His bullshit energy drink would be more wisely labeled "cocaine in a can"—drink it down to feel like you took a bump...or ten.

"My dad wasn't abusive, but do you even know Cherry? The shit she's been through? Keep your jokes to yourself when she's around."

I turn to look at him, placing a lid on my cup. "Like you said, she's *a big girl.* I'm not going to walk on eggshells." Her demons are my demons, and I don't need to validate that for him.

Bang! Bang!

A harsh sound from outside strikes me with the force of a lightning bolt. My gut twists sideways, and my lungs are stripped of oxygen. The noise ricochets beyond the building's windows, knocking me to my knees.

As I slide to the end of the counter, I peer around it. Panic drains my blood from my face.

No, fuck no!

Fuck this town. Not again.

That was a gunshot. Holy fuck. Fuck.

That was a gunshot, right? *Right?*

Breathe. Fucking breathe, dumbass.

Where's Cherry?

I don't see anyone in the parking lot. The tail end of a faded green long-bodied car drives away, and I find Cherry and Wes in the SUV, casually chatting.

What? *What the fuck!*

Shifter's hand on my shoulder shocks me into realization.

The car backfired.

The fucking car...backfired. And I took cover.

Fuck me.

"I'm fine," I insist, standing up.

"You got shot. That's how you died," he replies without sympathy. Not even the slightest undertone.

Does his empathy only exist when it comes to *his family*?

"Yeah, it's not a big deal. Watch out." I knock my shoulder off his, forcing him out of my way. "I want to pay for this and get the fuck out of this town," I mutter under my breath.

He follows me to the next aisle toward the register and pulls on my arm, forcefully gaining my undivided attention. He's lucky he didn't make me drop my coffee. This little—

"They killed me."

What?

What in the actual fuck is he talking about?

"The mad scientists. Intentional or not, I'm the second zombie they created." The air thins between us, creating a plateau where we have reached an understanding within two sentences. "Second string." He shrugs before his smirk falls from his face. "I'm not okay." His words turn raw with a sliver of a smile towing the side of his mouth.

In his attempt to relate to me and show compassion, he has become another person I'm expected to feel sympathy for. I can't do it.

I turn away from him, walk to the cashier, and set my coffee down. Without hesitation, I walk back to him, take the Buzz Energy from his hand, return the deadpan grimace he's sporting, and add it to the counter next to my drink.

"Looks like we need some caffeine today," a short and skinny kid with flat jet-black hair so fucking wonderfully greets us. His braces have those rubber band things. What the fuck are they for? He looks between the two of us, and they stretch with his smile. His lips quickly pull together, and his smile becomes more strained.

Are we making you uncomfortable, kid?

With the tip of my tongue, I trace the corner of my top teeth and hold in my amused laughter. Shifter and I both blankly stare at him.

The kid rubs his elbow, not pussyfooting to open his mouth again. "Is the blonde single?" With the flex of my jaw, I look him over once more. This kid has some balls; I can give him that. I'll play.

Shifter steps up next to me, and I roll my eyes to the side. "She has a boyfriend," he replies, checking in with me. I give him a subtle nod.

"Oh, who's the lucky guy?" I knew he would ask—little twiggy shit. He's a fucking baby. He couldn't be much more than eighteen. *Oh, shit! Hah!* I know what he reminds me of now. That movie character, uh...*McLovin*! Ah, hah. He has the confidence to back it up.

"He is..." Shifter thumbs toward me. "And I am...and the big guy, too." He takes the corner of his marbled circular glasses frame between his pointer and thumb, adjusting them upward. The kid's eyes widen and it's clear he's going to ask another question.

"How does that...I mean, *sorry*. Is that everything?" He blinks away, pointing to our drinks.

I press my palms against the counter, lowering my voice. "Three holes, three boyfriends."

"Sharing is caring." Shifter winks.

His jaw hangs obnoxiously, and he tries closing his mouth twice before taking a step back. His eyes fall to his register's screen.

Fucking shit. This is hilarious.

I straighten, burying the laughter that begs to escape my throat, and slap a fifty down, sliding it to him. "Keep the change."

As I twist toward the door, he calls out. "How did you meet her?"

Did he bother to look at the cash I put in front of him?

I gravitate back and lean over the counter. "I gave her a reason to want me dead." With that, I return to the door and push it open until the bells chime.

He's already texting his goofball crew as his left hand pinches the fifty-dollar bill.

Shifter smacks my shoulder with the back of his hand. "That kid died a little inside," he laughs.

"I was waiting for him to ask which hole was mine." I continue walking parallel to him.

"If we stick around long enough, he will. Guarantee he would ask to watch."

"Better than asking to join." He laughs. "Wait." With one word, he stops me feet away from the pump. "Wes doesn't know." He glances over at the vehicle. "*That I'm a zombie.*"

I take a slow sip of my coffee and try not to burn my flesh. "It's none of my business."

"Cool, cool, cool." He nods vigorously. "And you didn't have to pay for my Buzz. I wasn't asleep for the last three—*three?*—years." *It's going on four years already—a few more months.*

I face the vehicle again, making my way to Cherry. "I'm not your savior. I'm taking care of this for Cherry. Plus, I have a lot of paper I can't take to hell with me." I study him for a second and start walking again. "What were you doing—to make money?"

"Teaching pottery classes at an art studio in Chamlin." He rushes to get back to my side as he talks.

"Chamlin is a thirty-minute drive. How'd you get there?" None of the rats had cars, and with someone clearly aware of their existence, I wouldn't expect any of them to be parading around with their IDs, catching Ubers, and signing up for background checks.

"I had a girlfriend."

As I approach, I notice the rear passenger window is cracked. Wes and his big mouth are clear as day. I lift the handle of my door, and it only gets louder.

"Baby *girrrl!*" He yells, mocking Shifter's *girlfriend* comment. "He couldn't keep a goldfish."

"Yeah, yeah, yeah," Shifter replies dryly, his amusement on the same level as mine.

"What? You had a girlfriend? When did this happen?" Cherry twists, glancing back at him.

"It was fun while it lasted." He has nothing more to say, and she leaves it alone. She bites into her egg burrito, dying to know where they met and how long they dated. Yet, she doesn't push it. Her theories turn into daydreams, and he chews in her mesmerized state.

Cherry catches me off guard as she awakes from her starry-eyed daze. "Why are you going this way?" She lowers her window about a quarter of the way.

"They have Main shut down for that bicycle race." Southern Whiskey is knowledgeable about more than food and bodybuilding. He keyed me in before we left.

"You're going to take Fisher, and then Water to get to the highway?" She begs for confirmation.

Is she off? Her voice is...I don't know. *I'm tired. It's been hard to sleep knowing I could be woken by Animal Control trying to capture me.*

"Yeah, unless you know another route."

She goes back to staring out the window, wordless. She fucking hates this town.

"Hey, Little Red. Don't look so lost."

A lazy smile follows her gaze. "A big bad wolf will always be close behind thinking he needs to save me. You don't need to worry, B. I've made it this far on my own."

"You're not on your own anymore, Little Red. You can talk to me."

"Nothing to talk about, B." Her smile widens, looping her gentle fingers between mine.

Does she believe her lies?

How do you feel about a split POV? I've been contemplating letting Cherry co-write. As much as we joked about it, this story belongs to both of us now. I want everyone—yes, you—to know her story. What's her character's name, again? I'll search and replace later. *She deserves to be heard.* She's picking a fucking pen name.

Looks Like We Have A Problem, Shifter

*F*uuuuuuck.

I lean my head back against the headrest, close my eyes, and exhale the *bullshit* out of my nose.

Cherry was dead. Never to be seen again. *Dead.* Will I ever wrap my mind around finally making peace with her disappearance as she reappears? I doubt it. This is wild. *Wild, wild.*

This is my life, though. Something insane is always coming out of left field. I used to be the kid with the divorced parents who got away with cursing in French during class at Wently Prep. Now, I'm a science experiment gone wrong, witnessing my vanishing friend show up more than three years after she went missing, or as everyone pushed me to believe—murdered—by the very male specimen she showed up—Bennett Larson—not to mention, who I walked in on her getting dicked down by. Hell of a reunion. My shock is more than valid.

Cherry has this...*je ne sais quoi*. Something. It's like she has it all figured out. She's always a step ahead of everyone else. I don't know how she does it. Neither does she. She doesn't see what's right in front of her face...ever.

"Chug that energy drink. It's too early for a nap," Bennett murmurs. I take a sip and continue looking out the window. His only concern is my lack of awareness. I need to be prepared for any occurrence, at least until we get away from this town.

Cherry thinks she needs to save everyone. That's her attraction to Bennett Larson, but he'll take more than a Band-Aid. She's always loved a project. I remember when I was on that project. I'm not an idiot. I could see how much joy she got from turning the pieces of my puzzle around until they fit, lining me up, and coating me in Mod Podge. I was her therapy, and she was my distraction, so I indulged because realistically, a little glue wasn't going to keep me from falling apart again. Every one of us—every single one—has a shitty story to tell. As narcissistic as it sounds, it felt good to be the one to put that smile on her face.

This little ghost resurfaced at the right time. I have these...uh, what do I have? *Seasons?* Yeah, yeah, yeah; seasons of life. Sweets arrived during a pretty interesting one.

The first season of my life was good—childhood—not much to complain about. I spent summers at Mom's and lived with Dad for the rest of the year. It was the only arrangement that worked since she moved back to Lille—as in France—when I was a few years old. I wasn't part of the plan when she came to the States. There's a lesson about drinking the punch at a frat party. Closer to season three, I became fifty percent of the supplier for that jungle juice.

In the second season—when Barbara became my stepmom—I was fifteen. I would butt heads with Dad frequently. That's all I choose to remember, besides my emo-punk era, which seems essential. The amount of glue I used on a weekly basis to keep my mohawk from moving...shit, that was great.

Season three...ahh, yeah. Season three was when I became nocturnal. As careless and free as I want to say it was, it ended with Dad kicking my ass out.

Season four—I found the lab rats. Dad wasn't a complete asshole. He set me up with this *job interview*. He had no fucking clue what exactly *this job* meant besides it including housing. That was the last time I talked to him. He used to call when he had my number. I'd screen him every time.

He was right. I don't think about anything long-term.

I've never kept a steady job or a girlfriend for more than a few months. I wanted to get the fuck out of there with no plan. Most of my friends faded when I moved because they were doing the same shit I was. We lived off our parent's money because they let us, and we had a good fucking time doing it. It's not like I had no direction at all. What are the odds of being a successful artist? According to Dad, it was a pipe dream.

Cherry was the last person I met at Trustinex. I'd rather call it *the lab* for the rest of existence. *Trust-in-ex?* Trust who? Trust my ex? Which one?

Man, when she showed up, standing in my door frame, I could have sworn someone lost their ballerina. She had to be a two-faced bitch. There was no way that her big smile was genuine.

I couldn't have been more stoked to be wrong. She spent the first five minutes asking questions about my paintings without muttering a word about herself. I had to put the work in to get her to open up. Cherry is one of those people everyone falls in love with in a different way. Even Ronnie admires her. It's why they butt heads. She's fiercely competitive, and Cherry would easily allow her to be the center of attention. And for someone who's been handed a lot in life, Ronnie hates that she's not superior by her own doing.

Looking back, I can't say Cherry wanted attention. I believe she tried to hide from it. It's a little shocking that she's on a big screen now. I guess she gave in—embraced her light. Damn, it's been a while.

Wes keys away on his phone. "Ronnie texted me. Charlie and Slow are fighting."

"What's new?" I mumble.

With a quick glance over her shoulder, Cherry laughs. "Some things never change."

Charlie remains a hothead. It's probably why his band dropped him, and he ended up in East Grenton as a science experiment to begin with. *Control freak.*

Cherry's chin brushes against her shoulder, and I catch the roll of her eyes as she looks back once more. "Tell Ronnie to do something instead of complaining to you. We just left. Is she always up your rear end?"

"Damn, sweets."

She's rightfully pissed but has no clue what it's been like the past few years. I haven't told her everything. It's a lot to unload in a few days. Bennett's a smart guy. He already knows I've been holding back. It's the only reason he invited me to go with them. Keeping me close is his wisest move. I'm not only knowledgeable of what's been happening around here—I'm also a threat.

"She's not that bad," Wes replies. He won't admit it, but he has feelings for Ronnie. I can bet they've hooked up a few times. I've caught them in some fruitful positions that they've played off. As if nobody suspects them? They're always at the gym together.

You have to find *someone* to do when it's hard to find a job. We can't exactly risk a background check. There is always a price to pay, especially when it comes with easy money and free living quarters. I wish I knew that back then. Dad was right. My impulsive, lack-of-thought decisions would bite me in the ass one day.

"Yeah, backstabbers are never *that bad*." Her eyes shift to the side.

At some point, she's going to find out my secrets and she's going to kill me. *Wait.* Nah. *Not sweets.* She would do something worse. She'd never talk to me again.

"What's the story with *Slow* and *2002*?" Bennett shuts her down before she gets fired up more.

"2002?" Wes questions.

"The guy with the pinched hat."

"Charlie," Cherry answers. "He was in a band for a few years before all of this. He's a talented drummer, but he's..."

She trails off, so I finish her sentence. "He's a hot head. Ka-boom." With the sound, I pinch my fingertips together and spread them as if they were the fireworks lighting up his prefrontal cortex.

Wes laughs. "But Slow—" His accent hangs heavy on the name. "Is stupid enough to rob the same mini-mart twice." That's not even the worst part. His mom is in prison for grand theft. That's why he's been in and out of foster care his entire life. *Moms is a klepto.*

Bennett's eyes thin, and the hairlines nearing them twitch before he looks away from Cherry and back to the car in front of us that's driving under the speed limit.

Wes continues. "The first time he put a fuckin' plastic bag over his head and held up a squirt gun."

I hold my laugh in. It's funny. Slow is the definition of a dumb blonde. I've spent evenings wondering if he would lick bird shit off a window if we ran out of paper towels. Okay, exaggeration. My guy does some stupid shit. The story of him earning his nickname over being the last to understand the joke is true. He's missing the common sense gene.

An airy sound leaves Bennett. "He did what?"

Welcome to the fuckery, *Larson*. You're not as special as you think.

I do wish I could master that straight face, though. While he's a solid brick wall, I'm smirking as I wait to see which one of these two is going to elaborate.

"He was like twelve," Cherry professes. "The second time he was sixteen and went to juvie."

None of us know much about his *deal*, only that he had someone looking out for him. He said he joined the military at eighteen after he got his GED. I haven't heard him talk about that too much or how he ended up with us. Slow tends to focus on the present.

"Did he use a squirt gun the second time too?"

"Knife," Wes replies with a smug grin.

The silence hangs for a long minute before Cherry's voice brings back a small amount of comfort. "Hey, turn here."

I do a double-take.

Wait, *here?*

"That's not the right way," he replies.

She knows Bennett's right. We don't want to go that way.

"I know. Turn."

Nah.

I let my head drop back.

What are you doing, Cherry?

At the risk of Bennett getting butt hurt, I gently grab Cherry's shoulder and swipe my thumb back and forth. "Are you sure?"

She looks right through me. I can't talk her down. She's made up her mind, and this is going to be bad.

"This is the street," she points out. "There," her voice softens. "That's the apartment complex I used to live in."

Bennett's eyes are about to expel from their sockets. He unknowingly delivered her to the place where her nightmares and dreams merge. When you're stuck inside a box for months with only the occasional escape, you become close with the people around you. I've heard the stories, and I've found my way to this street many times.

I can't believe she's alive. However, her leading us here—that's not surprising at all. I could be wrong, but I don't think this is a healing thing. She's harboring too much tension for that.

"Why would you tell me to turn this way?" He lowers his voice.

I can't tell if he's more concerned or pissed. Either way, he's not stopping her now. Cherry always has a plan. On occasion, she's as impulsive as I am. The shit they shot into our veins made it worse. It's like, whatever is in that stuff, it taps into parts of you that are already excessive and makes them ten times worse. I'm sure they didn't intend on that.

We all have a reason to be angry, to be depressed, to hold grudges. It's the obsession that fucks us all over the most. They're unpredictable and we never know they're going to happen until they take us. Now add anger and watch very, very, bad things happen.

"Motivation," she shrugs, looking through her window.

It's more than that.

"Slow down," she demands. It's the most unattached tone I've heard from her lips.

I frantically look around. An old guy with a hideous rug on his head stands in front of the apartment complex. The light brown mop on his head is shaggy, while the unmatched sides are short and graying. He's around six feet and had a few too many brewskies, by the looks of the egg strapped around his core. How's that nursery rhyme go? Humpty Dumpty—maybe he should sign up to be a lab rat. I know the diet habits I had no choice in kicking. Fuck, I missed salt and vinegar kettle-cooked chips. Whatever, man. It's not my business unless it's who I think it might be. Could it be?

"You're kidding me," she mutters.

She knows that guy.

She's pissed at that guy...And, uh, woman?

The woman watering plants in a dress so hideous it resembles a nightgown has a cigarette pinched between her thin lips.

I miss cigarettes, too.

No. Cherry's not even acknowledging her existence—just the rug doctor.

Oh, man...she has the look.

There's no way she would do anything. Not Cherry. She's not like us. She's centered and...sweet. I want to believe it. I want her to stay sweet.

This is East Grenton.

The street she hates.

Fuuuck.

I need to tell Bennett to push the pedal to the floor. We need to leave right now.

I scope out the poor structure and the foot of dying grass. A destroyed couch is parked in the center and trash is scattered about. It leads me to ancient planks of wood that make up the porch where the haggard fuck awaits.

He's her devil, and this has been brewing for too long.

"Bennett." I lean forward. "Bennett."

A heavily spray-painted building borders the left, and a dark alley—or small road, maybe—stretches between the right of the complex. I glance at a con-demned structure with tape surrounding it and reach for Bennett's shoulder.

"What?" He finally answers, studying Cherry's face.

Is it the same as she remembers? *Shit, this is East Grenton.* If anything, it got worse, not better.

This isn't how I grew up.

How many kids can say they spend every summer vacation in a foreign country? Mom is far from broke, working at the courthouse. I wish I knew what she actually did and if she still does it. The money she's sent me is nothing besides a drop in the bucket. It's how she's always solved our problems. It's not how I solved mine or Cherry solved hers. We buried them. We pushed them deeper than we'd admit. And now, we have no say when they'll spring up and turn us into mindless zombies.

Bennett needs to drive away.

I hesitate. "Cherry..." *We need to leave.* "It's him, right?" It's her mom's dirtbag ex-boyfriend.

THE CHERRY BOMB GOES BOOM

He deserves a fate worse than death. Please, allow him to become stuck in limbo, where he is given only one choice—to watch his body being dropped into the ground without a single soul sending their goodbyes *or* feeling his last breaths being stripped from his lungs, the suffocation taking him under over and over again. If one single loved one would show up at his final resting place, they'd fall into a grave of their own, and he'd have to witness that too. It's an effortless promise made when the man couldn't care for anyone besides himself.

Time is supposed to heal. It doesn't. Nothing healed. It was just a bunch of lies someone told you to make you feel better for the time being. It scabbed over, and I've been picking at that crusty little thing for years.

I blame Greg. It's his fault. Everything is his fault. It has to be. He deserves this. He will pay. I'm stopping him from making another child bury their mother. He'll never hurt anyone again.

Baby girl, my ass. I swear this is all his fault.

The colors fade around me until they've turned to gray, and the monster in red gawks, dumbfounded, as I barrel out of the car before it comes to a full stop, letting the door hang behind me.

If you smiled, you'd look so much prettier.

I won't smile when I'm not happy just to appease you.

I won't be a pet and fetch you a drink.

I'm a force, and only I can take back my peace of mind.

Only I can end this madness.

The smug piece of trash smiles, spotting me—a young woman he's met before. He's thinking disgusting thoughts about how I've *really grown up* or even worse, how I look like my mom.

I swing my coiled fist, abruptly stopped by Bennett's hand circling my wrist. It had to be B, by the way he grabbed me. Then, he spoke—the only sound to break through and temporarily return color to my blackened vision.

"Excuse me, sir. I believe you know my friend here. Could she have a word with you in private?"

"What's this about?" His dry voice gives me the worst gut-curdling sensation.

As I glance over my shoulder, the world shakes. *That odor.* With each inhale, the color Bennett called to the surface fades.

Of course, he didn't quit. He didn't quit! He wouldn't! He'll push his dirty lifestyle onto innocent children and screw their moms. He'll drive them to their death! He doesn't deserve my grace!

"It will only take a minute of your time."

"You have bodyguards now, little girl? I saw you on TV."

I lose all rationality as I lunge forward, pointing a finger in his face. "I'm not a little girl, pig!" Bennett wraps his arm around my middle and my wad of spit lands on the pig's boot.

What?

I search for him—for *any* familiar, comforting face. None of them come across clearly.

Did he say something to Shifter? I don't know. I can't evade my focus. I'm locked on the monster again with every intent on destroying him. I want his blood on the floor—his ashes in flames.

My legs move, but it doesn't feel like I'm walking. B is pulling me through the building. He pulls me through the hallway to the second floor, and I'm—on clouds or...gliding over ice?

It's hazy. *Where's the*—the door comes into view. That's it.

1-1-3.

Where is he!

As the switch flicks inside my head, it sends gallon after gallon of fuel at an alarming rate. It sparks the greatest rage I've felt since the day I set out to destroy Bennett. The tiniest remnant of myself is gone. Any chance of regaining control has disappeared.

I shove past Bennett and Shifter. The haze thickens as I make impact. Each time I pull back, my arm becomes heavier. I become more numb.

"Cherry! Fuck!"

I want to scream at Bennett—I can't let go.

"She's not going to stop until he's paid the price." Shifter is right.

For the first time, I couldn't say B was the calmest person in the room. He fears my unruly, foolish decisions will ruin our plan. I'll derail it and destroy us all. I'll take his peace.

My arm is twenty-five pounds—a heavy weight that drives forward over and over as the angled blade clenched painfully tight in my fist slices the man pressed into the cheap commercial-grade carpet below me. His round cheek spews a crimson river.

"Take back your control, Cherry."

I abruptly snap back to Bennett. He looks down at me, a foot away, knowing better than to come between me and my mission.

"I am in control!" I'm lying.

As I stare at my tremorous hand—the tiny dull blade that peeks between my fingers like brass knuckles—I drop the sharp object. My legs shake under the weight of my body, and I crawl backward, away from the bloody excuse of a man. The dingy carpet obscures my vision. It sails back to my shaking extremities, and the empty shell painted in blood beneath me. The rhythm of my chest switches constantly—deep and shallow, then panting in panic, and even out again. It's as if my conscious meaning is catching up with the shadowy storm.

I try to stand. My legs break like a newborn deer, and I stumble forward. With an upward glance at Bennett and Shifter, a new layer of this nightmare takes me—embarrassment. I shuffle to my feet and run toward the bathroom, barely keeping my balance as I fall into the bordering walls and hang on the doorknob, pulling it closed.

I twist the lock, and no sooner do I make it to the sink than I vomit up the breakfast sandwich that I ate fifteen minutes ago. The chunky yellow mixture turns my stomach again, but I hold it back, wiping the tears from my eyes, and with it, my liner smears over my cheek. I try to blink the moisture away, continuing to swipe under my lashes with the side of my thumb. When I finally look into the mirror, crimson splatters cross the bridge of my nose and smudges over my jaw—the little flecks covering my face like freckles in the heat of a July afternoon. *I'm the only heatwave to cross California this month.*

I grip the side of the ceramic dish, puking up the remainder of the contents from my stomach. My throat burns as much as my eyes, and my abdomen hurts from heaving forward.

What's wrong with me? Why me? I don't want to be like this. "I'm a good person. I'm a good person!" The thought bursts out of my mouth in an unexpectedly high pitch.

I tug my hoodie off over my head and flip it inside out as fast as my unsteady body will allow.

"Cherry," Bennett's voice carries through the slab faux-wood door. "Darling...I...if you need me, I'm here."

"I'm fine," I yell back.

I twist the clear plastic knobs, turn on the faucet, and cup my hands. I vigorously scrub my skin far rougher than I should as I splash the water over my face. The off-white dish blurs in my dead stare, a crystallized glacier that holds me in place. It's one of those fixated stares that I'm sure is going to ruin my vision one day while the world becomes bleak and gloomy.

"Hey..." Bennett's tone is less consoling this time. He's over the dramatics and I'm an inconvenience. "Uh...he's—"

"Don't fucking tell her," Shifter interrupts. His whispers would wake a snoring Yeti.

I twist the lock and pull the door open. Both of their attention shoots to me and the unexpected invitation.

"Don't tell me what?" I snap.

Shifter rolls his eyes to the side and presses his tongue to the inside of his lower lip.

"Tell me." I drift between the two, becoming impatient as they both refrain.

"Bennett," he hisses. "Brought him back."

As my face contorts, an overwhelming emptiness lifts my stomach. He saved the life of a terrible human. The disgust I felt when I saw what I had done should make it logical, and yet I'm conflicted. The world is piling cement blocks on top of my lungs and telling me to keep moving forward as I struggle to retain any O2. And against my will, my brain keeps a mental list of all the tasks I need to accomplish in the next two hours. I lost control.

"We either cover up a murder or we go find the scientist. We can't fucking do both," Bennett says, rubbing his brow.

She's a doctor, but he's right. If Bennett didn't dig me out of this hole, we would be set back a day, risk exposure, and potentially alert the ones seeking our captive. It doesn't mean I have to be happy about it.

"Whatever. I just want to get out of here. I need to get out of here," I mumble.

He doesn't waste any time—a man of stone—as he walks out of the narrow hallway and back to the open room.

"You have, uh…" Shifter's fingers kiss my neck, barely touching my skin and his thumb swipes across my jaw in one swift movement. "A little something." He leans in front of me, rinsing his hand in the sink.

What could I possibly say to justify what I did? I strategically told B to turn onto this street. I told him to stop the car. I got out. I got out knowing—knowing!—exactly what was going to happen. I wanted to do it, and I left myself. I'm worse than Bennett. I'm a premeditated monster.

Shifter wipes his hands dry on the sides of his jeans inches from me. The tiny, crust-covered bathroom doesn't allow for much personal space. I glance around, taking in the drab walls framing us.

"Is it like you remember?"

"What?" He captures my trance. "Um." I exhale and close my eyes for a moment. "It feels different, but also the same. That probably makes no sense."

"It makes perfect sense." His eyes dance over my face.

"Is there more?" I lean around him, attempting to find my reflection in the mirror. I wipe at my skin before he has a chance to answer.

"No, no, no. You're perfect."

"*Perfect.* Did you see what happened in there?"

"Your skin is perfect, sweets. It's a mess out there. I'd take your time." He nods and turns towards the door. "I better see if Bennett wants me to do anything."

I find my reflection and nod in agreement. "I'll be right out."

"No rush."

Baby girl, we are born fighters. We fight till we don't want to fight anymore. I press my head against the eggshell-coated drywall behind me, whispering the words once more as my voice cracks and uncontrollable tears take my cheeks. One more emotion I refused to rein in, allowing it to break me apart.

I miss her so damn much. Time doesn't heal anything, and I hate the asshole who came up with that saying. Time does nothing, but give a reason for miserable people to tell you it's about time you move on. What the hell is moving on? Pretending the pain doesn't exist? Is that the answer? Am I supposed to push it down and act? To save everyone else, maybe I should. Push it down.

I rub my fingertips across my eyelids and over my face, exaggerating a sigh. *I need to get out of here.* I dry my eyes and salvage what's left of my makeup by patting it back in place and fluffing my lashes with the side of my pointer.

I call out to Shifter, and his presence is immediate. He hangs on the door frame with his fingers curled around both sides.

"I need to get out of here without..." With a pause, I run my thumb over my ring. "I need to avoid that."

"Don't worry, sweets. Bennett is more creative than I wrote him off for." He flicks his chin to the side and walks back to the main living quarters.

I anxiously follow his lead. As I calmly lift one foot after the other, the burn twisting in my stomach grows. My underarms dampen, and I take the final step into the living room.

"B," I whisper.

Written across the wall, Greg's blood spells out a three-letter sentence. *I BEAT WOMEN.*

I find Bennett next to the coffee table. It's covered in pills. He drops a bag onto the pile as his lips part and then draw together tightly.

"Where is he?" I inch myself forward.

"I can't bring him back twice. I won't be able to do that, darling." He takes my hand and holds it against his chest. "The sad excuse of a man is going to call the cops himself. He's going to confess, and the medic might make it here before he bleeds out from the wrist. Karma came delivered by a bunch of rats today." He squeezes my wrist, pressing my palm tighter against his cotton shirt. "Do you feel how calm I am? Do you hear the drum as it thumps against your hand? I need you to swear you'll match it. You'll be level-headed and think before you act despite the boiling rage ripping through the curves of your brain." His thumb flicks over the back of my hand. "You're capable. I can't keep covering up your tracks. It's too risky. Someone is watching us—everyone is. There are eyes everywhere. Everywhere, Cherry." He drops my hand and glances at Shifter. Shifter peels back the partially broken window blind with his pinky.

"Send Wes," Bennett orders.

He nods and walks out.

"Wes is going to babysit until the lights start to show up. Then, he'll get out and meet us around the block. Shifter is already fucking all the minds he can find that may have seen us. We were never here and nobody will question it."

"Where is he?" I ask again.

"Your pig is in the kitchen."

The second I twist at the waist to walk away, his hand clenches around my forearm. "Cherry. Did you fucking hear a word I said?"

I whip my arm back, losing a battle as he reels me into him. His chest forces my chin up. His eyes split, the color draining out of them.

"Let me speak my peace, B."

"You speak your peace with a blade, Little Red. If I can contain my wolf, you better fucking get yourself in check. I'm serious. I think you need to recenter or whatever it is that you did before to gain control. We're done here." He lets go of me, and I rub my arm, taking half a step back.

His fingers thread through his dark fringe. "What's fucking happening, Cherry?" The confusion disguises his face. "This isn't you.""You've known me for five months. I'm not hollow.""You've known me for five months. I'm not hollow.""You've known me for five months. I'm not hollow.""You've known me for five months. I'm not hollow."

"You've known me for five months. I'm not hollow."

"Are you saying I need to get used to this? One outburst after the next?"

"Did you forget where all of my demons came from? It's this town."

"Run away with me, then." He laces his fingers between mine. "Fuck this town."

My sight falls on Wes as he opens the door while Bennett doesn't move. He follows me with his eyes, and there's something safe in it. His composure blankets me in calm.

"Ya'll ready?" Wes asks.

Without saying a word, I nod and walk past both of them, out the door, and into the hallway toward the steps.

Wes closes the door, and I envision him helping B drag the piece of trash from the kitchen floor into the living room. B plays his mind games while Wes skeptically watches with amazement as the pig calls the cops on himself, confessing his sins.

Does B cut him? Does he convince the pig to do it to himself? Is Wes phased, or does he get the reality check of how much damage Bennett could do?

The stories always make you believe that the worst monster you could meet is a vampire. That's what I've always read. The charismatic, beautiful, fast, and deadly creature of legends. We're not a made-up story. We're real people who signed up for a medical experiment. The world doesn't expect us to exist. It's not a blip in their mind. I can't say I'll ever meet a bloodthirsty vampire or flesh-eating zombie, but I have met monsters capable of killing, controlling, and seducing. One monster in particular that could rule the country—maybe the world—and part of me is exactly like him.

As I exit the building, a little girl draws with chalk on the sidewalk. I fake a smile, admiring her pretty purple sunflower dress and little dingy one-inch heels. Her frilly scalloped socks make them cuter. It hurts my heart that they're falling apart. The little girls who live less than a mile from here in Rebecca would never.

They're far too wealthy for shoes bearing worn soles. I spent some time in that area with those ugly relatives I was condemned to for a few years.

What am I doing with this existence—fighting when I could be helping little girls like me?

She's probably five or six. She can't see this. She can't be there when they bring him out.

At the end of the sidewalk, I meet Shifter.

"Have you talked to her yet?" I thumb toward the woman and little girl.

He shields his eyes from the sun, using his hand as a visor over his glasses. "Not yet."

"Tell them to go inside."

"I'll see what I can do."

"No. You'll make them go inside." A heaviness washes over me. "You're capable of convincing them. Spare the kid, Shift."

"Okay."

A single, simple word. His reply is with all of the understanding I would expect. I've missed him. I'm not the same woman I was the last time I was here with him, and every time he looks at me, he tries to hide exactly how much he relates. I never truly left East Grenton back then. Now I know what it's like to feel free outside of this concrete hell.

"There's always a new one," Shifter says.

"What?"

"A new problem to solve."

"I didn't mean to—"

"You're not the problem, sweets."

"You don't have to lie."

"I do have to lie—about pretty much everything, except this."

I open the trunk, shoving my balled-up hoodie in the corner behind our bags. I move Bennett's laptop case that's on top of my bag. Unzipping my duffle as far as I need, I pull out a clean black sweatshirt. Most of these are from B's closet. I doubt he noticed.

"There's a lot we haven't talked about. Too much to really get out, ya know." He rubs the stubble above his lip, his rings catching the sun. "We've all fucked up."

"Yeah." I nod, tugging on my lip. "Here comes B. Let's go."

Bennett Is On The Outside

S ilence cloaks the three of us as we take in the sirens. Cherry's blue eyes meet mine and quickly retreat as she notices I've caught her.

"Talk to me."

That piece of *worthless* shit. I want to strangle the fuck out of him for her. In a different place and time, I wouldn't have wavered.

"Talk to me, Cherry." I take her hand. The little abrasions from the blade lining her finger must sting. She's always pulling weapons out of nowhere.

Say something, Cherry.

I fucking hate it when she's quiet.

Before I met her, my life was fine. Now it's a shit show. I couldn't stop the death grip she has on my soul if I wanted to. Fuck. I don't want to keep overanalyzing this. I'll let you do that for me. It's too late. I'm here, in deep, and regardless of what happens, I will help cover her tracks, run in circles, and jeopardize my career because, at the end of the line, I know what it's like to lose your everything.

Oh, B, you've come such a long way from the manwhore picking up random women at the airport and sleeping with your fans. Am I a good boy now? Or am I a fucking idiot who fell in love with a woman who might want me to give up these abilities that have changed my distorted life?

Fuck the headaches. Fuck the blackouts. Fuck—I don't want to murder. It's a waste of my energy, despite some of these assholes deserving it. I never wanted that, but I did it, and I don't feel bad for any of them. I don't know if this doctor can fix me. I'm more fucked up than any other test subject.

This is the type of shit for the comics.

Should I turn this into a graphic novel instead?

Could you imagine what life would have been like if I had these abilities in high school? I would have given Brayden Mayner a wedgie from hell, and Sarah—Annie's friend—would have been my prom date. I would have gone, instead of skipping it and getting trashed at the beach with the guys. I would have joined the cross-country team and made everyone purposely trip over hurdles for a laugh and then take the gold.

These past few months have put me in a deep spiral, often thinking about the guy I used to be in high school. Yeah, here we go again, but that's who I was for a long time. That loser traveled into my early adulthood. The wallflower of all wallflowers. Bennett, what are you getting at? Right? Well, I always had that group of friends that got me. I mentioned them before. I'm sure you remember the hit list guy at least. It's hard to admit my loneliness in the more recent years. I didn't appreciate them because I couldn't. I was in a good place when they were around, but solo...I only remember struggling. I hid it well.

Does the reader give a fuck anymore? Why would they want to hear my sob story? Shit. It's me. I'm the desensitized one. There's only one part of my story that truly hurts.

I would have turned into Bennett The Asshole a lot quicker if I had these abilities back then. I wouldn't have ever lost Annie.

My darling sister, how far can I raise the dead? What about you, reader? Do you think I can do it? Could I have brought back Cassie? Would she completely heal, or would it have been a waste of energy? Either way, it would have been a mistake. Fucking greedy cunt. She would have done anything to steal more money from me. Extortion. Sextortion. I could give her a fresh start, and she would take it for granted.

But Annie—

Could I bring my sister back from the grave?

Could I?

I'll never know, and it fucking sucks. The light Cherry has put back in me chases the shadows to their corners. It's just as much my responsibility to keep hers at bay. I miss Annie every single day. With Cherry, I can breathe again.

As for my friends, all of them moved on. Welcome to the real world. Everyone leaves you eventually. Why should I try to make new connections? Someone else is always more exciting than me. They all leave. While Cherry clings to the likings of her rats, I know we'll all split at some point. Fuck. I'm Bennett Larson and soon enough, she'll realize that she reflects me. We only need each other. I swear I'll burn the world to the ground before I lose another piece of my heart.

Cherry stares out the window without a glimmer of her sparkling spirit remaining. I hate it. I wish I could take that pain from her.

She relived her worst memories, didn't she? Fuck. Her mom and everything.

Don't look at me like that. I know you're picturing it the same way I am. Her mom is in that shitty one-bedroom apartment. I see her clear as freshly squeegee-cleaned glass, dangling from the doorway. She has blonde hair, a slightly lighter shade than Cherry, and her feet are bare. She's fully clothed in sweatpants and a loose-fitting t-shirt.

No. That's not right. She's on the kitchen floor. She's draped to the side and soaked in a pool of blood.

No. Wrong again. It was the tub. That's where she found her. She overdosed and drowned.

How bad is it that I want to know? I don't know if that's the human curiosity in me or the monster getting excited. If she's inclined to tell me the details, down to each out-of-place hair, I'd paint a mental image as she speaks.

"Do you feel alone?" Her voice comes out of nowhere.

Do I feel alone?

"No. Not anymore. I have you. You're all I need." I reach between her thighs, take her hand, and pull her attention from the window. "Cherry...What happened in there? I lost you for a minute."

She chokes back the sorrow, rubbing at her eye as the door behind me opens. Wes hops in, exhaling one heavy breath as the door slams shut.

"All clear. You didn't kill him," he says jokingly, sharing the same dark humor that exists in all of us. It's not a rat thing. It's a coping mechanism.

Cherry stares at the dash, finally finding her words. "I did. B brought him back."

"What?" He asks with amusement in his tone.

"Yeah." She gazes intently into my eyes, devoid of any trace of heartbreak. "B can raise the dead."

What is she fucking doing?

The sweat clinging to the steering wheel reminds me that I'm driving, causing my heavy scowl to leave her.

"Huh. That makes me feel a lot better now. Ya'll can revive me if I get taken down. We're fuckin' invincible now, baby."

"I can't guarantee that." I put a stop to his victory dance and look in my side mirror. There's nothing to see, and I put the car into drive, pulling out. In my peripheral vision, Cherry gives up, letting her glare fall. Then I spot Shifter's hand on her shoulder.

She observes him before returning to the window. I stiffen, not wanting either of them to know I'm watching, an unusual stance for me. Call it curiosity—I need to know what her boundaries are with him. His thumb sweeps two or three times, and he retreats. I hate this hidden code they share.

Hey, you can't tell me that he doesn't secretly want to fuck her. We're on the same page. And fuck, Whiskey, with his knees in my back, would take it if offered. Oh, he's like her brother. I don't buy it. Excuse—No, shut up. Shut the fuck up. I'm not jealous. It has nothing to do with jealousy. I have nothing to be jealous of. I'll remind you, now that I've reminded myself—I'm Bennett Larson. I'm a fucking go d.

Their connection is nothing more than circumstantial.

My phone buzzes, vibrating my leg. I press my weight into one foot and lift my hips to shimmy the device out of my pocket. When I glance down, I see it's Justin calling me once again. My unconscious and exaggerated sigh is too much for Cherry. She may have held her tongue when it came to prying into Shifter's business, but my darling can't resist poking when it comes to me.

I told you. I'm the God—superior.

"Who was that?"

"Justin. I didn't answer my editor's email yesterday. He's chasing me down to get an update for her." Cherry's eyes roll around and quickly land on the floor, where she stares blankly and heavily. She puts the pieces together, flicking her thumb across her ring just long enough that I notice. "My editor has me scheduled for the first round of edits on this book and I'm not even close to having it ready for her. I have a week to get it to her, and because of my history, she wants to know if I'll have it on time. I didn't reply," I swiftly chuckle.

She's quiet again, but it doesn't last long. "Are you gonna have it done?

"I'll figure it out. I always do. I'll push it back if need be."

"I'm sorry," she murmurs.

"Don't be," Shifter inserts. It's an endowing reminder that those two are in the back seat, listening to every word I say.

You know what, if he wants to talk, he can at least give me some informative information.

"What's your story, Shifter?" I purposely lower my voice to get my point across. "Or is it David?" He catches my devious smirk in the rearview mirror. He leans back, and I can't read his face. His body language tells me enough that it doesn't matter. I'm making him uncomfortable. His shoulders are back, and his chest rises. The little tilt he did with his chin was noted. Hmm. Does it make him mad when I call him *David*? "How is it you got that nickname, *Davey*? Shifter—it's interesting."

"High school," he answers, sapless.

I press him for more. "Care to elaborate? It must be a good story if it stuck this long."

Cherry looks over her shoulder at him, and he loosens.

Well, that's fucking annoying.

"I was the only one with a manual transmission. Real nice bright blue WRX. I loved that car. But there's a learning curve with a clutch. I stalled it out leaving school enough times that one day I said, fuck it. Power over and dropped the clutch, burning it up through every gear on my way out of the parking lot. I was threatened by the principal a few times and pulled over twice, but—" He shakes his head with a short, breathy laugh. "What were they going to do? A kid getting used to driving the stick shift he owns? It wasn't like I was speeding or endangering the public."

"You were a rich kid, right?" Sounds like something a rich kid would say; *what were they going to do?*

"When your mom lives in a different country, she tends to overcompensate, *enfoiré*," he blusters.

"French? And I'm going to assume that wasn't very nice."

"As nice as I can be when someone is desperately trying to pull information out of me that they can use later." I meet his chin rise with an airy laugh, pushing it out my nose.

"If I wanted to use something against you..." I glare into the mirror. "It would happen right now."

"It's funny." He sucks air in between his lips loudly as if he's waiting for me to question him.

"What's funny? I could use a laugh." What could he possibly think is going to piss me off? "Huh?"

"That...with as much monster we are, you're a jealous, insecure bully. The legend isn't all he's cracked up to be. It's just a fluke that you took out the lab staff. You latched onto rage bait and went to strangulation city."

There we have it. We both know why I'm an asshole to him, well, an escalated asshole compared to everyone else. I hate their connection, and good ole Shifter isn't giving it up.

"A fluke?" My deep chuckle stirs through my lungs. "That's why your girl left you. You tell too many fucking jokes. I like a good laugh, but you're kidding yourself with these grade school quips."

"Number one: any girl would love to have a guy as hilarious as me catering to them. Numéro deux: she didn't leave me on her own free will."

"You—" He fucking told her to leave? Is he saying he used the mojo and mind-warped her into leaving him? "You're not as intelligent as I thought."

"Keep talking, jellyfish."

"I'd rather sting."

"You had a girlfriend?" I glance over at Cherry as I hear her sweet voice.

I hope she can handle this trip—and everything that comes with it.

"Yeah. You would have liked her. Real down, never afraid to leap, girl. She matches my energy, but between you and me, she's a lot smarter," he snickers.

"What does she look like?" As Cherry picks Shifter's brain about his mystery woman, I take a hand off the wheel and stroke her thigh. The softest smile tugs at her mouth, and she turns back to Shifter. He laughs, tucking his chin to his chest, and his eyes stay down.

"A goth princess." Another medium chuckle draws a slightly bigger smile from Cherry's lips. Shifter leans in and speaks slowly. I hold onto Cherry and continue to side-eye them. I hate the way he's looking into her eyes. "Her body looks like a canvas, painted in like a falling angel. She always wears deep purple eyeshadow, like an eggplant-y color, around her chestnut brown eyes. That's her favorite color...and she's so *thiiick*," he exaggeratedly groans humorously, and he returns to check my scowl in the rearview mirror. "With a huge *heart*. Really, really, big heart."

Shut him up. Painted in like a falling angel? This isn't a romance novel. What does that even mean? Does she have skulls and daggers tattooed on her skin or a deformity? Fucking wiry poet.

"You still want her." Saved by the voice of a goddess. "Maybe after all of this, you can find her and prove you deserve another chance."

Shifter pulls away, looking straight into Cherry's. Hah, this fucker. Straight into Cherry's gorgeous blue eyes!

"I'm not good for her." He adjusts, leaning back into his seat. *That's right, back the fuck up.* "I can't ever give her the life she deserves. Not like this."

"We're gonna change this, Shift."

Shit, am I the asshole? She's this positive light, set on helping everyone else find their happiness, and what am I doing? No—I'm not. I'm here, going out of my way to help her. This is the part of the story where I'm supposed to realize I'm in the wrong, right? I'm possessive and jealous and all of those other dominant manly words that are both toxic and attractive. Darling, I've always known who I am—it's not jealousy. It's determined.

"She's an angel and I...can't undo the things I've done," Shifter admits. It's as if they're in their own little world. We, myself and Southern boy over here, are nothing more than lawn ornaments.

"You gave up this *angel* selflessly," Cherry consoles him. "You couldn't be as bad as you think you are."

"You couldn't be as bad as the big bad Bennett." My deep chuckles awaken the vehicle. I do take pride in being this cold.

"I think you need a drink." Wes burps, holding up a silver flask.

"Where the fuck were you hiding that?" I ask.

"You have open liquor in a moving vehicle?" Cherry mom-schools him.

"Didn't you hear? Bennett is a God. We can do whatever we want," his vowel drags.

I attempt to knock him down a peg. "I am a God, but don't get ahead of yourself."

"You'd let me die?" With wide eyes, he laughs.

"I think we all know, anyone that Cherry cares about, I'm going to attempt to keep alive. These doctors played with fire, and look what it got them. There is no telling the effects on people when I bring them back. I've only done it twice and up until a few weeks ago, I didn't know it was possible."

The car goes silent. It's almost as if they're wondering who the first person I brought back was. They certainly wouldn't suspect it had anything to do with Cherry. After witnessing her beating the life out of a grown man, I'd put it on the table. To them, she's still too sweet to put a body in the ground. I've seen her dig the hole, drag the body, and stomp away.

I reach for the dial to turn the sound up on the radio, glancing in Cherry's direction. Her eyes meet mine before she swallows and clears her throat.

"B, you're nose is bleeding." She faces Shifter. "Reach behind you, my hoodie is back there."

It only takes him a few seconds to find it and hand it to her. The gentle touch of her hand takes the inverted sleeve to the skin beneath my nose, cleaning the few drops that ran.

"It's not that bad," I assure her.

"It's not good either."

We're about an hour and a half outside of Phoenix on our journey to find a doctor to soothe our nightmares. We only stopped once, surprisingly. I rack that up to everyone napping on and off. None of us intended to start our trip with emotionally taxing memories and bloodshed, but each one of us felt it, black hearts and all. That's what happens when you've all been through your own shit—their trauma triggers yours.

As much as I want to know their stories—the writer in me craves—it would be wiser to stay detached. When Cherry spilled her licorice trauma, as she called it, I became weak. I felt empathy for the first time in years. I swore it was only her. She was the exception—and the rule.

With each passing day, I find myself more concerned with what we'll find and who will make me weak. I refuse to be marginalized and overlooked, as I once was. The world knows Bennett Larson. You wouldn't be reading this if you didn't. If I were another Joe in the coffee shop, you'd impatiently await my exit in order to have my table and go about your day, chatting with your girlfriend about pop culture and new book releases. If Bennett Larson sits at that coffee shop and you walk in, you're whispers turn into stares, and your plastic cups become signature boards. You're day is made.

Wouldn't it be oh-so selfish if the artist you love dearly disappeared?

"Ice cream!" Wes shouts, startling everyone.

What the fuck?

I recenter, raising my forearm from the door card and grasping the steering wheel with both hands. A sign signals the next rest stop is a few miles ahead. It's the first marker I've seen in an hour. "How the fuck did you wake up and immediately see that billboard?" Shifter tiredly asks, rolling his neck against the headrest.

"Have you ever been to a rodeo bar?" He asks.

What in the fuck is he talking about?

"No," I blurt out. "And I don't want to."

"I bet you never did a shot from a dixie cup."

Is that an insult? "I did shots straight from the bottle."

"Alright, we're stopping then. You get groupies, and I get buckle bunnies. We're not so different. Ya know?" His attempt to stay on my good side is random—and expected. "That's what I like about a hometown bar: low drama, cold beer, and red meat."

Cherry stretches her arms above her head as she squints from the blinding sunlight beaming through the windshield. The sunset is at its most brutal point.

"How do you eat everything in sight and look like you're about to walk into an MMA ring?" Cherry asks. The rasp in her tone reminds me of the first night she slept next to me and the morning that felt overwhelmingly natural. That stupid, fluttery butterfly feeling hits me square in the gut. It falls just as fast when Southern Whiskey opens his cakehole.

"Octagon, please," he exaggerates. "I live in the gym and love my protein. Plus if I have a heart attack, now your boyfriend can bring me back to life."

Doesn't he fucking listen to anything? I'm not his personal defibrillator.

I run my fingers through my hair, combing the strands that hang by my eyes to one side.

I'm tempted to turn the radio up and drown Shifter out as he joins in. "Who says he'll do it?" He refers to my monster tendencies, letting Whiskey's heart stop for good. I take my eyes off the road, facing him.

"My favorite sweet psycho," I wink. "She's why you live." I point to Cherry. "*My* sweet *psycho.*"

The reason I'm here in the first place and the only reason I'd save her dumbass friends. Her eyes send in a full circle. She liked that one.

My weak chuckle is enough to make her lips pursed again. "What about when we're cured?" *Cherry always has a plan, and I'm not looking forward to losing my abilities. The goal is for this doctor to stabilize our moods, although I think she would be fine with being normal or as normal as it gets. That's what she believes. To me, going back to before isn't going to make anything better for her. Would the side effects go away? Sure. You tell me, would the scars of her past be erased? What about the people she hurt while in the skin of a monster? Will she be able to separate that part of her and move on? It would take years. What if we didn't have years? It's unpredictable what will happen. She already has an idea of how this should play out. If it doesn't, what will disappointment do to her? What does happen if we're cured?*

"Then I guess I have to use my brain again." Wes shrugs.

He checks his phone too much.

"You have a brain in there, scarecrow man?" Shifter pokes the bear.

"Brains and big as fuck brass balls. Maybe I'll let you borrow them sometime."

This is getting good. What is, uh, hashtag...hashtag Team Wes. If I created a Cherp profile or whatever it is—that app that replaced actual face-to-face conversations and gave people balls as big as Whiskey's brass cojones—the fucking cyber bitches would beg me to spare them. I'm talking about the trolls shitting on my work, not the conspiracy bros. I like running them in circles on the forums.

That wasn't what I was getting at.

Delete everything after hashtag Team Wes.

What was I saying? Oh, yeah—*I'd make a profile on Cherp just to hashtag the piss out of Team Wes and put Team Shifter to bed.*

"What's the first thing you're going to do when we get cured, Shift?" Cherry weaves her fingers through her hair, pulling it back into an invisible ponytail and letting it fall to one shoulder.

"Uh...I don't know."

"Are we talkin' *no side effects cured* or *basic human cured*?" Wes asks. "Bennett would like to continue bossing Hollywood around, so we should aim for the first." He's on the fence about being cured, too. He's finally hit the nail on the head, finding something we have in common. I raise my brows at the thought and glance to the side in hopes that Cherry doesn't notice.

Shifter butts in with a suggestive tone. "How do you do it, Bennett?"

How do I boss Hollywood around? I'm not the one hiding my ability to influence minds, *Shifter.* I thought they were a *family.* They certainly keep secrets from each other, at least Cherry and Shifter do.

"I'm sure you could figure it out."

"I have scarecrow brains," Wes amplifies and his sarcasm only thickens from there. "I can't figure it out. Let me in on it."

"At least you have a heart," Shifter mocks. His scorching grimace burns the side of my head like a lit bud with his beady fucking eyes. "The Tin Man is heartless."

Cherry's fingers trail mine. "You're not heartless, B."

A thickness in the air takes over the vehicle, capable of suffocating everyone. I can't say I'm as excited as Wes is for ice cream, but I need to get out of here and away from them for ten minutes. If you want heartless, I'll deliver.

"No, darling. He's right. I'm fucking heartless. I convinced people to work over ten hours a day. They work until *I'm* tired. Despite not giving a shit about money, I've hired people for well less than their worth. I—"

"You fucked the actresses, right?" The four-eyed fuck interrupts my speech.

"No. I'd usually find a woman in the city of my project and make her my live-in ass for the duration and then end it when production closed. I'd have a few *run girls* on the side." I slide the flat of my palm across the wheel and let my fingers curl over the leather material again.

Cherry has a smile tattooed on her face like nothing I could say will make it falter. I'm aware my words could hurt her. Pissing off Shifter is more important right now for me to consider the consequences.

"Mommy issues?" She asks, knowing the answer.

Hah. That humor.

She leans to the side, mimicking my movement to get closer. I grip the steering wheel with one hand and tuck her falling hair behind her ear. "I needed someone to put me in my place. It could only be you."

His angry glare gets lost, pissing his frustration out the window. His attempt to make Cherry see me for what I am came up short.

As I press my lips to her forehead, I kiss her and take the wheel in both hands again.

Stop.

Don't fucking do that.

That "Aww, B. Forehead kisses." Yes, that bullshit. Do you want to love a killer? You don't. Are you capable of forgiving him when he talks about the woman he's fucked before you out of spite? I understand that it wasn't directed towards her. You can make up any excuse you want. You can't glamorize my love story, darling.

It's mine, and it's a mess. Shifter is the one you should adore. The pain in my ass is your catering knight.

"Ya'll kill my appetite," Wes grumbles.

"Right here's the exit."

"I change my mind. My appetite is alive and thriving."

"Are you capable of putting your phone down for more than five minutes to eat?" I badger.

"I won't miss a beat if you hand-feed me. FYI, I'm a finger licker."

"He prefers toes." Shifter smirks.

"If you were a better stalker, you'd know I've stated slurping is more appealing than licking."

"I can be a loud eater," Wes nods.

"I adore this little bond you've guys made overeating etiquette," Cherry giggles and swings her door open.

New Mexico, 11:02 PM

After driving over thirteen hours today, I'm desperate for a skin-melting shower. I want the water so hot that my epidermis is squealing for a savior that will never come. Bennett, you masochist.

Bing! Bing! Bing! That's the sound that will haunt my dreams. Shifter tapping the alert bell at the front desk to a made-up drummer-boy rhythm.

As I leave the check-in desk, I hand Wes the key to Shifter and his room, walking toward the elevator. "Don't touch the fucking mini bar."

"You got it, captain."

He's going to drink it dry. Asshole.

"Here's your bag," Cherry says, lifting it from the floor.

I take it from her, then grab hers from her shoulder. The elevator doors open, and I tuck my hands into my pockets, walking inside.

"Today was a lot." I'm itching for her to talk to me alone. She only nods, pulling her lips tight in agreement. "Did you mean it?"

"Mean what?" Her thumb moves back and forth over the ring on her finger. She knows exactly what I'm talking about. I wouldn't say it out loud. Not here.

"How long did it take you to decide to stop at that apartment?"

"The minute I saw the street sign," she admits. "Yeah, B—" Her heavy gaze settles on me. "I knew what was going to happen if I saw—" She abruptly stops, blinking away. "I knew it. I meant it. And I don't regret it."

"You sound like me." I chuckle and adjust the strap of her bag to keep it from sliding off my shoulder.

"That's exactly what I'm trying to prevent."

"What happened there? I'm a monster again?"

"B, you're not a good person," she deadpans. "You're an asshole, especially to Shifter, and you're a—" Cherry looks around at the cameras as the elevator jerks to a stop. "You're good to me, and I love you. I love who you are with me. Only me. Can we leave it at that?" She sighs. Then, a soft smile tugs at her lips. "I'm tired."

I grasp her upper arm, stopping her as she steps out of the door. "You can tell me anything. Whatever you need...or want, I'll make it happen. Tell me about your demons all night, if you want."

"If I want something, you'll know, Bennett." She pulls away, walking off in a random direction.

"It's room twenty-three." She looks around and continues leading.

Watching her walk away is terrifying. I can't let anything get between us. I won't lose her.

CHERRY, PLUS TWO

I want solutions.

I want answers.

I want something to occupy my mind aside from selling me insanity.

As I paging through social media, I roll from my stomach to my side, propping my elbow against the mattress. I stop on a tabloid boasting the inside scoop on Maggie Moronay's wedding with a photo of her lacey gown. I can't imagine they have the real details of the crossover country star's nuptials. A few quotes from guests seeking their five minutes of fame and easy-to-snap photographs from hungry paparazzi.

I blink away from the celebrity gossip when someone raps on the door. My heart sinks briefly before I stand up, leaving my phone on the end of the bed. As I slowly flip over the top lock and then the one on the knob, I pull the door open. Shifter looks over the top of his glasses with a big cheesy grin, soothing all my worries.

"Can I come in?"

"Did you forget this is also Bennett's room?"

"I didn't. Can I come in?"

They've been fighting to be the *alpha or something* all day.

"Uh, yeah," I nod and step to the side. He walks in and stops at the end of the king-sized bed with his back to me.

"Wes is already snoring."

I relock the metal clip along the top of the door and spin around. His eyes scan over my body and stop at my chest, twice. As I cross my arms, it dawns on me that my nipples are noticeably hard in my ribbed tank top.

"Where's Bennett?"

Oh look, he found my eyes.

"He's in the shower."

I thought I could get a minute to myself to decompress. I thought wrong. Shifter will always hold a dear place in my heart, but I've made peace in my lonesome these past few years. It's the quiet I need at the end of the day.

Shifter's here for a reason. I couldn't push him away when he needs me. Plus, it's almost midnight. He wouldn't have shown up—hoping I was alone—to hang out after a long day of driving.

It's bizarre how nothing can drain you in a similar sense as eight hours of hustling like being in a car, stuck in the same position for hours upon hours can. If we can spare the small talk and skip right to what's on his mind, I'd be exceptionally grateful.

"What aren't you telling me, Shifter?" I walk past him to the right side of the bed and sit down, slouching forward and crossing my legs. "What's the thing that's bothering you?"

"You know me too well, sweets." I close my eyes, waiting for him to complain about Bennett. The bed sinks, bouncing me around in the slightest while he makes himself comfortable next to me.

"What is up with you and B?" I ask.

Bennett and Shifter got along fine a few days ago—or was I imagining it? Did I miss the steam rising before the water began to boil? It's complicated to be present when you're brain keeps wandering off, sometimes in the past and sometimes the future.

"I'm not here about him. The raid...I knew it was coming because I've been tracking them."

"Them?" I finch. "Who are they?" I close my eyes for the second time, bracing myself as I draw my brows inward and try to comprehend his words.

Since when does he shy away from anything? A heavy sigh exits my lungs. Expecting everything to be the way it was almost four years ago…I should know better. I was dead to him and he was gone to me. We are not the same people.

I do this thing where I bury any fragments of torture, instantly—to the point where I don't process them. I accept what's in front of me without questioning it. I pretend until I can't pretend and then I purge. We are not the same people and I can't pretend this time.

"I'm sorry I didn't tell you sooner."

"No." I shake my head. "You don't owe me an explanation."

"I wanted to tell you."

"I have to earn your trust again."

"You don't. It's me, sweet."

"It's both of us. Please—I'm listening."

He leaves my face, a daze taking his hopeless expression. "His name is Ronald Hyderton. He owns the lab and had a stake in the experiment." I don't blink, letting my vision blur as I stare deeply into the ugly white comforter. "He's had a team in place for months keeping tabs on us. I can guarantee he saw the two of you going in and not coming back out like all of the other explorers do. He sent in his goon squad to save you, not knowing who you were."

"Does he know who we are now?" I ask without a movement.

"I don't think so. Either he thought you were in danger and wanted to save you, or he was looking for any moment of weakness to take us down. If we're devouring human flesh or torturing them for answers, it's the distraction they've been waiting for."

The abrupt snap of my neck reconnects our eyes and I'm annoyed, to say the least. "He's tracking all six of you? So you're saying he could bust us at any given second?"

"No worries, sweets. I gave them a distraction." He shrugs and rubs his finger along the bottom of his glasses frame, over the darkening bags that hang below his eyes.

"What *kind* of distraction?" I press, stiffening throughout my body.

"One I'm not proud of," he nervously laughs. "I panicked when I was cornered." He plucks his glasses off, dropping them onto the bed. His thumb deepens into his temple while he covers his forehead and eyes with his palm. "Put a rat in a box and he'll chew his way out," he mutters, refusing to lift his hanging head.

"You killed one of them?" I deadpan.

"They're willing to take our lives for a science experiment." He finally lifts his head and puts his marbled glasses back on.

"You put a target on your back."

A smirk rises from his mouth with a quick side-to-side shake of his head. "I put a target on my back the day I signed on the dotted line. You did the same." My jaw tightens. It irritates me that he's right. "Charlie gave them the run around disguised as me. They'll be searching everywhere, giving up the upper hand."

"Charlie? His heart is going to explode with that much pressure on his shoulders." I stare at the ceiling. "While I've been trying to find a way out of this, the rest of you have been hiding."

"What were we supposed to do, Cherry? Jump back into the world like nothing happened." Acid takes his words as he continues. "Yeah, we all had that motivation when we got here," his sarcasm slaps me in the face. "We're a group of misfits, lost in fucking hysteria." This conversation should be more irate and aggressive, yet neither of us lets it escalate. No matter how much I'm appalled that he also has blood on his hands or how many of us are going to snap and take a life before we find a fix, I don't let it take me.

"The worst part is we know these things we do are wrong and there is still a part of us that says *they deserved it*. Are you honestly happy living this way?" A chill raises bumps across my skin as I swing my arms up and drop my palms back to my thighs. Beneath the appearance, I'm warm to the touch. I'm borderline sweating.

"Sweets, I don't want to keep doing this. I'm…it's…I'm glad you came back from the dead. It's just really, really complicated now."

"What can I say? I've always been destined to be an honorary zombie." He has to see my exaggerated eye roll before I flop backward and lace my hands on my stomach as I stare at the boring ceiling.

"Zom-bae."

Whaaat? A smile twists my lips, taking me back to our stupid inside joke.

"Hey, bae. I love your hat, bae. It looks so much better on me, bae," I mock.

Shifter drops to his elbow beside me. I snatch his black beanie off, lean forward to tug it on my head and fall back again.

His vocal pitch raises two notches and I can't handle his valley girl persona. "Bae, you should come hang with me tonight because like I have so much to tell you about you know who." He falls to his back and stares at the ceiling. "She's a little skanky-snack," he whispers.

I giggle uncontrollably and give his arm a good shove. "How pissed would Ronnie get if we did that before we left?" Making fun of Ronnie and her favorite televised show used to be routine.

"She might have torched the place." He steals his hat back. My hair flies outward and I tame it back down while he drags his beanie back over his dark side-swept hair.

"She shouldn't have watched that stupid show every week."

"Tuesdays at nine." His rich eyes light up when he winks. "You don't watch any reality TV these days?"

"I don't watch TV period."

"I don't do much of that either." His exhale is heavier than normal as his face turns stony. "Seriously, sweets…I'm glad you're back. It was…it was—" He clicks his tongue against his hard palate. "Rough, without you."

With a blink, I try to shove my heart wrench into the shadows. "That's why you stayed."

"I guess it's part of it. I had this hope for a while that you would somehow show up, but then I accepted it and I couldn't leave. They held me up when I never let them see how much I was…" The tip of his tongue rolls across his lower lip. "Hurting. Then, they needed me. They just didn't know how much."

I roll to my side and wrap my arms around him, pinning his arms to his body as I pull him tight and hug him. "I missed you too." He loosens, embracing it. I let him go, pushing myself back up to sit. "When did they show up?"

"The rat wranglers?" He asks. "The first time was about a year ago. I caught them on the cameras I set up. I suspect they have been monitoring us long beforehand." He lightly groans, pulling himself up.

"What happened after that night? *The night.*"

"The night Bennett turned the place into a blood bath?" With a brow raise and a heavy exhale, we both picture it.

"Yeah, B did that. That wasn't him. I mean it was…He's not that…" How do I say I'm still trying to accept that he's both the monster that slaughtered sixteen people that I vividly see in red and at the same time he's the man that carried my bag up to our room for no reason other than wanting to carry it for me, the man who covers my tracks, and worships my flaws?

"You know what he's capable of. Why are you so sure he's not going to rampage again?"

"He has a heart that beats under that psychotic flesh. Bennett has spoken of selfless love and heavy pain. When he mentions his sister, his eyes light up and turn dark at the same time. He's complex and damaged and I wanted to kill him. I intended to…" I hide my face in my palms.

"You—You went there to kill the icon?" His mouth rests between shock and unbelievable hysteria. "You never fucking change," he laughs.

"You don't think I'm a monster?"

"Not at all. You'd do anything for someone you care about, but your overwhelming thirst to save him took over. You saw something good and in sweets fashion, you had to doctor it."

"I couldn't unsee the good. I couldn't unsee *him*." Do I look like a sap with a hand over my chest?

"You care that much about him? What does he have that another man doesn't?" I shake my head and practically sit on my fingers. Anything to wipe the love drunk away and sober up.

"Acceptance." I scratch my brow, hesitating. "I've done…some terrible things, Shift. And he doesn't want to fix me. He appreciates that I'm imperfect."

"I accept you and appreciate you. He's not the only person that loves—that cares about you." He swallows.

"I know, Shift." I smile and squeeze his shoulder. "When I lost—*when I thought*—I lost your friendship, it was hard. It was excruciating. You know how I am with touchy feelings. Don't try to pull it out of me."

"I would never."

"So what happened?" I hop an inch closer.

"I wasn't there."

"What?"

"I took off. I couldn't handle it. I had like a panic attack or anxiety attack, that shit, and I split. I walk around the woods, trying to get the sounds out of my head. Once they disappear, I came back. It was an hour or something later and you were gone. Bennett was gone." He rubs his jaw, avoiding my sight. "I saw Ronnie cry for the first time." His spontaneous laughter eases the darkness. "I didn't think it was possible. Dragon lady, rawr." He dips a shoulder to mine. I missed his smile. It fades too fast. "She's human, Cherry. I know you hate her. I would be pissed if she stole my man too and it was shady, shady."

"He wasn't my man," I blurt out. "She's a bad friend. I don't trust her."

"You don't have to trust her. All I'm saying is, she's gone through it too. You know her story."

"She's a bitch." I cross my arms over my chest. "A spoiled rich kid that pissed mommy and daddy off."

"Yeah, yeah, yeah. You're stuck in the rage zone. I judge you not, my sweets." His chest lifts and his sigh bothers me. "She was the first person I saw when I walked down that hallway." He looks at me with those gentle, doe eyes. They're no match for the frigid scowl he's staring down; mine. "Do you remember...how bright it was and somehow ridiculously dark?" Every time I let my mind free. If I don't keep busy, one of my ugly memories creeps back in to haunt me and they only get worse and more consistent lately. I nod but refuse to let the images escape the shadows. "Her back was against the wall, her knees tucked close to her chest, and she held herself tight. Nobody was comforting her."

I drop my arms to my sides and unintentionally lean forward. "I'm not going to feel bad for Ronnie."

"I'm not trying to make you. Let me finish." Flicking my wrist, I palm towards him and relax. "Charlie's hair looked extra greasy. He never could balance his hair products." His smirk tugs upward, fading as fast. "He paced with his jaw on the floor and his fingers pressed to his scalp. I can't forget that." He rubs his jaw. "It's like the fine details of a portrait. Every small stroke makes a difference. Seth was leaning over that tall square table that used to have magazines and books anyone could take to read, smoking weed. He wouldn't make eye contact with anyone. Wes and Slow were arguing about something. They shut up as soon as they saw me." He goes to rub his eye again, but I grab his forearm, stopping him. He takes me in and shakes his head before his fingers hold both sides of the back of my neck. A glossy sheen beats from his gaze as his thumbs stroke the softness above my jaw. "I asked where you were and they just hung their heads."

As I let go of him, I rapidly spin my ring in circles. He uncomfortably drops his hands and looks down. "Anyway, I'm not the most brilliant guy, but anyone can set up cameras—and turn them off." He tucks his chin. "Someone had to be watching. I proposed to not touch a thing, leave for forty-eight hours, and come back. I was sure it would be cleaned up." Tugging at his beanie, he adjusts the sides that didn't need adjusting. "It wasn't. Shit on Shifter. Take six exhausted and overstimulated, impulsive drug-induced rats, and put them inside a box of death stench that they have to clean—and it was *your* idea to leave. Yeah, shit on Shifter season began."

Uncontrollable giggles wrench out of me. "I'm sorry," I apologize, fanning the emptiness in front of me. "Where did Seth get the weed?"

"Oh no, don't ask how much bleach it took or how many hours we spent digging holes in the woods," he spews sarcasm. "Ask for Seth's ganja hookup." His laughter joins mine.

"This conversation could use some."

I smoked it twice in my life and both times it was with Shifter. The anxiety I felt letting go of the slightest amount of control fades quickly in my safe space. I couldn't let a plant or anything else affect my clarity outside of the comfort in the two men who can't stand each other.

"I bet there's a blunt in Wes' duffle." He smirks.

"Wes?" I ask in surprise. "Since when?"

"We've been through it." He shrugs. "Naa. If he does, it's because Seth put it in there. He spends all his time lifting iron. I heard that lights up the feel-good nerves. He's being over the top because he knows Bennett has money and will pay for it, you know?"

"He would be a good trainer. He has a lot of patience."

"It's kinda hard to fill out a job application without an address." He yawns, stretching his arms up.

"Charlie should be a line cook and Seth would do well as a car salesman, and Slow...Slow needs a sugar momma." His laughter compliments mine.

"Did I miss the joke?" Bennett walks out of the bathroom—shirtless, with dark grey sweatpants hanging off his hips. He dries his hair with a towel as he stands in the doorway. The inviting v-contour pulls my attention for the third time in seconds as I glance over the ridges of his taut core.

"We were talking about how Slow needs a sugar momma," I assure him.

"One that likes blond bimbos," Shifter adds.

"What's that smirk?" I playfully backhand him in the abdomen and he cowers over.

"Nothing, blondie," Shifter continues. "They have to be a felon, too," he dramatically drops his chin. "You're a smart blonde. You'd never get caught."

"Yeah, smooth save. Now I won't kick your rear end."

"We can all agree on that," Bennett consents, making his way to my side of the bed. I lean back, resting my head on his legs, and stretch my arms above my head, clasping my hands together. A hushed, but inelegant moan involuntarily barrels out. His thumbs glide over my bare shoulders and I tip my head astern to look up at him.

"Does your back still hurt?" He asks.

"I don't heal as fast as you."

He inspects Shifter. I don't move, continuing to take in the angles of his jaw from below. "What do you know about those bullets?"

"They're designed to stop, not to kill." I can feel his attention moving between me and B. He already caught us mid-action. I can't see how my staring at Bennett with hungry eyes would make him uncomfortable. If anything, it's a sign our conversation is nearing its end. "They want us alive."

"Who are they?"

I stop myself from being swept up in the thought of twisting my tongue around the barbells splitting through Bennett's nipple, listening to Shifter repeat what he told me.

"A team hired by the lab's owner, Ronald Hyderton. He has money beyond means. Owns a few companies that I couldn't find a lot of information on. He's been watching us and studying our moves. It's why I had to quit my job."

"The pottery instructor thing?" Bennett asks.

I interrupt before Shifter replies. "You gave up your dream job to protect them? You're stupid. You're a hero—and stupid."

"You would have done the same thing." He squints at me.

"You're right," I reluctantly admit.

"Okay, dumb and dumber." Bennett's jaw tenses. "How much trouble are the other rats going to be in?"

"Wes has been checking his phone every five minutes since we left. That amount of trouble. I mean, me and Charlie gave them the runaround, but it's only a matter of time."

"Maybe you should have stayed back," I argue.

"They have the camera access and a new protocol. And honestly, sweets, we need control of that lab. There is no point in this plan of yours without it. They can hold it down."

"What's the possibility that the doctor is involved?" Bennett's asking questions we should have had answers to before we started this trip. Shifter should have told us about all of this right away.

"In video games, you always want to understand your opponent. What move are they going to make next? Stay one step ahead and if that doesn't work, shoot like there's no tomorrow."

"Are you saying you know what they're going to do next?" His forehead creases. If it's confusion or disbelief, I don't care, as long as Shifter doesn't drop a second bomb on us.

"I don't think she's going to be a willing participant."

"Good thing I don't care." Bennett heads toward the bathroom, walking through the open threshold as Shifter replies.

"Then, we're on the same page," Shifter mutters.

I grab my phone from the table next to the bed. "Are you driving tomorrow?" I ask.

"Yeah, if you need me to?"

B returns with a dental pick and Shifter's eyes steady on him, waiting for confirmation. He casually nods and tosses the pick into the small plastic trash bin next to the desk.

"You should get some sleep then." I smile. "We don't have time to clean up a mess if you fall asleep at the wheel," I joke.

"Says the girl who—ah never mind."

Shifter can't hurt my feelings. "Say it. The girl who went vigilante this morning."

"Vigilante, darling? You went Mrs. Smith," Bennett says.

Mrs. Larson would be more accurate.

I shake my head until the smile takes my lips, and my giggles break the quiet. It's all for a dark laugh right now. In a few hours, I'll wake in sweat, fighting my racing heart.

Cherry Spiral Incoming

As the heat of two sets of eyes burns a hole in my back, I bury my face in my palms.

"What was it like?" I jerk up, glued to Shifter. "Dying."

"Uh, who are you asking?"

"You."

"Yeah, yeah, uh...I don't really remember anything." He strokes his chin. "Clinically, I was dead for two hours...Yeah, I don't remember anything."

"Was it calm or...peaceful?"

"It was nothing. It was fucking black nothingness, Cherry," Bennett interrupts. "People like us don't move forward to whatever plane you think is out there. We get stuck in the black abyss." His words sting. They're not what I wanted to hear.

I bet he doesn't believe his sister is drifting in the dark. In his heart, he thinks she's somewhere beautiful and free, and he'll never reach her. I don't know if I care if I reach the magical forest or if I'm in the black abyss. If I don't have to keep running from the demons in my head, either one would be better at numbing the pain.

My heart races like I'm running on a hamster wheel as I sit steady. I'm not on the wheel. I'm in the plastic ball, stuck in a corner, and pieces of tape are being slowly and strategically placed on the air slots.

Shifter doesn't want this life either. He wants to be alive again and not a zombie trying to find the next meal, the next step in the maze with no exit. I want that for him. He deserves to be free of this. He deserves an escape.

The pout on his face makes me want to help him in the way I help B. That's an unlikely thought. Not him. He's kind and sweet. I'd be lying if I tried to convince myself that I'm he's unattractive. Am I being selfish? Is it for me or is it for him—the way my body warms and my core tightens? The little flex in my hips tells me he needs me, and I could use him.

Bennett is more than enough. I don't need Shifter. Not for that.

Did he come here hoping for more, believing he'd never get it?

His long eyelashes flicker as his gaze runs down my chest for the millionth time. The gap between my lips closes and parts again before I confront him. "Why did you come here, Shift?"

"Uh—to tell everything I've been keeping."

"What else are you keeping?"

"I don't know what you—"

"Do you want me?"

"What?" He squeaks. His dark brows rise, and he clears his throat.

"We could die and fall into the black abyss tomorrow, right? Like B said. If tonight was your last night, who would you...*do*?" I pronounce clearly.

"Do?" His eyes could stretch to the ends of his frames with how boldly he opens them.

In the time I've known him, I've never once made a pass at him. I put him in the friend zone, and that's where he stayed. That's where he had to stay. I'll never feel romantically inclined to seek deep everlasting love within him—only the depths of a sempiternal friendship. This isn't the life we shared four years ago. Everything has changed. We've always done this little flirty thing for fun. We have no problem walking away from each other like the gravitational pull doesn't exist. It's a myth.

"Look, sweets—"

As I crawl to the end of the bed, I press my hands on his thighs, lean in, and quiet my words. "Would you let me hurt you, Shift?" Nothing can get me off the wheel. I'll drag a spool of thread with me as I run and watch it tangle around me.

"Hurt? What exactly are you into?" His vision travels to my mouth and back, making my heart speed up. It's exciting—the tease, the temptation, and the electric current.

Dancing my fingers back and forth, it's easy to forget. Erasing everything horrible that happened today, like it never existed. It's the same as erasing chalk from the chalkboard—a leftover cloud will always hover. If a wet sponge appears, it'll take ten passes to make sure those chalk lines stay invisible.

"How often do you have blackouts?"

"Too often." His gentle tone softens.

"What if I told you I can control how fast you see those stars? I can do that. I can give you a *mask of peace.*" I cautiously bat my lashes, fishing for a reaction.

"You crack me up, sweets," his laughter is short-lived. He stares at me with a sudden hostility. "Do it," Bennett's demand calls attention to his presence.

Is this what I've secretly wanted? To flirt with Shifter to provoke Bennett? I want to watch his pupils turn stark white and icy. I want to see how far I can push him. It excites me. Somehow, these sick games have replaced any form of thoughtful coping. It's funny, and it's not. I think I lust for the dramatics.

"How well can you follow directions?" His smirk lifts his cheeks, and his gaze drifts to my parted lips.

"You're not serious."

"I am."

"Sweets." He glances at Bennett. "You two are fucking kinky."

"You're jumping to conclusions. Let me show you. Lie down, facing that way." I point to the bottom of the bed. The position makes it easy to keep my eyes on B. If he's going to kill one of us, *uhm, Shifter*, I'd at least like to see it coming.

"Fine."

I pin his arms above his head and smooth my hands down the ridges of his arms, as the folds of his t-shirt pleat. My movements become hesitant, and the warmth of his skin invites me to stay.

With a glance, I eye his tight black jeans that are loosely scrunched above flat-sole shoes. I dip forward to his chest, running my fingertips over the skin peeking from the hem of his shirt.

"Are my hands cold?" I toy with his jeans, tugging at a belt loop.

"They're fine."

I'm not sleeping with him. I had opportunities—late nights falling asleep beside each other. I couldn't cross that line. I never wanted to. We're containing each other's monster. That's it.

My thighs rest along his sides, and my knees dig into the mattress. His breath shallows, and mine mirrors. With the trace of a finger, I draw down his jaw, and with the same ease, I wrap my hand around his throat. Pressing my thumb into the tender ravine below his chin, Bennett's heavy glare rests on me. I tighten my grip, rolling my hips forward with the arch of my back, grinding into Shifter's lower abdomen.

The hostility in B's face from across the room matches mine. And I love it.

I tilt my chin up, refusing to let either of these men go.

It's a high I've thirsted for. The way he watches me move above him has me hungry for his thoughts. Does he want to know if I'm wet? If I'm turned on by the life slipping away below my grip. Each breath exits his lungs with a more shallow one to follow. Will he stop me?

Benny? *It's Benny again, isn't it? Standing there, watching me without the balls to make a move. If I taunted him aloud, he would surely snap.*

I drive both of my hands around Shifter's neck and listen to his lungs lose oxygen.

Come on, B. Stop me.

Shifter's hands grip my thighs. It's the stars—that's what he sees. They blink in the haze as the walls disappear and his body separates from his mind. Everything is stripped away except freedom.

Below the scrunching fabric of my top, his fingers dig into my exposed skin. They start to slide, his conscious state fading quicker than B's does. Bennett fights back harder.

Shifter's hands slip from my body, and I immediately let go of him. As I hold my hand over his chest, the slow, steady rhythm beats against my palm.

He's alive, blacked out.

I climb off of him and slide to the floor. With every intention of setting Bennett off, I walk over to him like I did nothing wrong. The line is thin, but it was nothing more than innocent fun. I didn't kiss him. I didn't feel him up. I didn't sleep with him. It was harmless.

My smirk challenges him, quickly met with a glare from hell-glazed eyes. It only ignites me, dropping my chin lower and pressing my tongue to the corner of my mouth smugly. His sudden movement takes my breath. His fingers press into the hollow space vaguely above my jawbone, pinching my skin, and pulling me an inch from his mouth.

"What the fuck do you think you're doing?"

"I—"

"Don't." He forcefully presses his thumb to my lips. "Don't roll those pretty blue eyes at me." I jerk away, curling my lip. His fingers never leave my skin. "You use me to escape. Not him. You *had* to fucking bring him into this. I—" He shakes his head in disagreement, and my divided smile teeters. That deep, airy chuckle rolls through his throat, taking my half-baked superiority and replacing it with a scowl as he lets me pull away. "What the fuck were you thinking?" He firmly captures me again. His fist tightens around my neck, and I swallow hard against his skin. As I wrap my hands around his arm, I yank until he decides to loosen his hold.

"He needed it."

"Lies."

"He needed me."

"You needed it! You wanted it. You want him."

"No, I don't."

"Don't do this shit. Stop telling me lies."

"Fine! I was thinking about how you wouldn't be enough to stop me from myself, and I was right. You didn't even try."

"Wha—what does that mean?" His eyes narrow, and it only draws me in more. I want him to bend me over and fuck the life out of me. I want him the same way I wanted him when I tied him up in the basement of his house. His venomous chuckle takes the air from my lungs. "Am I not enough?"

"It's not about you."

He releases me, and something changes in his eyes.

"Enlighten me, *Cherry*," he scoffs, throwing his arms open wide. "Because you're talking in tongue and we don't do this. This isn't us. You tell me every-thing that's wrong with me and I tell you the truth."

I take a step back. "You didn't stop me."

"Is that what you wanted? I don't think it was. Nobody can force you to do a damn thing. You're the most stubborn woman I've met, and I've made my way through all types of personalities. You want me to read your fucking mind. That's what you want. Here's my call then, darling. You want him—and you wanted me to watch how much that turned you on, squeezing his windpipe. And yeah, *Cherry*," he overly pronounces. "It turned me on." He towers over me, pressing his chest against mine. "I'm turned on."

Each rise and fall is exhilarating. The simple movement against my body creates a pulse between my legs—a lusty warmth. "It was *fucking* hot watching you. Your hands warmed around him. Your body controlling his. Your eyes on me the whole time." Between the depth of his voice and the certainty of his tone, the tug of my lips falls and reappears over and over while I drift back to his light eyes, trying to hold myself together instead of grabbing hold of him. "You knew what you were doing to me. You want to do it again." The pressure of his fingers hugging my lower back deepens as his lips skim my earlobe, and his whispers make me die for his body. "Like a little slut, begging me to watch. Telling me to wait my turn." He brushes the hair from my face, and I smack his hand away. He's too quick with a counter and holds onto my wrist.

"B—"

"If he ever touches you without my permission, I'll kill him. I'll cut off every single digit, one by one, including his dick, and torture him as he bleeds out. Tell me you understand."

"What if I touch him?"

"I can't stop you. I'd hope you only wanted me and if you feel compelled to be with someone else, give me the respect of the truth."

"I want you to read my mind now."

"You're not selfish, darling. I don't need to take a guess to know that."

We both glance over at Shifter, lying on his side. He slowly looks up at us, and my heart sinks. What was I thinking? Bennett *would* kill him, and it would be worse than what he did to Ames. If I'm not selfish, why did I allow Shifter to be in this situation? There is a part of me that my dear friend doesn't know. I should have kept it that way.

In Bennett, this intense, abnormal earthing to hurt him—to let go—to empty my pain while creating pleasure is accepted.

"She'll be the death of you." He turns to Shifter. "If I were you, I wouldn't cross the road between the friend zone and I've seen you naked." He lets go of me as his deep laugh sends chills up my arms. "My little devious slut," he mutters to himself. "I'm a fool for thinking this wouldn't happen."

CHERRY CHEWS THE BOYS UP

I take a few steps back, and he traipses back. He takes me by the shoulders and spins me until my back is slammed into the wall. The motion happens so quickly I couldn't have foreseen it. I cringe in pain as a sharpness shoots down my side. The damage from *the dart thing* that I was shot with has yet to heal.

"It fucking hurts, doesn't it?" His lips pull wide. "Don't ever tease me with him again."

I laugh through the pain. "Do you think you could stop me?"

His slow smirk pulls upward, and it means trouble. He slams my arms to the wall above my head, and Shifter hops up to the side of the bed.

Don't be a hero.

"No, darling." He sighs. "I don't and I wouldn't try." He chews the skin of his lip, coaxing me to lean forward, reaching to take his lips into mine. One slow, soft, intense kiss shuts him up, and then I let him have it. I bite down on his bottom lip, sinking into the soft tissue until I taste the metallic crimson.

Ah! Asshole!

Shooting pain courses through my back again as he slams me to the wall once more. His chest heaves and his body pours over me. His glare pours down at me, his eyes gleaming with bad intention. *And I smile. An insidious smile.*

"Fucking—"

"Say it, B." I remove the space between us. "*Fucking slut.*" For all that is unholy, say it.

He keeps my arms extended with one hand, while the other trails down to my ribs. His fingers glide down my tank top to the waistband of my shorts and don't stop until he's between my legs. I squeeze my thighs together, but his fingers continue slipping over my wetness.

"You like it when I call you a dirty little slut? Tell me you do."

"I'm a slut for you, B."

"That's right. He couldn't give you what I can. You're mine. I fucking *love* how he's trying to hide those glances over here. He knows you'll always be mine." He drives two fingers into me, scolding me. "Don't!" My inhale halts, and I press to my tiptoes. My body is on fire, heat coursing through every thought. "Don't you dare fucking look at him. Your eyes belong right here. Your pussy belongs right here. You are mine, darling." His foot forces my ankle out, and I fall back to the soles of my feet. He kicks at it again, forcing my legs open.

"Tell me, what do you want? Wait—no." He stops me with that mischievous, breathy laugh. "I'll tell you what I want, for once. Turn around. Keep your arms up." As the noise of shuffling shoes catches me, I attempt to peer over my shoulder.

"You're going anywhere," he orders Shifter.

With blunt force, he changes his mind and drags my hips, turning me around. I want him to take every square inch of my body and destroy me until I can't move.

He yanks my shorts down, and my heart pounds against my chest cavity. With my face pressed to the wall like this, my audience of one watches B's run down the curves of my ass. My thong stays in place as he drops to his knees.

His demanding hands take the smoothness of my thighs, caressing and massaging my skin. The pillowing of his lips nuzzles the inside of my knee, and I hold my breath for a moment before it shakes violently out of me. His teeth sink into my ass cheek, mixing pain and pleasure to the level that makes my body quiver.

I have bruises all over. They temporarily scar me with a reminder of him.

Lost in the feeling, I realize he stood up. His gentle touch startles me. He brushes my hair to one shoulder and kisses the back of my neck. Bennett is destructive to my body while being tender at the same time, knowing exactly when and where he can push me, keep me whole, and only break what needs to be broken. Then he pulls back, delivering a princess treatment that I tell myself I deserve.

"Touch yourself," he whispers.

No. This is my game. I won't do as he says.

"Do it," he orders again. "Or he goes in a body bag."

It takes everything in me to fight off a smile and even more to resist the urge to challenge him. As I pull the fabric to the side, I reach between my legs and slip my fingers over the slick skin. With a slow motion, my middle finger runs over my clit.

"Play with that tight pussy." He drags my hips towards his body, earning the arch in my back as I press my ass into him. "Don't touch your clit." His teeth tug at my ear before he whispers against it. "One finger."

"I hate the tease."

"I know." His hot breath caresses my skin. "Could you handle both of us inside you at the same time?" His lips hum along my ear. "Was that a thought in your head? Have you wondered if we can stretch that pussy out? I bet we could." I drop my head to his shoulder and moan, hating the agony. "That's it, darling."

Oh, God...

He shoves his finger in my mouth, waiting for my lips to wrap around it. Forcing my neck to stretch, he holds my chin. "Look at me." I peer at him from the corner of my eye. "Beg me." With narrowed eyes, I consider my words before I speak. "Cherry, ask me if you can have him too." His lips press heavily to the corner of my mouth as he continues. "Do you want to feel *him* inside you? *Fucking* beg me to allow it." He gently kisses my neck and whispers. "This is how we both win."

"B," I murmur. My direct gaze climbs to his. "Please."

"I said whatever you need, or *want*, I'll make it happen."

"You're serious?" *We shouldn't.*

"You only do what you want—as stubborn as they get." His soft lips deepen into my jaw. "You'll always be mine. Don't forget it."

"Are you—"

"I'll hate his hands on you." The texture of his voice swallows me. "And if you kill him, don't expect me to bring him back."

He pulls my hand from the wall, lacing his fingers between mine. I step around my shorts as he guides me toward the bed.

"Do you want to fuck her?" Bennett tilts his head, unaffected. His hand warms mine, refusing to let go of me. Shifter follows the length of my legs as I subtly gaze at the outline of his noticeably hard package. "It's not a difficult question."

His doe eyes narrow. "It actually is."

"You have two seconds to decide." B's jaw clenches to the point where he could break a tooth. He hates this, and it makes me want him more. The animalistic urge to tackle him to the bed and ravage his body down to every scar, tattoo, and piece of metal he's added.

"I, uh...Are you sure?" Uncertainty could paralyze Shifter.

"It's just sex."

"Yeah...yeah, yeah." He brushes me off.

I'm going to break him. He's going to wish he never came to my room tonight.

"If you can handle it." A teasing grin tugs at my mouth.

"I'm in."

With his confirmation, I suck Bennett's lower lip into my mouth, kissing him with a starving passion that makes my thighs wet. He lets go of me, and I step between Shifter's legs. He doesn't shy away as I near him. His hands trail down my ribs, hold briefly on my hips, and then abruptly squeeze my ass, lifting me to his chest. As he walks to the side of the bed, his gentle eyes relish my body and avoid my face. He tosses me onto the bed and tugs his shirt over his head.

He stands between my legs while B remains stiff at the end of the bed. This is my story. I'm in control. Everyone does what I say. *They worship me.*

With profound confidence, I reach for Bennett's hand, drawing him closer. He leans inward, pinching my mouth between his fingers. "You know I love you, right?"

"I know." I nod.

"Good, because those pretty eyes won't get you out of this one. I hope it's what you wanted." His hand falls to my neck.

"Kiss me."

His deep suctions and flicks of his tongue remain after he pulls away as I take in Shifter's naked body. He wasted little time, removing his sneakers, socks, and jeans. He handcuffs my ankle, sliding his long, artistic fingers over my skin. With the opposite hand, he strokes down the curve of his dick.

It's bigger than I expected, not that I thought too deeply about the structure in his pants. I hadn't considered a comparison either. B has these two veins that pop out along the top of his shaft. Shifter has this deep depression on the underside that I can't take my focus off. Each pump of his hand slowly slips down his length and back up, rolling his thumb over his reddening head.

I fidget with the strap of my top, calculating my next call. The ache between my legs stutters to my stomach. I can do whatever I want. I can make them suffer, push their bodies to the limit, and mine. I squeeze my knees together, gripping my muscles tight as the blood rushes to my horny core.

Shifter takes my other ankle, letting his dick jut out from his hand. He pulls me closer before placing his palm to my stomach. His fingers wrap my ribs and flip me until I'm face down. I profusely giggle, amused.

"Hey, B," I taunt, tipping my head back. He glares down at me, standing above my head, across from Shifter with his cock in his hand.

"Sweets," Shifter calls, pulling my attention back to him.

His doe eyes became faded. They've ice over as cold and white as Bennett's. On a throne of pillows, two breathing, living dead zombies hold my body as if I'm what they've been starving. "Don't think I'm going to take it easy."

He grabs my hips, jerking me up to my hands and knees.

"Oh *fuck*," he moans with an amused laugh. "You're going to kill me."

"Tomorrow isn't promised." *And I'm okay with that.*

"We give a new meaning to that phrase." His brows jump. A smirk tugs at his lips igniting a feral urge within me. "Hold these." He tucks his glasses on top of my head.

I reach up, securing them behind my ears like a pair of sunglasses. Nothing matters to me when I'm in this place—lust intoxication and blurry from the real world. Nothing. *I don't care.* He's a warm body.

Shifter kneels, looping his arms underneath my legs and hoisting my thighs to his biceps. I jerk as the flat of his tongue takes my clit, conveying more giggles I can't hold back.

"Oh, my god," I moan.

Realizing the words that escaped my mouth, I glance up at Bennett. He takes my jaw between his fingers.

"Right here, darling."

I stare down his erection. My jaw hangs, and the curvature of my back deepens until my forearms are against the mattress, forcing Shifter to work harder between my legs. Moans slip away from me again, this time without any coherent words. As Shifter pulls away, a chill meets my wet skin with the involuntary widening of my knees.

"Hey," I groan, wanting him to return to his position.

"Easy, sweets." He pays no attention to B and yanks me until my toes touch the floor. The tip of his cock presses against my clit. He rubs it up and down my slit, coating it with my wetness and what remains of his saliva.

A panic flushes over me. I search for Bennett, certain he can see the worry in my eyes and the pouting of my lip. As I abruptly sit up, I plant my hands into Shifter's solid chest, shoving him back.

"White irises don't make you superior. Neither of you."

"Easy, sweets. You know, I kinda like this side of you, but you haven't met the other side of me yet. I'm just as scary as your boyfriend." As his hand takes my throat, I inhale through my nose. "Did you like the way I spread that pussy with my tongue, sweets? Am I being a good boy?" The heat from his mouth coats my lips. "I knew you would taste *fucking* sweet." He shoves me back by the neck. I jolt backward into B, rubbing the indents below my jaw. "Yeah, yeah, yeah." He quietly laughs. "You'll be my death, but I won't be unworthy." As I glance up at him, the change is obvious. He's not the same guy I had a clothed conversation with. A dark smirk sticks to his face; ravenous eyes stalk me beneath heavy brows and a slouchy beanie.

"Oh, darling." Bennett's laugh vibrates against my back. "You want the monsters, you win." The mattress sinks under the weight of his knee. His sparse, dark-haired thighs brush my arms as I lean back. His hand wraps around my throat, and he chuckles again. The side of his finger dredges beneath my chin, tilting me back. "You got what you wanted like you always do." He slaps his dick off my cheek twice. "Darling, I know you're thinking about it. Don't fucking bite me."

"Slap me in the face again and I'll tear that barbell clean out; coat my face in blood for the second time this week."

His tongue plays at his lip as his dark glare holds me. Saliva pools in my mouth as I wrap my lips around the width of B's length, gripping the base, and easing him in from this position. In suffocation under his weight, his thighs line my face, sliding in and out of my mouth as I fight the urge to gag. He pulls back, continuing to stroke his length.

"You don't mind the metal in your throat?" Shifter asks.

"Eh uh." I lick my lower lip, tugging at the supple skin with my teeth. "Does it intimidate you?"

Bennett twists at the wrist every time his fist nears the tip of his dick, continuing to stroke over his piercing.

"No."

"B—come here, lie down," I order. As I roll onto my knees, I crawl to the center of the bed. "You too, pet. Lie down on this side." I point.

With a quick movement, I kick my feet to the side, slip off my panties, and toss them to the floor. Cunning laughter shakes through my throat.

"What's so funny?" Shifter asks.

As Bennett tucks his hands behind his head, my sight travels across the inked lines banded around his lean muscles and cording veins in his hands. "It's not her laugh, you should worry about." His focus never wavers from my body. "Show him how fucking lucky he is to be alive, darling."

"I know how lucky I am."

"I wasn't talking to you." Bennett's core tightens. "Tell him, darling."

"The first time I slept with Bennett, I tied him to a chair, I threw a vase at his head, I sliced him with a knife, and we ended up naked in the woods. He put in a lot of effort, and nobody could measure up to him. I wouldn't choose to go back to mediocre hook-ups."

"I promise, you won't be left unsatisfied."

As I stand up, I hold my arms out like I'm walking on a balance beam. I step over him and lower to my knees. Straddling his thighs, I trace my thumb over the notch on the side of the protruding vein, handling his cock for the first time.

"You take my breath away," Shifter's voice trails.

"You're funny," I laugh because it's the accurate truth.

I brace against his thighs, dip forward, and sink my teeth into his bicep.

"Fuck!" He flinches, pulling his arm higher above his head.

"Taking your breath away would be far too kind now." I lick the blood dotting his arm. "Do you see the bruise on Bennett's ribs? You understand how quickly he heals. *You're not like him.*"

"I can be."

"No...you can't." The tip of my tongue trails down the center of his toned abdomen. I stop at the base of his dick and look up at him. "But it's okay. We can still have fun." I hold his trusting eyes, taking the flat of my tongue in one slow sweep over his shaft. "I need you to do something for me." I crawl up his body, find his lips, and inch my mouth directly above his. Reaching the delicate skin, I trace the outline of his lower lip with the rounded tip of my finger. The heat of his breath mixes with mine as I stem my elongated nail over his gentle flesh.

"Anything, sweets."

I dip lower, a hairs-length keeping my lips off of his. "Stretch me," I whisper. His tongue darts into my mouth, claiming my lips with a savage kiss. I pull away, replacing his lips with Bennett's.

"You heard her," he hums and his Adam's apple turfs out. "Better listen before she whips out a fucking knife. My money's on it being under the pillow."

"Wait, how many times have you pulled a knife on him?"

"More than once." I tilt my head back, forgetting where Shifter's glasses are. I lift my shirt over my head, and they fall off beside me. As I pick them up, I unfold the side that turned in and slide them on his face. "You're clean right?" I don't know how I looked at him a million times and never wanted to fuck him. Now he's naked between my thighs with that black beanie and those sexy, big round glasses, looking like he needs to be corrupted, but we both know none of us are innocent.

He nods, and I trust him as much as Bennett. It seems like a foolish question for one of us. I can pretend a lot of things—that I'm invincible isn't one of them. It's equivalent to B with his natural peanut butter. He ate as if his life depended on it and smoked like his existence was sempiternal.

"I could slit your throat if you'd like to go quicker." B's crooked grin doesn't concern me. That would never happen, but it's too late. The scowl on Shifter's face says it all.

"Shut up, B."

"Fuck you, darling."

"Fuck you."

"Fuck!" Shifter moans out as I rub the head of his dick through my wet pussy lips and slide down on him. Rolling my hips, I rotate to take him deeper. My hands bulldoze into his chest, clawing his fair skin with pale marks that instantly turn red. He lifts my ass, dragging it back down. The second time he tries it, I don't let him, falling forward and pressing my wet pussy onto his abdomen.

"Enough," B calls out. He clasps his hand around my forearm and pulls me on top of him. "You still want me to stop you from yourself?" He shoves me back, latching his finger behind my knees. As he pulls me forward again, I take the base of his dick, and no sooner lining it up, he drives into me.

I shriek, gasping as the pain of hand-to-ass contact echoes off the walls. The sound bothered me more than anything. He does it several more times, reddening the skin, and I've become detached from the repetitive action; it no longer fazes me. How many times has he hit me? How many times has his palm scorned my skin? His thrusts are rapid, one after another, sliding in and out of me with such force. With each lift of his hips, his thighs meet mine, his pelvis rubs my clit, and he gets lost in the motion.

He takes his thrust deep, holding it. I moan and twist, squeezing my walls around him. His hips relax on the bed, giving me enough time to welcome back reality. I stop tugging at my lip and smile nefariously at Shifter.

Bennett's fingertips press between my breasts, shoving me backward. I catch myself with my hands, gripping the bed sheet, safely straddling his thighs as his cock soaks inside of me.

"The sacrifices I make for you, Cherry bomb."

I crawl up his body as fast as I can and reach beneath the pillow beneath his head. He grabs my wrist, and I fall to my elbow with my chest meeting his. I couldn't imagine more than four of his seven inches fill me while hovering over his mouth. As I pull my hand up, his hold breaks, and I press the side of the knife, swinging it open. Without hesitation, I hold the blade to his jugular. Shifter jerks. B deeply chuckles, letting it cut him as he inhales.

"You need to find more clever hiding spots, darling." He lifts my hips, pulls out, and pushes me off of him. He rises, and I take his hand, pressing my lips to his palm. "I know how much you love twisting your tongue around my dick, flicking my barbell around. So, why don't you do that while he fucks your cunt." For the first time, his eyes slowly draw upward, off of me, and onto Shifter. I dive forward and press the tip of my blade under his jaw. As I gain control, he freezes and holds his breath.

"Still want to play?" I taunt.

"I never run."

I snap my knife closed, sitting back. B cups my jaw, kneeling on the bed above my head, and fills my mouth. His stainless apparatus taps my soft palate every time he slides away. I quickly roll to my side and let my lower backrest on the mattress.

Shifter widens his knees below my bent legs, smacking his shaft off the inside of my thigh once, twice, then a third time, as if I need a warning. I attempt to glance up at him, but I don't move too far with B's fingers threaded into my hair, and duress my attention.

Shifter watches B fuck my mouth, stroking his—*oh*...his fingers take me. One, then two, then three...four. *Four*.

I let my knife fall free from my fist, pushing it out of the way. He delivers, spreads me open, and unknowingly gets me ready for both him and Bennett. I want both of them. I don't care if it has an unfortunate ending, it's all I can think about now. One at each end of my body isn't going to cut it. I want the kind of pain I can only foresee taking me once.

"Are you always this wet?" Shifter mutters. "Fuck, don't answer that." His doubt messes with his head. He thinks this is wrong—we shouldn't be doing this. It's going to ruin our friendship. It could if we let it. We won't. *We won't.* It's just sex. Incredibly hot, fucked-up sex.

My brain is as flooded as my pussy, and the squealing noises I hum over B's dick are luckily muffled. It excites him, and he gives me more. The farther back he enters, the more I gag. I push to my elbows, and his fingers take my chest, another blow exerting me back to the mattress.

"I fucking hate you right now."

He pulls out long enough for me to spit a few words. "Fuck me like it then!"

Shifter takes my hips, wraps my thighs around him, and widens his legs to match. He presses into his knees and drives into me. With a gag, B's return cuts my moan short. The thrusts keep coming. Pressure upon pressure layers in my core turned on their attack on my body more than anything.

"You're easy to forgive." Bennett's hand locks around my neck.

The tension isn't what I'd expect from him. It's...gentle. His hand slides over my chest, toiling my nipple between two knuckles. Another rush of desire crashes over me, sending waves of an uneven tide in my stomach. I clench hard around Shifter's dick, close to reaching ecstasy. It's bliss teetering at the edge of intense satisfaction.

Shifter's balls slap against my skin and Bennett's tip grazes the top of my throat. His body stiffly jerks as his fingers tug on my hair. His hand tightens around my neck, and a warmth coats my throat. I choke it down, drowning in arousal and adrenaline. His cock paints my lips with a salty coating, and he exhales a heavy breath, narrowing in on me. The restrained scowl eases with the abrupt grab of my shoulders that hoists me up. The motion drives Shifter's actions. He pulls out, curiously locked on B.

"Lie down," I order Shifter. His dick glistens with pre-cum balling at the tip of his shaft. As I straddle him, I lick the bitter, salty bead, tracing my tongue over the center of his head.

"If you make it to hell before me, send a postcard so I'm not walking in blind," Bennett says with a smirk.

He pulls away, and I scold him. "Mine." With both hands, I coil his wrist.

He wanders my naked body, settling on my lips as his mouth curves upward. "Can we fit two in there, Shift?"

"I'm willing to try anything once," he replies.

I shake my head, giggling almost as sardonic as Bennett. As I reach out, I slap Shifter across the face. Stunned, something amused exists in his white eyes. He comes alive, and he smacks my thighs. It prompts me to steal his oxygen away, choking the air from him as quickly as I can. My mouth curls into a smile that burns my cheeks. As he begins to fall backward, his eyes roll, and I let go, cutting my fun short before he passes out. He struggles, gasping for air, and coughs in starvation.

"Come on, lightweight. Come back to me." Satisfied with myself, I smirk before I turn, swinging my leg over him, and reverse straddle his chest. I lean forward, lick him once more, and his fingers pace between my legs. One, then two, then three. In and out. The dousing sounds that come with it have both of them humming along to my moans.

B presses his pointer finger and thumb under my jaw until my eyes steady on his. "Take him first. It'll be easier." The ice covering his eyes doesn't erase the neediness. He wants me to confirm. He needs to know I heard him, I see him, and I want him.

"Okay," I murmur, soaking in his dauntless face. "He's first."

I clasp around Shifter's wrist, replacing his fingers with his cock as I slide him back in.

"Are you dripping?" Bennett closes any distance between us, straddling Shifter's thighs. His lips take my chest bone and his hardened package presses to my pelvis. "Your heart's racing."

"It's because I need you, B. You can't come this close and expect anything else."

"You know you're making a mistake."

"My life was built on disaster and destruction. If this is a nightmare, at least it's by my own doing."

I have two men worshipping my body. They allow me to use them as my outlet, and this is the type of controlled pain I crave. I built the walls I survive in.

Bennett sucks my hardened pink nipple into his mouth, pulling it to a point. He lifts, and I gaze down his body. His thick fingers pump his broad length. Will Shifter feel his barbell? It's one hell of a turn-on, these two intimately touching to give me what I want. For all that is unholy, broken, and lost, we will transcend this realm and discover euphoria.

Shifter slows his pumps, lifting my ass from the bed. "I'll stretch, you slide," he exhales. B runs his tip over my clit, putting tender pressure in one direction as tension increases at the lower end of my opening. I suck a breath in through my nose and hold it with the burn.

"Hey." I find B's eyes. "Exhale." Warm air blows from his lips, heating my skin. "If I could slam it into you, I would." My shoulders fall farther back with the sound of his voice. "That would be your last exhale." He pushes in farther, and I breathe out. "It doesn't work like you think it should." Shifter doesn't move, letting B take control. "There's a balance to keeping the two of us in a tight place." With a scrunch of my nose, I remind myself to exhale. "You okay?" He mutters against my ear. I nod, and he inches deeper, stroking half his length inside me against the man he'd rather kill than touch cocks.

The positive pain eases up until one of them slips out and my muscles contract. The shock sends a different type of adrenaline over me, one that taps into anger. My wetness lathers both of them with each pump, making it easier on all of us to move simultaneously. Their bodies trap mine, destroying me with heat and lust.

My knees fall as wide as they can, and B reaches back, squeezes my ankles between his hands, and tests my flexibility, lifting forward and using my legs as a crutch. Shifter braces his weight against my thighs, wrapping his fingers around them. They both rail me with more force and as deep as they can manage without losing connection.

"Keep going," I pant.

A hand takes my breast, toying at my nipple. It's overwhelming and intoxi-cating, boiling heat through my core as it turns my breath shallow and my heart expedites. I incoherently ramble through moans and whimpers, losing track of bodies.

I twist at the waist, smacking my hands to the bedsheets and ripping at the fabric until my fists are full. The sensation rips through me over and over and over, crashing through my entire body, dividing me into an exhausted and limp, breathless being held up by the two men who refuse to stop.

B lets my legs fall and reaches for my jaw. As he slowly pulls out, he clenches my throat in his hand. My hard swallow is painful against the pressure, yet it's barely noticeable above my overwhelmed senses.

Shifter thrust slowly once more, holding deep pulses against my g-spot. Ben-nett's gentle lips embrace my face, kissing below my ear. "I hope you're fucking happy," he whispers in my ear. His hand stays in place and his lips linger, tethered to me as Shifter's hand squeezes my breast and his slow thrusts become irate. The groans of my good friend pushing his cum into my g-spot build me to the edge of orgasm, falling flat as Bennett's lips leave my jaw and his hand disappears.

Shifter quickly stands up, and I fall to my side, lying drained on the bed in my spent skin, exposed and vulnerable for the first time. I close my eyes, trying my best to stay in the moment, but it's too late. It's over. The world has returned to its miserable fight.

B grabs his shorts from the floor, tucking his erect dick in as he pulls them on. As I glance at Shifter, he's milking any remaining cum from his dick on the blanket. Housekeeping will be ecstatic to find the comforter tossed to the corner of the room.

"We're not using this blanket tonight," I mumble. He smirks, buttoning his jeans.

"You can have mine."

"I have plenty of sheets and body heat."

I should get up, but I don't. I fold myself on my side, watching Shifter pull his t-shirt over his chest. He adjusts his glasses and tugs at his beanie along his ears. I can't believe he wore that the entire time.

The unlatching of the door's lock draws my sight to B, standing with his hand on the knob. "Let's go." He waves his hand in the direction he wants Shifter to walk. "You're driving tomorrow. Get to sleep."

Shifter's doey eyes cling to my face. "So, we're—"

"Good. We're good," I answer. "Right?"

"Yeah, yeah, yeah," he nods endlessly, rubbing his nose. "Sleep tight, sweets." He turns and walks toward the door without a glance in Bennett's direction as he turns down the hallway.

Before I can blink twice, the door is latched, and B is standing between my legs without giving me a chance to run to the bathroom. He's quick, grabbing my knees and ripping them apart. My heart jumps as he looks from my swollen pussy up to my eyes and back again with heavy brows. I close my gaped lips, swallowing. I knew that was too easy.

He taps my inner thigh twice with the back of two fingers, oddly similar to Shifter's warning. Unlike Shifter, though, B makes me jerk and squirm, especially as he dips them inside me. Removing them, he brings his fingers to my mouth.

"Taste your victory." He shoves his fingers into my throat angrily. "Tell me, how is he?" I sink my lips around him and suck them clean, tugging away.

"He'll never taste as good as you. Is that what you want to hear, B?" Gripping onto his arm, I pull myself up to him, nibbling at his lip. "Nobody will ever taste like you and that's the truth."

He snatches me by the jaw, jerking me away. A deep sigh mixed with a growl-like groan floods warmth against my cheek.

"I want every trace of him gone." He walks around me to the clean side of the bed, lying back on the bed, and propping three pillows behind his back.

"I can do that." I straddle him, lick my fingers, and touch my pussy, separating it for him to see. He dips forward, sucking my nipple between his teeth as he tugs back.

"You want more?" I continue rubbing in circles. My pussy has a heartbeat at this point. "Wash him the fuck away and I'll let you touch your clit." I clean my fingers in my mouth and circle over my worn pussy once more. The swell against my fingers only reassures the tender strain. His pupils haven't returned to blue yet. "That was a one-time ordeal, Cherry."

"I'm happy with only you." I inch closer on my knees. "Just you...and maybe a toy...some other night."

He shakes his head. "You are going to be sore as fuck tomorrow."

"I'm okay," I insist, widening my eyes, despite already feeling the consequences of my choices. "I'm not done. You didn't finish."

He yanks at the waistband of his shorts. "Get off me or pull these down." He toys at his waistband.

"Asshole," I sneer and slide down his legs, dragging his shorts with me, and toss them to the floor. His strong hands take the lowest part of my hips, pulling me over his lap. I slide over his length, shaking as I take him down.

Mm, shit, shit, shit. Screw the pain. Screw tomorrow. Tonight is all that matters. I don't see my demons or a monster in the mirror. I see Bennett and paradise.

"When we get out of this, I'm finding that toy of yours and shoving it right up there with my cock, way harder than Shifter could ever fuck you."

"You plan on doing a lot with me when we get out of this, it seems. What if we don't make it out? Live for the now."

"Live in the now and plan for the next." He sucks my lip into his mouth. Letting it go, he replaces it with a soft kiss. "If loving you is suicide, cut my wrists and watch me die." His thumb traces my lip. "I thought you were going to be a lot more brutal to him, you know?"

"Wishful thinking." I sigh. "I wanted to be." I draw my chin to the ceiling. "B..." The serenity overtakes my voice.

"Yeah?"

"This is a serious question. Okay?"

"Okay. Ask it and maybe I'll have a serious answer," he so smugly replies.

"I get the tattoos, but what made you get the piercings?" He flexes, and I lift forward, slowly sitting back down.

"I fucked a piercer who talked me into it."

Ah, what?

I tuck my chin, and my heavy bloodshot eyes dig into him.

"I'm joking, darling." He squeezes my waist, his dick still soaking inside me. "I can be a funny guy…That's what you like in Shifter, huh?" His brows rise. "I liked the way they looked. I didn't wake up from being dead and run to Hollywood, darling. It was rough. The lights were on, but I was inside avoiding the windows. It's uh, kinda a blur. My guess would be around a month—it was around a month where…I was just pissing my life away. I had most of my sleeve done in that time. I got the piercings. I drank and smoked and…"

"Fucked hoes," I answer for him.

"Hah, no. Licorice trauma? There is a healing process nobody talks about. It wasn't all bad. I wasn't going out drinking every night, and I started to write my dreams down again. That's when I found out how well Red Tape was doing. It feels like that was yesterday."

"So, what you're saying is, your dick jewelry saved your life," I nod in amusement.

"No, you saved my life." *Please.*

"But I'm suicide, *meh meh*," I mock.

"It's possible to be both. My savior and my suicide." He takes in the sight of my naked breasts, dropping his gaze lower before returning to my lips. "It's possible to be both."

Bennett Is Your Alpha & Omega

Why did you do it, Bennett? "It's not about you." It clicked the second she uttered those words. It wasn't about me. It was about her desires. That's why I told her it was fine fucking dandy to wrap her fingers and pussy around someone—Shifter.

Have you not learned anything by now? A desire to be a normal person may ache in the back of your head for a while. Eventually, you move on or, put simply—become bitter. We don't move on. We relish and thirst and starve. We become obsessed. It wasn't him—Shifter—either. It was the idea of two men she trusted to be herself with. In my mind, that's how I saw it. It's the only reason I let him touch her. I doubt he'll be quick to return for seconds. He heard her.

Can I swap all "Shifter" names to "Shitter" or would that get flagged in editing? Someone would have words, but in my opinion, it's an upgrade. Shhh—Shwifter? Shwiggler?

Dennis "Shutter" Monnie.

"You can touch him, but if I touch anyone, *she dies.*" My airy chuckle covers my frustration. "I see what you did. I went with it. That's on me, but you can fucking stop acting. *Fucking stop.*" I throw my duffle on the bed and unzip it.

Welcome back. I've started an argument. Why, Bennett? Last night was last night. It's over. It's morning and she's sore, tired, and bitchy. That should set the tone. Think hangry, except you stubbed your toe. We both know there's more than sexual obsession that pushed her to fuck her longtime bestie, and I want her to talk to me about it. With Cherry, the worst thing I could do is pity her. She'd rather I laugh. It's difficult to do that when she won't let me in.

"I'm not," she proceeds to argue. Cherry walks out of the bathroom, standing behind me.

"That's a lie." I find a pair of jeans and slouch against the bed, tugging them over my ankles and up my legs.

"Fuck you, Bennett."

See, hangry with a banged-up toe. Now that I think about it, she's been doing a lot of that lately. The swearing. What happened to the good girl? Wait, I know. I happened to her. I pushed her over the edge, and she shoved back. I take it as a compliment. Nobody sees this side of her except me. I'm the only one who knows that she's drowning.

That's a tad egocentric? I call bullshit. It's a like-minded connection that magnetically glues us hand in hand. I'm her judgment-free zone, and she's my secret harborer.

"Fuck you," she repeats.

Not bothering to fasten my button, I rush her. "Fuck me?" I hold her to the wall by her neck. "Fuck you. *Stop*, darling. Stop fucking smiling," I groan.

"I'm not—"

"Try harder."

"It meant nothing. Why are you being—"

"No, fuck! You're using."

Shit. Wrong word. That's not going to get me any closer to the truth. Why is she lying?

Her eyes are massive. "Excuse you. *Using.*"

"You *use* me to feel better, to expel the pain you can't hide from. We have our mutual understanding and discussions. That's not what I'm talking about. You use me like you've used other men—for sex. It's your choice of relief. I know it is because it's mine—kinky sex. It's not a pill or potion. It doesn't have to be.

It's just as addicting and alleviating. You know it, I know it, and for fuck's sake, Shifter knew it. Is it the asshole who—the asshole from the apartment?" With my thumb, I trace her jaw. "Why won't you tell me what's going on?"

You want to know what happened since last night, right? I let it go then. Am I obsessing now? Has B gone full-on psychotic again? Don't call me B—besides the difference between night and day, we did the cuddle thing. We slept next to each other. I refused to spoon a woman until Cherry. Spooning leads to catching feelings.

And yes, darling, that's what it did. I got in my feels and tried to be the good guy. I asked her if she wanted to talk about it—yesterday morning, not the threesome. I'll point out, my dick was bigger. It blew up in my face. She's impossible. She refused to open up to me.

She's a loose cannon for a reason. Walking around only knowing what torture is, always having to watch her back, and being afraid to lose everything good because it happens over and over. And you want to know what scares me the most? It's not that she could snap and go on a murder spree. It's not that she could expose us to the world. It's if she's not telling me about the demons dancing in the streets of her think space, then she doesn't trust me. If she doesn't trust me, when will she question her love for me?

She has let me in just far enough that I can see the concrete damage, but not enough to heal with her. I want to be her safety, just as she is my home.

Pop quiz. Who was I in high school? Do you remember? I was the fucking weirdo, the outcast, the quiet guy. Now, Cherry, she's the popular girl. I longed for her in my teenage years, drooling as I scrolled her MySpace page. I don't care who she was back then. In my mind, she was a cheerleader and was friends with everyone. She's the schoolgirl. Yeah, here I go. I'm back on my Benny bullshit. Hah. *Last night I felt like him. The popular girl fools the weird kid. If I told her, she would have given me some line about how she's seen every stupid daytime movie and she doesn't fit the criteria. The popular bitch in the movies always had her secrets, granted they were usually more superficial.*

Was I wrong to let her bring him into our bed? Was the obsession an excuse to mask my foolish decision? What was I fucking thinking? She wasn't in the right mind, and she wanted someone to tell her. She needed me to tell her "no". Instead, I challenged her. It was fucking hot seeing her unravel beneath both of us. I wanted to watch her in control. I could tell her all day long the rules of dating Bennett Larson, but Cherry would protest until her dying breath.

Am I convincing myself I'm not in the wrong or the reader?

Fuck. I'm taking this story back. It's about me, not her. Why are you on her side? I'm the walking dead guy and I'll remind you ten more times if I have to.

"You're being ridiculous." She finds the full-length mirror next to the desk, behind the trash bin, and clips her hair back on one side, sticking the needle-like pins in a slanted row to hold it in place.

"Come again." What the fuck?

I'm willing to gamble on everything for this woman, and she closes me off.

Fuck Shifter six more times, if it'll give you the will to talk to me. "You wholeheartedly think that a scientist is going to fix you or save you or fucking help you cope. It's a damn lie, Cherry. If you dig the hole ten feet deep and bury the truth, it will find a way to crawl out from every layer of dirt. You're fighting human demons, not ones of monsters." Buttoning my jeans, I grab my shirt from the bed and walk back into the bathroom to brush my teeth.

She stares at me blankly, then turns back to the desk, picking up a cotton swab and cleaning her nose ring.

I love her as desperately as I hate her. I want her to have the world. She's going to get the world. This world or another, I won't stop burning bridges until she gets it. That's the difference between who I was and who I am. Benny would leave everything right now. He'd be afraid of failure and denial. So, he'd steer clear of it, opting to surrender before facing disappointment. I refuse. I don't want to be cured if it turns me back into him. It scares me, and not much does.

That part of me will always exist. Each day I spend with Cherry, I begin to realize that he comes out more and more. Empathy, compassion, and consideration. It's a recipe for disaster and disappointment.

"Alright, what's goin' on?" Wes spits his gum out the window and rolls it back up.

It's hard to avoid the cold silence. He twists around, looking to the backseat, between Cherry and me. Shifter is hunched over the steering wheel like a granny, paying little attention to him.

"Nothing. What's going on with you?" Cherry barrels back, rolling her thumb across her ring. She almost forgot it this morning. I found it next to the sink when I went to brush my teeth.

"Ya'll have been quiet all day." He stretches his broad arms over his head. "I know what's goin' on."

He has no idea. He lived with these two for—I don't know how long—and they never hooked up. The last thing he's thinking right now is how Cherry selfishly fucked both of us last night, and nobody wants to talk about it. She said it's just sex. Sure seems like it.

To sum it up, Shifter is burying his head in the sand, upset that my dick is more exciting than his. Cherry used him to cloak her lacerations, and he knows that he was an idiot for accepting the invite when he has romantic feelings for her.

The grandma finally straightens, entering the conversation. "What's that?" He asks.

"Hold on," Wes replies before pulling out his phone. He takes his good old time scrolling or whatever, tapping the volume on the radio.

Tell me he's not going to sing a "pissing in my beer, my girl left me, and I'm drunk in a country bar" song.

He belts out lyrics I've never heard. *Fuck me.*

Cherry joins him. *She knows the words to this?*

"*Noo,*" Shifter groans, and for once, I agree with him.

"You just need a little Alan Jackson." Whiskey hoots a *yeehaw.*

Is my jaw on the floor? It's on the fucking floor, and my eyes are protruding to their limit, but there she is—blue eyes full of joy, wiggling in her seat, and singing along.

She dips forward, meeting Whiskey Boy between the front seats, and they sing in unison. *Fucking goobers.*

"Dance with me, B."

Not happening.

"I'm not dancing to this."

She wrinkles her cute nose. "Party pooper."

Don't pout.

"Wes has you," Shifter calls out as the third wheel popping his two cents into play.

"He's the only one in this vehicle that hasn't had you," I mutter under my breath.

Say it! Bennett, you asshole.

Cherry stops dancing as Hell crosses her eyes and they roll upward. The corner of my mouth plucks into a smirk.

Can you feel the warmth in my smile, darling? Hah.

"Language, Mr. Larson. Watch what you say." She cautiously holds my brace. Blood rushes to her cheeks and her teeth cut into her lower lip. She blinks away, letting her fingers dance above her head.

Oh, beautiful. Even the darkness declining from her under eyes suits her. I like what she did with her hair today too—a full clip, pinned to one side.

Slipping my phone out of my pocket, I open the camera, snapping a shot of her. I don't try to hide it.

"Did you take my picture?" She presses the palms of her hands under her chin, framing the jaw of her heart-shaped face.

"Yeah."

"Why?" She follows her question with another nose scrunch.

"Next time when you're acting like a psycho, I can open it and remind you of who you are."

"A hot mess?" She nods confidently.

"No," I deadpan, taking her jaw between my pointer and thumb. "A force of light."

"A fireball," she asserts.

"A comet."

"They're the same thing." She cocks her head to the side, full of attitude.

"Well, Fireball." I run my fingers up and down the cotton material covering her thigh. "It's one hell of a wake-up whisky."

"Is it reserved for special occasions like the Irish coffee?" Her brows jump.

"Every day with you is a special occasion." Her mouth hangs, fully insulted as she should be. Luckily for her, nobody else knows what we're talking about. "Ms. Cherry Kaas, the walking impetuous fireball."

"It's better than the, what was it…"

Oh, the tabloid. I don't know half the names of the people who work for me. Everything that has to do with Cherry seems to stick naturally. "A talentless whore?"

Both Shifter and Wes glance backward, completely out of the loop and concerned…Or, you know, waiting for her to deck me.

Her jaw chutes to the floor while her lips retain a smile. "Rude!" She scolds.

"That's what you said, wasn't it?" I cross my arms over my chest.

"No, that's what *they* said."

"No, that's what *you* said. They said something along the lines of you using your lips to get a role." My devilish grin is well-received.

"Same thing," she continues to argue.

I bear my shoulder against hers and whisper against her ear. "You're a dirty girl, Ms. Cherry Kaas, but they got it wrong. You never used me. You just abused me."

"What's this movie about?" Wes erases the thought I had twisting between my ears, giving me an opening to brag about my art.

"Oh, let me tell him," Cherry insists. She scoots forward as much as her seatbelt will allow. Her excitement is adorable.

Adorable? I swear that word didn't exist a few months ago. Sexy, wild, and dirty. Perhaps cute. Adorable is…it's a magnitude I couldn't foresee wanting.

"I play Samantha," she continues. "She's amazing. She was born into this high-class family of dirty money and has to uphold its reputation, but she's a mess underneath and does a lot of crazy stuff to make sure she's the one who is next in reign over her brothers. She's constantly put on a pedestal and expected to marry into a family for business."

Wes points, matching her vibe. "What's his name, uh…" He snaps. "Ames Heart! Isn't he in it?"

"You did your research." Her eyes tighten briefly. "Yeah, he's Samantha's love interest, Jensen."

"He was in *Raceway*. We snuck into the theater to watch it," he laughs. "Seth and Shifter, fucking—" The guy has a contagious laugh. Cherry starts giggling before he spits out the story. "Seth got stuck in the fucking window and ripped his pants. I told him cargo pants weren't cool."

Shifter eyeballs him. "No, they were cool...as in air-conditioned."

"He was too high to give a fuck."

Cherry's curiosity takes over. "Is he growing that stuff?"

"You're behind, sweets." So there's more he hasn't shared. "We have an entire indoor veg and fruit garden and yeah, the special garden." They laugh among themselves like it was a long time coming.

Wes tips his baseball cap up. "Didn't think a bunch of degenerates could be green thumbs, did you?" He trails off, humming *Dr. Greenthumb,* and I almost spit out the swig of water I sipped. I drink it down, tighten the cap back on, and set it in the center cup holder.

"Don't sing." Shifter cuts him off. I wouldn't have guessed Southern Whiskey would be educated in '90s hip-hop.

"They're a bunch of party poopers today." Cherry side-eyes.

"Right?" Wes agrees. "We're in the wild! Where's your spirit?" He latches onto Shifter's bicep, shaking him.

"We'll be in the wild if you do that to him again." I clear my throat. "They didn't call you Shifter because you're a good driver. You're supposed to stay between those two lines." It's hard enough to get any sleep with how much he jerks the wheel without Wes fucking with him. I was dick-deep in Cherry until the early morning hours and then spent another hour writing before I finally passed out.

"Never claimed to be." *Fucking four eyes.*

"Will you two kiss and make up already?" We both stare at Wes. "Is it like an alpha thing? If anyone is alpha material, it's these puppies." He lifts his arm, flexing the muscles. Cherry coos, running her hands over the ridges. I don't like it.

"Ronnie is more alpha than you, hush puppy," Shifter replies. For once, I agree with him...Or is that the second time I agreed with him? Whatever.

"Fuck you, Shifter."

"*Uhhhh, yeaaah*," he moans in exaggeration. It must be normal to Wes, but Cherry's eyes widen, and I've lifted my chin so far to the left, I look cockeyed. "Wait, wait, wait. I'm celibate." He waves a finger.

"Since when?" Cherry laughs.

"Since one AM." His face stones over and Cherry looks as confused as I am.

"Since you jacked off on the toilet and got your tool pinched in the seat when your sweaty legs stuck to the seat? Yeah man," his long *a* drags. "I heard you in there cursing up a tornado."

Shifter scratches at the scruff on his chin, keeping his eyes on the road. "Stubbed my toe."

"Sounded more like someone stabbed you in the gut."

"Wes," I interrupt. "Have you ever killed?"

Yeah, I said that, and they're all as shaken as you are. Why would I ask such a question? What the fuck is wrong with me? First, you already know the answer. Second, sit down, and you'll find out.

"Rabbit...and squirrel." He rocks in his seat. Uncomfortable? Imaginably, since I slaughtered the lab in front of him. The muscles don't make him *alpha*.

"Okay, then nobody else has done the things I have, correct?" I calmly look around.

"Um..." His fingers take his chin, and he shies away. "No."

"I think that makes me alpha."

Keywords. Right here.

"That makes you a murderer," Cherry bites.

I was hoping she would. It earns her a devilish smile. "We're all capable of murder, aren't we?" I squeeze her thigh.

"Yeah," Wes answers. "But so is a human *without* the syrup shot into their body."

"I'm not like them and I'm not like you. As far as I know, only one of us can revive the dead." I hold onto Cherry, glancing back and forth.

"Alpha," he nods. "You're the alpha."

I squeeze Cherry, smile, and straighten in my seat.

"Just because you can, doesn't mean you should," Shifter runs his mouth.

"I shouldn't kill the bad guys and save the good?"

"Some things aren't meant to be played with." He watches the road, clutching the top of the steering wheel with both hands.

"You're telling me that if I had the chance to save my sister, I shouldn't?" I lift my ass enough to tuck my hands in my pockets, waiting for a load of bullshit he's about to shovel out.

He blankly looks between the road and the rearview mirror. "You can't predict the outcome."

"I bet *you* could. You seem to know a lot about my abilities," I taunt. "How do you know them so well?

"B," Cherry reprimands.

"He can fight his own battles, darling," I counter, unfazed.

"No. You're not starting this." I stare at her with an exaggerated gap between my lips onward of licking it away and nodding.

"Wake me in three hours and I'll drive." If I can get *any* shut-eye.

"Mood killer," Wes mutters.

Spare me another eye roll, Cherry.

I look away, quickly doing a double take, as she falls to her side.

"Cherry? Cherry!" My seatbelt latch pings off the window as I unlatch it and throw it backward, sliding over to her. I lift her limp body, holding her head in my hand, and brush the hair from her face. "Hey, open your eyes."

"What's going on?" Shifter swerves, looking back.

"Watch the fucking road," I bark. "It's a blackout." I tuck her head against my bicep and grab her forearm, pressing two fingers to her wrist. "Her pulse is slow."

"Should I pull over?"

"For what fucking reason? CPR? Fuck no. She doesn't need that kind of help. She needs this fucking doctor to fix her side effects. Keep driving." I unlatch her belt and push her onto her side, resting her head on my lap.

"She didn't tell me about this," Wes hesitates. "Did you know?" He looks at Shifter. His mouth gaps without words. He nods, swallowing hard.

Six minutes of stillness. Six.

This is the first time I've seen it happen to her. She left me in the woods when she witnessed my blackout. My pulse stopped, though...She didn't know. With all of the variables, how are we going to find an answer, a solution? What were they trying to do? Fuck. None of this adds up.

Her knees pull up to her chest and her sleepy eyes blink rapidly as she looks up at me.

"Welcome back, sunshine."

Cherry Or Chérie?

It's been nearly a week of pavement and too much time for my thoughts to wander. It's exhausting living in my head.

"Wes." I gently squeeze his forearm as I hold the door of the rear passenger open. "Hey," I greet him when he blinks. "We're here."

The day I blacked out, Wes didn't ask any questions. If he did, it would've been hard to answer them. It was only the third time—that I'm aware of anyway—that it's happened to me. The first was a few days before the massacre, over three years ago. I told Jack, and he sent me to the lab for blood work. The second time happened on the first day on the set of Samantha. I couldn't admit it to myself. I pretended like it never happened and that rescuing the turtle was my sole reason for being late.

Despite my failures, I'm here, standing outside the building that holds the woman who has the power to change my life. The only thing that stands between Dr. Romberg and me is the security at this lab. It's not surprising that she found another laboratory job. She spent many years in education and training for a position like this. It also makes it easier to find someone when they stick to the same habits.

You can find out a lot about someone on the internet. If she wanted to hide, she did a poor job at it. She's single, as far as I can tell, and her cat, Goose, is her only roommate. She has a beautiful voice and spends her Saturday nights at a karaoke bar not far from her apartment. Her only traceable sibling is a sister, Ellery. She's in upstate New York and has been since long before I became a rat. Their parents can't seem to stay put. I'm guessing timeshare properties and retirement funds to blow. Her bestie, Resh, is my only concern. I caught two of his live streams in the last five days, and he's quite the opposite of her.

Several websites list her place of work, and a quick search revealed her address. In a matter of minutes, I found out Ms. Feather is about my height, has curves for days, and has the most luscious dark locks that I'm tempted to ask what products she uses. I'm hoping she's not as "tanned with a paint gun" orange as she appears in some of her photos and prepared for color transfer at the same time. Look who's talking. The number of hair products applied to my hair on set could light my head on fire with one spare ember. Unfortunately, I couldn't have side effects that included never parched skin and a blemish-free chin.

I don't care why Feather's single. I'm glad she is. One less complication.

It had to be traumatizing—working with a patient every day who turns around and slaughters your entire team. Ronald Hyderton seems like a piece of work to stand by and do nothing. Those doctors or scientists had to have families waiting for them. I wonder how much he's paying her to keep quiet...or threatening her with.

"Where's Bennett and Shifter?" He stretches his arms over his head, asking me through an air-filled yawn. I try to hold back from joining him, yet his contagious yawn catches me.

"Doing as boys do...Peeing behind the bushes." I glance across the parking lot in the direction they went, and his sight follows. "I haven't seen her yet."

"Cherr...what if she makes us worse?"

"Move over, teddy bear." He slides down, and I sit next to him, grab the door handle, and pull it closed. "I want to tell you something that you've probably predicted by now. I did something really bad," I tell him. "And I don't want to do it ever again. I can't lose control of my anger."

"That guy deserved it." He nudges my knee. "It's the obsession for me. Can I tell you about it?" It's written in his eyes, the melancholy.

"I'm listening."

"Ronnie liked this guy at the gym and in Ronnie fashion—" He smiles. "She asked him out. He said yes." A hard gulp bobs down his throat. "I stalked him for weeks, sent him anonymous threats, and eventually he switched gyms and ghosted her. I knew this man's routine like the back of my hand."

My brows force together. "He was your obsession?" I didn't mean to sound harsh.

"No. You don't get it?" His eyes are downcast. "Woman…" His head falls back with an exhale. "It's Ronnie…And the only thing she wants from me is an occasional hookup. I'll never be able to let her date anyone else. I'll hold onto this fantasy of us, chasing her like a lost pup."

"Why don't you tell her? Maybe she thinks all you want is to be friends with benefits."

"She couldn't possibly love me." I reach for his hand, stroking the side with my thumb.

"You do love her, or is it the obsession? You're worried about what's going to happen if we get a cure. You might find out you don't love her."

"Yeah." He rubs his face down. "What if I do love her and she doesn't want me?"

"Build more walls?" I flash him a big movie star smile. "And it's only a suggestion, but brick blocks tend to work better than glass."

"That's not funny." His laugh lies. It must be a little funny. "Bennett and Shifter are at each other's throats because they both have feelings for you."

"No." He doesn't know what he's talking about. "Shifter does not have feelings for me. He's attracted to me. That's human nature. He cares about me like I care for him, but he doesn't have romantic feelings," I insist.

"Big shot movie star, and you don't see the big picture right in front of you."

He glances out the window, and I copy him. B and Shifter pass each other, rounding the vehicle, and find their seats up front.

"Hey guys, nice piss?" Wes jokes.

"Beautiful. Superb relaxation. You should give it a go." Shifter winks.

B stretches back, dangling his arm along his seat's upper bolster. "Other than the main door, they have two emergency exits. Those two are locked from outside entry, and the front has security. Waiting for her to come out is our best shot." Bennett runs his fingers through his hair, brushing the loose pieces back that frame his face.

Wes pulls out his phone before I get to mine. "With the intel I've gathered, it's wise to assume she gets out of work between four and five," he says. "It's three forty-eight."

"What does she drive?" Bennett looks to me for the answer.

"I don't know. Public information only took me so far. None of the pictures, including those she was tagged in, gave me an idea."

He nods. "Cherry and I will stay here, and you two can spread out near the door. You showed them her picture?"

"Rightfully so, boss man. Sent it to their phones. We're set."

Wes and Shifter head to their position, and I climb up front as Shifter shuts the front door. As I push the automatic button to drop the window, I call to him. "Hey! Be careful."

"I'll be careful if you pay attention." He smirks. *Don't get off in the car while you wait* would have been clearer, but we all four know what he meant.

"Some things are more important!" I call out. "Very few. This is one." The entertainment takes his face again as his gaze drops to the ground, and he hustles to catch up with Wes.

"Can we talk?" B asks.

When does a conversation with "can we talk?" ever end well? His tone worsens it.

He does that thing where he tucks my hair back behind my ear, and then as soon as he's not looking, I shake it back out. "What do we need to talk about?"

"I don't like anyone, Cherry. I fucking love you." *His calm is a shelter. Once he opens the window, the barrel of a rifle will stick out of the cavity. Bennett serves as a protector to a few, a safe space, and an ear for listening. He thinks I don't understand how privileged I am to have his sanctuary.* "That's huge. Why won't you let me in, and you know what I mean. Like...really...in."

"Love the descriptive words, best-selling author. *Like, really.* What do you want me to say, B? I had a hard life, and I don't like talking about it." I twirl the string to his hoodie around, dropping it in a huff. How is he not warm? "I like dancing with you, and cooking with you, and doing other extracurricular activities with you. You know more than most. Can't that be enough right now?"

He bats my hand away, and I push my lower lip out, scowling.

"Five, six—whatever the fuck—how many days ago, you beat the shit out of a man at the drop of a dime. He was dead. The damage you did to him didn't even heal completely. If I didn't send Shifter around to mind-warp the passersby, we would have had cops coming for us. You're messy. I deserve to know what else I'm walking into and you—you have someone you could tell the most foul, hideous acts to ande—"

"That's one way to get fame."

"I don't think you want fame or getting caught." He exhales. "I never wanted fame. I wanted someone to see me."

"I see you."

"Yeah, I want to fucking see you, but I can't because you refuse to let me." He stares at the steering wheel in a brief silence. It's long enough to wash a wave of calm over both of us. "Why did you do it?"

"That was days ago. Can we just move on?"

"Please, Cherry."

"You did the same not long ago to Ames."

"He called you a whore for fucksake." He shakes it off. "That's not the point. What's going on with you?"

"I saw him and...I couldn't leave without giving him what he deserved." I snatch the bottle of water in the center cupholder and twist the cap.

"Why did he deserve it? Fuck, come on. This is like edging, only to leave me with a cliffhanger that permanently hangs."

I take a huge gulp, letting B continue to grill me with my *sudden* inability to reply since I'm *so parched*.

"You're telling me it wasn't a big deal and fucking Shifter wasn't part of the Band-Aid?"

Tucking the plastic bottle back where I got it, I give him very little. "I was horny."

He digs his finger into his hair, rubbing his scalp in frustration. "I told you I hated you. Horny doesn't conceal those words."

"You always fuck me with hate."

"Wrong. I fuck you hard, and it won't stop if you talk to me about it. You can lie to yourself about it. You can't lie to me. I already made you promise not to do that shit."

"Promises, hah." I chuckle, mirroring one of his.

"Do you think I'm going to tell you that you're not allowed to wrap your hands around my throat? That I'm going to bitch out when you tell me something normal people fear? That I'm not going to fight for the upper hand and let you take it so I can steal it back again and again? I'm not saying, let's sit here and discuss twenty years of your life in two minutes. I'm saying...if you're on the ledge, call me. Lean on me. Not Shifter. *Please*," he overly pronounces. "Don't make me kill him. It'll be a bitch."

I ugly laugh, tears welling behind my eyes. As I choke back whatever is happening to me, I search the front of the building.

"Look, look!" I point, taking the door handle so fast that I lose my grip the first time.

"Let's go."

I stumble out of the car, slamming the door shut harder than intended. It doesn't matter. There she is, my ticket to everything. I get ahead of Bennett, running as fast as I can. Before I reach her, I slow down and inhale hard, barely letting it out when I question her. "Feather Romberg. Are you Dr. Feather Romberg?"

"Yes? What is this?" Her confused gaze shifts between me and the two guys standing off to the side, not far from her.

"Do you recognize me?"

With a quick glance over my shoulder, B has caught up. He stays to my right, not passing me. Feather starts walking backward nervously, pulling her slim tan suitcase tight to her chest in both arms. Her flared black slacks fluctuate along the pleats with each step.

"No..." She shakes her head. "How are you here?" Intently mindful of B, she doesn't falter for a second.

"You recognize him?" I look between them. My heart races, fearful of her body language.

"Please, leave me alone," she cries.

"We're not here to hurt you." I try to reassure her, but it's too late. She knows who Bennett is or—what he is—and she's petrified.

"Leave me alone!" She takes off, sprinting back into the building, and the door latches behind her. Wes tugs at the handle, but it doesn't budge. It's locked.

I run over and pull on it, jerking it ballistically over and over. The glass doesn't budge as the side of my fist pounds into it.

"What the fuck! Why didn't you stop her?" I pace the floor. As I cup my hands around my eyes, I press them to the glass, trying to see inside. It's tinted and I can't make out a thing. The annoyance sends me.

"Calm down."

"No, B! You calm down!" The lack of sense doesn't stop me from shouting. "She's my last chance!"

"We're going to get her. Look at me." He holds my jaw still. "Look at me. You have her apartment address, yes? We're going to go there. She has to go home eventually." Bennett takes my hands. "Breathe. One. Two. Three. Four. Five. Six."

I empty the air from my lungs and count in my head. One. Two. Three. Four. Five. Six.

"I'm going to get her for you, do you understand me? It's not over." I nod as his lips meet my forehead. "Shifter, take Cherry to the car. We'll be right there."

"Let's go, sweets."

"I'm fine. I won't get lost walking to the car."

What is he doing? I don't—I don't even care.

Shifter walks next to me through the lot, talking the entire time. His words are nothing more than the chirps of a bird and a creaky swing. Only one sentence makes it through the wind.

"For the record, I'd rather hang out with you than be Bennett's lackey."

I'm tempted to turn around and slam on the door until someone opens it. As I reach what feels like my detainment, I duck my head against Shifter's hand, and I sit in the back seat. I'm on lockdown...with a tracking device.

He runs around the car and gets in beside me. He's better than me. They all are lately. I'm the one who climbed the ladder little by little to get to Bennett. I spent every spare moment I had learning to control my abilities, and where did it get me? I'm losing it. All of my control and precision. It's vanishing! It's PMS times one thousand, and I can't blame my ovaries for this catastrophe.

"How you doing?" Shifter gently nudges me.

Bennett thinks—Shifter has—Wes says…They have to be wrong. Shifter doesn't have romantic feelings for me. He's not in love with me. We're friends. We care about each other. He's not only here as a friend. He doesn't want this lifestyle either.

"Shifter…" I swallow the saliva pooling in my mouth.

"Yeah?"

"Never mind."

"You sure?"

No. I'm not, but I am… "I'm sorry." I clear my throat.

His smile is comforting and only makes me feel more guilty. "Don't be."

Unlike a cherry bomb, when I snap, the damage is substantial. "Do you…"

"What is it, chérie?" He grins.

"Do you have feelings for me? Past a friendship."

His lips become flat. "You know that I do."

The rhythm of my heart picks up, pulsing to the music in my head that I use to block his answer with.

No. Hell…no. I did not. We hung out all the time. I cleaned his brushes for him and tossed popcorn into his mouth while he painted. We were the best friends we could be. He was my *best friend*…and he was in love with me the whole time? Or half of the time? How long? It doesn't matter because I should have known.

"I didn't…honestly. I didn't know and I wouldn't have…"

"I'm in love with two women and I can't keep either of them. It's not a *one-that-got-away* situation, sweets. I love you and I love Raven."

"I care about you…a lot. You have no idea, David, but you never had me to lose. I always have one foot out of the door. I never unpack."

"That's gonna bite you in the ass and you'll be alone like me."

"You're not alone." My eyes send in a circle.

His face remains flat. "I'm not okay, sweets." Shame chokes his words back for a moment, letting go with a sigh. "My mom sends the same message every time she sends money to my account—toute peine mérite salaire—all suffering merits salary. She believes that I'm working a custodial job at the lab to make ends meet. That's what they—my parents—believed since I signed on. You know how I grew up. I'm like Ronnie, except my well-off parents didn't disown me. They showed me the way. I walked away."

"If we're making comparisons, you are far more like Bennett than *Veronica*," I scoff.

"Pick my poison?"

"Yeah, *well*," the word hangs. "None of us are okay."

"About that thing we did, you did, the three of us did?" A short guffaw breaks up his reflection. "That was all okay, right?"

None of us has mentioned it since. We moved on like it never happened because it meant nothing. It meant nothing to me.

"Y-yeah." I brush my hair to one shoulder. "Nothing to worry about unless you have something to tell me?" I swear, if he has crabs, I'll stab him.

"No, no, no, but like…" He rubs his neck. "Are you two always over the top? You're both into that stuff?"

Always. I want to say something, but I pinch my lips together, finding B and Wes approaching us. Their doors open, then latch closed.

"Address?" It takes me a moment to escape the brain fog. "Baby, I need you to focus. Those clouds that are fucking your thoughts right now, push them away and look at me. I need the address."

I nod, leaning into the center, over the leather console, to key it in on the GPS.

Shifter tucks me into his arm, covering me in soothing relief. He stretches, flexing his shoulder, with a wince.

"Are you okay?"

"Yeah, yeah, yeah," he mumbles. "It's a headache."

"In your back?"

"A headache and a backache." I lift the hem of his shirt until I find the bruise below his shoulder. Dropping his shirt, I don't say anything. What could I possibly say? Question him for not telling me he took one of those bullets? I'm not entitled to know, and I'm a bad friend that I didn't notice while he was naked beneath me several nights ago...when it had to be ten times worse.

Should I give him another apology that means nothing? What's done is done. I say nothing. I lean into him and let our bodies comfort one another. That's all I can do as I ignore the scowl on B's face. It's not like I expected them to bond over that night. If anything, they've been less chatty than snarling at each other. However, it would be better for everyone if they could get along.

"Shift..."

"Yeah?"

"Do you know anything else about those darts?" I wonder out loud.

"I bet the doctor does."

We've been sitting outside the apartment complex for hours, and I can't get out of my head. I'm a monster walking among humans, fitting in seamlessly. No matter what I do, I can't escape. Not permanently, anyway. I hurt everyone—both the bad and the good. Sometimes without trying.

I keep trying to retain control...to stick with the plan, and nothing stays level. My plans keep falling apart. The high followed by the crash...over and over again. I don't know why I'm here. I can't save myself; how could I ever save anyone else?

And this is when everything ends and where everything begins.

This is where I started writing my story next to Bennett's. Remember? It went a little like this...

If I can't be the hero I want to be, I'd rather be dead.

"I don't want to do this anymore."

"Do you see the house tucked away up on the hill? I see it."

"You know I love you, right?" I ask, not sure if I'm questioning him or myself.

"Enough to leave Shifter out of our wedding?"

A lot has happened in the past few weeks besides making decisions that I can't take back. Everything I thought I knew—the reason I even met Bennett—turned out to be meaningless. Jack and Ronnie. How stupid could I be? Greg. What I did to Shifter—I wish, so desperately, that I could forget. I want to erase everything—not just the last few months or years, but everything. I'm supposed to create my happiness. That's easier said than done when all that I know is burning buildings and bleeding hearts.

"Can we go over the plan?" I interrupt.

He slowly centers back on me. "The plan is there isn't a plan. We go in and if anything—and I mean anything, Cherry," his voice deepens, defining his point. "If anything is off, we get the fuck out. Otherwise, the goal remains. Attain her without harm."

I eagerly wait for the unknown, drifting my sight amidst the three men towering around me. The elevator pings, jolting as it comes to a stop, and the door opens. Bennett grabs my hand, pulling me into his chest.

"When this is over, I want to dance on a rooftop with you and forget the world." His fingers take the side of my neck, and his thumb drifts over my jaw before gently swiping over my lower lip.

"With perfect posture," I smirk and kiss the pad of his thumb.

"Fuck the posture. As long as you're in my arms, anything goes."

It's...crazy.

That's the only word I can think of that truly describes it.

A few weeks ago, I was in Bennett's bed, forgetting the world around us, and in the months before that, I was spending my time getting lost in him when I never wanted to. Everything happened so fast.

I could walk away with him right now and find a rooftop of our own, far away from here, but the past would always haunt me. We can escape. We have to do this for everything I've overcome and for the lab rats—for Shifter.

I know, I'm losing it. One minute, I'm on a self-destructive path, and then the next I'm trying to play the puzzled-together superhero, ready for action. It used to be pretend. Now it's my reality. Karma's a bitch.

I stand inside the door, softly closing it behind me.

I've only seen apartments like this on the Home Network channel. The living room stretches to the kitchen, wall-to-wall faux wood flooring—a grey variation—and a plush white rug separates the two spaces.

"It's clear." Wes returns from the bedroom. "She's not here."

"Then, we'll wait." Shifter flops down on the sofa, kicking his feet up. It's boxy and doesn't look comfortable at all—likely why it's lined with throw pillows.

Everything is pure white, and I couldn't spot a nick in the drywall if I examined every square inch with a magnifying glass.

"He's right," B agrees. "Enough chasing. She'll show up."

Wes dips head deep into the refrigerator as he shuffles around containers. "Oh, leftover General Tso's."

You can't take him anywhere.

Bennett agrees with my eye roll, sharing a quick glare in his direction.

I gingerly pace the room, certain it couldn't hurt to look around. The paintings on the wall are very Art Deco. I pass them, strolling toward the kitchen, where I hear the running water. "She has a turtle," I mutter. "Benny!" I call out. "She has a turtle."

It's around the corner, close to what I'm assuming is a bathroom. From the kitchen, it's easy to spot, but coming from the living room, it's hidden from plain view. As I squat down, I follow the red-eared, fist-sized turtle up to the surface. He must be hungry.

"Look at that. She does."

I smile up at B. His hands are tucked away as usual, and his face is serious. I know he's thinking the same thing I am...or what he's hoping I'm *not* thinking.

"Cherry..."

"B." I scrunch my nose. "Who's going to feed it when she's not here?"

Is it a coincidence that turtles seem to show up at significant places or points in my life?

"We're not taking it with us," he presses. "Do you honestly think it will survive the drive?"

"I don't know," I sass. "Shifter." With a call for his attention, I lean backward until his eyes slowly drift to mine. "While you're looking at your phone, search how long captive turtles can go without water."

After less than twenty seconds of silence, he replies. "The experts say..." With a dramatic pause, he bangs a pair of invisible sticks on an air drum. "About eight hours."

"I didn't know she had a turtle...just the cat," I mumble.

"Turtles symbolize protection, healing, and transformation," Shifter fact shares.

That's interesting...hmm. "I don't believe in *signs.*"

He shrugs and goes back to his phone.

"Is this that cat?" Wes walks around the island as the gray fluffball trails briskly behind him. I must've spoken louder than I imagined. The cat rubs its chin on its leg.

"Goose! Hello, you big furry floof."

"You know its name?" Wes laughs.

"Isn't he cute?"

"No," Bennett butts in. "Absolutely not. *Cherry,* did you already plan on taking the cat?"

"Nooo," I exaggerate. The writing is on the wall or on my face. *All over my face* because, for the first time in years, I can't wipe a smile off of it. I've never had a pet. "I've always wanted a cat."

His long, thick fingers mess up his side-parted hair, and I sigh. "I'm sure she has a friend who can keep the cat while she's out of town."

"Put the cat and the fucking turtle in the elevator for all I care. Someone will pick them up. We're not taking either of them with us."

"Don't be so cruel, B."

"You two are going to be great parents," Shifter snickers, still holding his phone in front of his face.

"What makes you think that's even possible?" B bites. "If I thought there was a chance of that happening from dead *men*, I'd make sure it didn't. Wrap the snake, rubber band a sack." His teeth grind. "If she wants a cat or a turtle or a fucking tarantula, she can have it once we get out of this."

"Shifter," I groan.

With a half-full mouth, Wes joins in. "I want kids someday." He takes another bite.

With his feet crossed and the rectangular container balanced on one hand, he props himself against the counter.

"With Ronnie?" I faux gag. "Don't make me vomit."

"You'd be a good dad." Shifter shuffles his phone between his fingers as if it's something to fidget before almost dropping it.

"You know what? He's right. I hope you get that, Wes. I hope you get to raise a kind little boy who loves playing in the dirt and burgers on the grill, who makes friends everywhere he goes, and tries his best to be a good friend...I hope you never have to worry about him. I pray he has the life we've all wanted, and I know if anyone is going to make sure of that, it's you."

His gentle smile says more than he could verbally express.

"Four. I want four. They don't have to be all sons."

Bennett Loves Games

"Come here," I pull Cherry closer.

I listened to Whiskey Boy talk about his four kids, two dogs, and his dream of owning a gym for the longest and most excruciating forty minutes of my life. Excruciating. It was somewhere in that time frame that I saw Cherry's smile fade, return, and melt away several more times. I can't predict the future, yet I guarantee the idea of children would never cross my mind. I only want her, and for a fraction of a second, I've let myself wonder if I'll be enough on my own. In great timing, I didn't have the empty time to overanalyze it.

The doorknob rattles, kicking all of us in the chest cavity as it rips me out of the chair. Cherry takes off in the opposite direction, and the guys scatter. With the most logical choice, I slip behind the door. The moment she shuts it, I wrap my hand over her mouth and hold her arms tight to her body.

Yeah, this part was expected. She goes mad-cow crazy. She screams and wails around, but she's nothing compared to my woman. It's not much of a struggle for me. In a scary movie, the doctor would be one of the first to go. She fears for her life, rightfully so, irrationally letting it overshadow her intelligence. Wailing around like this is going to get you nowhere besides tired and overstimulated.

"Why did you run!" Cherry gets up in her face, yelling.

Fuck me.

"Wes! Get her ass."

The last thing we need is Cherry losing it. If she would, uh, fuck...nothing. Damn it.

Shifter takes the doctor's arm, dragging her to the recliner. I let go of her as he pushes her to sit.

"Shut up!" He yells. "Stop fucking screaming." He slams his hands down on the armrests. "Do you see her?" He points at Cherry as he squats to her level. "You're afraid of the wrong person." Huh...okay, Shifter. I could pat him on the back for finally showing the fuck up. "That's a woman who is on a mission, and you know what that means." He stands up, fixing his hair. It's the first time I've seen true rage come from him. "She's more dangerous than him."

I crouch down in front of her as she sobs. "Look, darling. We didn't come here to hurt you. We need your help."

"I can't...help you." She's not entirely comprehensible. Black tears stripe her face, covering it in her eye makeup. She foolishly tries to get up and make a break for it, but Shifter shoves her down, pinning her between his arms. His jaw flexes in place.

Am I...Am I the good cop in this good cop/bad cop skit?

"You have *no idea*," his voice deepens. "What I have been through." With a heavy exhale, he falls forward. "Were you there?" He presses his forehead to the high of her cheek. "Were you there when they stuck that last needle in my arm?" He growls, and for the first time I'm...*fuck, I'm afraid.* He could fall apart in the worst way when we need her on our side, and it wouldn't be easy to stop him.

"Shifter," I calmly search for his attention. "Hey." I squeeze his shoulder and pull him back. "Move the fuck out of the way. We don't need to do this." He's wasting his energy anyway. We have the power to make her cooperate.

He steps away, casually walking toward the kitchen, and leans against the door frame, crossing his arms over his chest and staring at her like she's a divine meal.

"Look at me." I take her hand, squatting down in front of her again. She shakes, expecting the worst from me.

That's where she's wrong. I do my best work when I'm not breaking necks. When I'm talking gingerly and informally, I'm in my most dangerous district.

"I have a lot of bodies to account for, right?"

"You shouldn't exist." Her sobbing is accompanied by anger.

"Well, I do, and you're going to fix me." I grab her chin, and she cowers, squeezing her eyes tightly shut. "You had a part in this. Don't you blame yourself a little bit?"

She blubbers, drowning her vision in tears as she opens her eyes back up.

"Look at me," I effortlessly remind her. "You poor little disaster." A rigid chuckle takes my lungs. "Are you scared?" As I run my thumb over her lip, I start reeling her in. Her eyes trace mine. I haven't done this in weeks, and it feels so fucking good. My veins are illuminated with the violence of a wildfire. The intensity of it all. "You don't have to be. I can make you feel good." With a tone I've only used to get women naked, I seduce her while Wes holds Cherry back and Shifter holds himself together. It's not exactly how I like to spend a Saturday night.

Wait...hah, did you think I was changing? I was evolving or...growing? That's what my character is supposed to do, right? I don't see it. Where's the big change, darling? If you're searching for growth, it happened when I fell for the girl. That's it. I swear I'm not going to do anything else substantial. You're crazy for accepting me this way, and crazier if you hold onto the hope that the living, breathing, killing machine will become some kind of exceptional vigilante. Now, darling, step to the side while I get little miss "you shouldn't exist" to do as I say.

"You have to let me help you. A beautiful, hardworking woman like you couldn't desire to be all alone forever."

"You don't know anything about me."

"Is it the fear that's holding you back? *This fear?* My face showing up at your doorstep, ready to take everything from you? I'm not going to do that. I will never do that. I like who I am now." I smirk. "If you're ready to find peace and move past this nightmare, I'm your only hope. You need me. I know you want to help me and repent for your sins. Trust me. You want to let me help you. You'll never have to worry about me or your part in this disaster again. I can make it all disappear. That would make you feel better, right?"

She nods, relaxing into the seat.

"That's right. I'll lead you, darling." She's not going anywhere.

As I turn around, I find my future Mrs. with a grimace stuck in place.

Cherry...come on, don't give me that look. I walk over to her and bend down, waiting for her to forgive me. *Don't pout.* Claiming her protruding lip with the pad of my thumb, I stroke her jaw.

"This is me, baby. It had to be done."

"I know." She pulls away. "I'll be fine."

"You don't have to be." I sweep up her body, catching her eyes in my dark gaze. I love when she locks her fingers into my hair and her eyes melt my black heart.

"I'll be fine, B. It's the only way."

"Wes," I call. "Escort Dr. Romberg to the bedroom and help her pack." Without a glance in his direction, I continue. "We'll leave in the morning."

"No, we're leaving tonight," Cherry insists.

Clasping my hands around her forearms, I remove her hands from my body. "We have to tie up loose ends. What happened to saving the turtles?"

"Nobody else cares. Why should I?"

Is she saying, *fuck the turtles*? Something is off about that, and yet, I relish in it. I flick my tongue to the corner of my mouth, deepening it into my teeth. She was sunshine kisses on the skin. Now I see murder under the blood moon. *Fuck.* She's getting worse, and I haven't succeeded at being a hero in this lifetime. What am I going to do?

"Real smooth," Shifter mutters.

"Excuse me?"

I meet him halfway between the island and where the living room dissolves into the kitchen.

"You know what I'm talking about." He slinks inward.

"Do you have an opinion now? You didn't when I let her fuck you."

"You didn't *let* her do shit," he sneers. "We both know Cherry does what she wants."

"She wouldn't touch you behind my back. She wanted my approval, not yours." My dark laughter separates the air between us. "I knew it. When you walked in on us the day we met, I knew that you wanted her. You'll never have her like I do."

"You'd sell your soul and your *dick* for her?"

"Hah. I'd sell every fucking limb, better yet, I'd dice a thousand men and sell their limbs for her. She's worth it."

"You don't deserve her."

"None of us do. We're not good people. We're fucking kidnapping a woman against her will, *for selfish reasons*," I add, continuing to chuckle. "We all know what we're doing. She knows who she's with."

"Do you really think you could only have one woman for the rest of your life?" He's desperate, trying, and saying anything he can to spike a wedge between us.

"I wouldn't be here if I didn't. You have no fucking idea who I am. Like everyone else, you see my name on movies and my pictures on the bullshit websites for the likes of dull women to discuss something exciting. I spend every day working and writing on set, and I find pleasure where I can. I was doing fine. Do you think I wanted to fall for the crazy woman who killed my ex at my feet? It wasn't on my to-do list, but you know her. You see the same thing in her I do, don't you?"

"What?" His expression turns sour.

"Mind your fucking business."

"No," he protests. "Did you just say Cherry killed your ex?"

I look back at Cherry, unable to close my mouth.

Ahhh...Fuck it. He was going to find out eventually.

"Guys," Wes emerges with perfect timing. "She said she's not going now."

"Looks like you lost your charm." A smug grin plays on Shifter's face. It's about as entertaining as golf at the country club on a Wednesday afternoon. I'll never do that again; not for Clint, Tim, or Martin.

"Impossible."

"Yeah, yeah, yeah." He laughs. "How about I do the job and save you the embarrassment?"

"You're good...*Shifter*." He narrows his eyes, scowling at me like I pissed in his cereal. "But you're not me." I dig the message deeper—I'll always be her first choice. "Hey, Wes," I call. "Shifter has something to tell you." Holding my tongue to the tip of my canine, the devil's grin is on full display and at work.

"Huh?"

Shifter doesn't answer him. His lip twitches, still locked on me.

"Oh, he's being coy," I ridicule. "Don't worry, I'm used to being the center of attention." Cherry's delicate fingers forcefully take my arm.

"Bennett, can I talk to you? Now." I wickedly eyeball him with stifled chuckles as she pulls me backward.

"Your master is calling," he sneers, and I immediately go flat.

"What?" Wes questions him, wanting to know what I was going to let him in on.

"Nothing. Let me talk to her." They stroll to the bedroom simultaneously, with Cherry cutting off my view of them.

"What are you doing?" Her tone runs low. "Are you threatening to tell Wes that Shifter's a zombie?"

My arms fly out to my side as I drift backward. "He's a fucking asshole. It's time to air out his secrets."

"He is not."

"No, he is. Shifter is only nice to you because he's in love with you. Admit it."

"There's nothing there," she insists.

"Cherry." I rub my brow and quickly comb the hair back in place. "I'm growing tired of these games."

"You love games, B."

"Haa. Oh, oh, darling. No. Fuck no." She grabs my stubble-covered jaw, trying to shut me up, but I keep going, swatting her arms down and holding them. "I love a single game with a woman for a period of time, not a lifetime of trying to figure out what the *fuck* is going on," I raise my voice.

"It's his to tell," she reminds me. "It's not a game, B. It's his life."

"And when are you going to tell me what's going on with you?"

She pulls away, showing me her back.

"Ya'll..." Wes steps around the corner, dazed-like. "Shifter," he slowly finds his words, thumbing over his shoulder. "Is a zombie...like Bennett."

Cherry's mouth gapes open as she looks at me, uncertain of how to respond.

"There's some cake in there." He points to the refrigerator, already walking in its direction. Eat your feelings in cake?

"You know he quit his job because he has the abilities the rest of us don't. He wanted to keep everyone safe." Cherry to the rescue.

"He's my boy, though, and he didn't tell me?" He forks a piece of cake and takes a bite while the fridge door hangs wide open.

"Cherry keeps me in the dark constantly. It's a common occurrence amongst lab rats."

"Fuck you, B."

"Fuck the turtle!" I yell back, grabbing one of the hundreds of throw pillows from the couch and throwing it to the floor. Why does one person need this many fucking throw pillows? "I need some air. When I get back, make sure she's ready to go."

"Go walk off those eyes," she mutters, stabbing a corner of the cake with a fork.

I debate whether I should entertain that comment, and after ten seconds, I choose the high road, walking out the door.

Fuck, I need a cigarette.

I dig through the door cards, along the seats, in the center console, and in the glove compartment—*fucking everywhere*—hoping someone didn't detail this car as well as they told their boss. Nothing. I reach under the driver's seat, and metal loops cool my fingers.

My notebook.

Ah, yeah. What's there to write about? The fighting or the fucking? Either way, why would anyone want to read this shit?

It fucking sucks. This entire book is trash. It's insanity. Nobody is going to read about a guy who was a little bitch, made stupid choices, got shot, came back with telepathy and photokinesis, made himself famous, and found a hot love interest, and then shit the bed because he's too fucked in the head. Now I'm rhyming.

Ugh! Fuck, fuck!

I slam the notebook off the steering wheel twice, pissing away my misery.

Damn it. Why did we go back to that town?

I slide my pencil from the metal loop and flip the notebook open, holding it in my palm and balancing the flat against my forearm. Knuckle to knuckle, I tap the pencil between my fingers.

I'll write about Annie.

I was lost without Allie in any lifetime. Then I met a fallen angel. Sometimes I think she was sent from above to put my feet back on level ground, and other times I have to wonder if she's really here to slice my throat and drag me to hell. She did the worst thing anyone could do to me. She made me fall in love, and then she seamlessly paraded away. The road that brought her to me was uglier than mine. It was darker than being a second string, sadder than being the invisible duckling, and grungier than every demon I have in my head. In my mind, I could die, and the world would be fine without me. In her mind, she was never meant to exist in the first place.

We fought through this existence with anger until it brought us together. My path stays the same, and hers fluctuates. Sometimes her anger becomes too much for her to control, and other times she seems sad. The type of sadness that can do more than derail her plans.

Too many people know our names to fuck up right now.

I never thought I'd seek invisibility again.

She is a powerhouse, lost in the confusion of black and white when the grey calls her home. The grey calls her to me.

CHERRY COUNTS THE CLICKS

"They have a mechanical bull." Wes is determined to make a detour. He doesn't get out much. "Come on, half an hour. I know ya'll are hungry."

He's right. I don't know how his nerves were intact to the point of being able to eat dinner and dessert at Feather's apartment. I barely swallowed one bite of cake after Bennett's fuse blew. On the bright side, Feather won't have to worry about returning to a moldy fridge.

"Is Feather a family name or something?" I didn't intend for that thought to escape my lips. Was it rude? As if being sandwiched between Shifter and Wes in the backseat wasn't enough.

It's around nine, nine-thirty, and we haven't made it out of the state yet. We could have stayed the night and risked something going wrong. That's why I insisted we leave tonight. Then B insisted he would drive through *the entire night,* and Shifter could take over when daylight broke. It felt more spiteful than intentional.

"No," she answers cautiously.

Between B and Shifter, they managed to calm her mind. I'm not sure what's going on with B, but I can tell he's concerned.

I wonder what it feels like to have your mind controlled. Are you aware and forget when it's over, or do you feel like you're in a hypnotic state, dreaming?

We shouldn't stop, and that's the realistic truth. B doesn't believe I'm being honest with him. And he's right. He was right. I was holding back...until I said I didn't want to do this anymore. I meant life—living—this being. He didn't understand. He assumed I wanted a different escape—a harder necklace, a deeper thrust, a quick cure.

The temporary escape never lasts. I'm back in the closet of that shitty one-bedroom apartment, covering my ears and squeezing my eyes closed until the red fades to black.

Rose and William.

Mom.

The break room at The Kitty, where I hid from low-life men who didn't care about age or consent.

The no-name daddy I never had.

Harley Harvey leaving me.

Greg. He ruined too much of my life. I'd kill him a thousand times.

No—Why am I like this? I'm disgusting. I'm a monster.

I think these ill, twisted thoughts. I plan the demise of flesh and blood—the slaughter of a human being. Or I don't plan them at all. I'm overwhelmed with a heat that boils over, and once the steam rolls out, I can't stop.

Like Cassie. A poor girl who, like me, was dealt an ugly hand and was only trying to make do with the opportunities presented to her. I took it away. She will never get a chance to change, to redeem herself, to find passion and love, and to build the family she may have desired. I stole that from her.

"It sounds like you're judging," Bennett interrupts my train of thought, and I quickly close my notebook, tucking it to my lap.

"No, I'm not. Thank you," I hiss and trace my ring.

His right hand holds the middle of the leather steering wheel, keeping the car straight. He props his fist below his jaw as his elbow rests on the door.

I want Feather to tell me a story. I need to hear the reasoning behind her name. It's that small something that'll remind me I'm human. A piece of humanity that coexists between women. Anything to keep my mind occupied.

"Take the next exit, B," Wes calls out.

Bennett drops his arm, looking over his shoulder. "What did you call me?"

"Shifter, help me out. He's hard of hearing."

"Nah, it's all you."

"Fine. I'll say it again, louder. *Ahhhyeeeah Beeeeee*," he moans.

I slap my hand over my mouth in shock. *Oh my god, Wes!* My laughter sets off a contagious echo. Shifter covers his smirk in the crook of his hand, trying to hide it. Bennett can't keep it inside either, his guttural laugh slipping from his teeth. Despite her situation, Feather can't conceal her grin. The noise was too humorous to escape.

"Stick with Bennett," B groans.

"Did I earn a half hour at the bar?"

"Call him daddy once." I pinch my lips together.

"Don't fucking call me daddy." Bennett swiftly pulls the brakes on *Daddy* being moaned. "We'll stop at the bar...for food *and the bull*. Don't fucking overdo it. This is still a business transaction."

"A business transaction?" I lip-back.

"Yes, Cherry. It's exactly that. She does her job; she gets to live. They do theirs, we all make it back in one piece."

"Sounds like a movie," I make a point of. "*In a world of ugly, one beautiful doctor holds her fate in her hands when a group of degenerates with wild abilities threatens her life with the task of fixing theirs. Will she be able to cure them, or will she meet the same fate as her associates?* Dun, dun, dun."

"What's it rated?" Wes asks.

"R—for rats likely to eject from the screen and eat you," Shifter answers. "*Obviously*. That's your zombie plug, too. *Eat you*."

"I know I'm the star and all, but I wouldn't mind being eaten by a zombie," I reply.

"Then how would I write a sequel?"

"I have a few ideas, B. We'll have a *brainstorming session* later." As suggestive as it sounds, it's not what I mean.

"We're still here," Wes interrupts.

For the next two minutes and seventeen seconds, I stare through Bennett. It may appear that I'm admiring him and thinking of that brainstorming session. I'm not. I want to talk to him about everything that's been weighing me down. The words have hit the tip of my tongue enough times, and only once have I been able to express something. He won't understand. He won't be able to make me feel better this time.

I trace every inch of him with my eyes. From his stubble-taken jaw, his strong nose, his balmy lips, to each dark piece of hair that caresses his temple, I trace every inch of him until I find his blue eyes. Will they stay blue, or will I wake one day with his eyes frozen in ice, glacier cloaked, and tired of living with someone like me?

I slide around the booth, crossing my ankles as I settle in. The crowd is lively in the bar Wes insisted we stop at. A few couples and single women dance across the hardwood. A paneled wall showcases neon signs, including one that reads "Country" and another featuring a cowboy hat.

The bull Wes raved about is off to the left, flinging women in tiny shorts around. It looks like fun. I just don't feel like it tonight. A massive American flag hangs between shelves of liquor and beer taps behind the bar where Shifter orders.

Wes joins us, walking across the bar from the main entrance, and he slides his phone back into his pocket. He scoots in beside me. "Hey." He looks directly across at B, chewing at his lip. "We have a problem." He hesitates. "Charlie called me." With a rub to the scruff starting to form a mustache under his nose, he bounces his leg up and down, jolting the table. "Ron Hyderton showed up at the lab."

"His guys were back?"

"No, well, yeah, but he entered unarmed with two guards. He wants to make a deal."

"Who wants to make a deal?" Shifter sets two glass bottles on the table.

"You should down that first." Wes points to the beer in his hand. "At least sit down."

Bennett slides over, pressing Feather to the wall. Having two grown men and a woman on one bench is pushing the limit.

"What happened in the time it took me to get three bottles of beer?" He lifts the bottle to his lips, drinking half of it in one shot.

"Ron Hyderton." With Wes' words, Shifter freezes. It lasts a brief moment before he slams the rest of his beer back.

I tighten my lips, snapping towards Feather. "You know who that is, *don't you?*" She has the worst poker face. "Did you call him?" I snap.

"Cherry, why don't you get some air."

"I'm fine, Bennett," I growl. His placid stature is unaffected, as if he thinks the death stare will convince me to follow orders.

"Is everyone okay?" Shifter asks, setting his empty bottle down.

"Yeah, fine," Wes confirms. "He said he wanted to talk, and *Charlie talked to him, alright.* You know how he likes to debate everything."

"He could talk you in circles for hours," Shifter agrees. "Doesn't shut up."

"*Ronald,*" He spurns. "Left a phone number and a threat. If he doesn't hear from anyone in a week, he'll be back."

"Back to do what exactly?" Bennett ends his silence.

I need to get out of here. "I think I will get that air."

I stand up on the bench and climb over the top of Wes, not bothering to wait for him to move. He holds his hands up in a surrender, letting me pass.

Wandering male gazes follow me as I rush through the bar with every hope that my aura is giving the *screw-off* vibe. Please, with all the stars in the sky, allow them to leave me alone.

As I swing open the door, a low breeze hits me, and I inhale. It does little to calm me.

The billionaire wants to reboot his little science experiment, and if he doesn't get his way, the people I care about are going to get hurt. I can't do it again. I won't.

I walk down the front of the building and pace half a foot, spotting a ladder along the shadowed side of the building. With each step, my fingers wrap around the cool bars, desperate for an escape. Despite the warmer climate, the rooftop feels cool as a gentle breeze wraps my hair over my face.

I drop to my knees, and it's as if the breath is knocked out of me. As I drop to my hip, I roll until my back meets the roof floor. I plant my feet and hug my arms across my chest, struggling to inhale. My eyes begin to water, unsure if it's from my exhaustion or if I'm actively crying.

It must hurt to be a star. You're always on fire.

Nobody can get near you without being burned. You're destined to live alone for a billion years, scorched.

I don't know what I'm doing anymore.

"*Fuuuck!*" A loud scream comes from below. I roll to my side and stand up, being compelled to meet the ledge.

"Sorry!" He says to a passerby.

Shifter? What the hell is he doing?

"Hey, buddy," he says to a nicely dressed man. "You look well off. I think you could spare a cigarette." The man hands the carton over without a word, almost robotic.

Oh, shoot.

I cringe, ducking out of view.

Did he see me?

"Nice night," he tells the man, then mutters something incoherent.

Speak up. I slowly look over the edge again. *Wait, is that B?*

"Where did you get a cigarette?" He asks.

"Coerced it."

What's he doing?

"You could spare another, right?"

I should trust my instincts. The man's stiff movement was a reaction to Shifter compelling him. He passes the stick to B.

"Thanks," he says dryly. B cups his hand around the tip as Shifter lights it. Then he takes a drag. Smoke rolls with the hollowing of his cheeks into the darkening sky.

Things are this bad that a cigarette is required?

"Where's Cherry?"

"I don't know. Hopefully staying away from people," Shifter slurs. "How do you do it?" He shrugs. "Stay detached? I should have left them long ago...I know people with money." While the tobacco stick rests between his lips, Shifter pinches the frame of his glasses, takes them off, and dusts them clean with the hem of his shirt.

"Is it your mom who has money? Do you call her that, or is there a word in French for *mom*?" A smoky cloud rises around them as they lean against the outside of the building next to the clueless man.

"Chienne prétentieuse..." He smirks at B. "Stuck up bitch. She still transfers money into my account four times a year. At least she believes I'm alive." He inhales.

"I get it, but I'm *the bitch* in my situation." *He did not admit that to Shifter. What did I miss when I left?* "My parents weren't perfect. They weren't as bad as I thought they were, either. Now it's too late for me."

"You're Bennett fucking Larson," disbelief in his tone. "You can't tell me they haven't seen you everywhere."

"They do. They don't recognize me. They think Benny died."

"You mind fucked your parents into thinking you're dead. Wow." He shakes his head. "That's next-level commitment to the rebirth and all. What about everyone else who knew you? Did you manipulate an entire town?"

"No. I'd deny it, do that trick you did to our tobacco supplier, and forget it happened." He takes another hit, ravaging it in his lungs and releasing it back into the air.

"Don't you think this shit that we can do will wear off eventually? I wonder about it all the time. How much longer can I hide, you know?"

"Yeah. I think about it. I didn't want to come back to East Grenton for that reason."

"Do you think about the bullet that killed you, too?"

"You're a quick fucker." B continues with hit after hit of the cigarette that's temporarily alleviating his agony. "I still hate you." Shifter flicks his chin up as if the feeling is mutual. "And a—okay...maybe I have some resentment or—"

"Man, you have PTSD. You dropped to the floor when that car backfired."

He did what? When was this?

"I do not. I'm fine on sets with fireworks, explosives, and dummy rounds."

"East Grenton has a hold on you?"

This happened in East Grenton?

Oh...that old car at the gas station. I didn't realize...

"This is fucking amazing, *Dr. David*," he sneers.

"Yeah, yeah, yeah. Shit on me all you want, but you know I'm the only one who understands being a zombie."

"Uh-huh," he nods. "You snapped back *there*." He points his cigarette out in front of him. "Dr's apartment."

Was that a sigh, or did he blow smoke again?

I crouch down, trying to hear them more clearly.

"That...anger, *rage*, that fucking burning desire to stab the person that did you wrong. I never saw Cherry being capable of that. She really killed a chick?"

He's cynical.

"Yeah." He inhales deeply, quickly letting it out. "I wasn't prepared for that either, or her trying to kill me...twice."

His chin darts in B's direction. "*Fuck*."

"She's dangerous. Not only to normal people...she's smart enough to take all of us down."

"Are you afraid of her?"

What kind of question is that? Bennett's not afraid of anything.

"Maybe of what she'll do if this isn't successful."

What?

My heart sinks into my stomach as it continues to beat in my chest.

"I'll do whatever it takes to find her cure," B continues.

My feet find the surface, floating my body away from the ledge as my fingers find my hairline and twist through my strands. A daze takes me away as I lose control of my movements.

Bennett is *afraid* of *me*. I'm making their lives hell. I shouldn't have returned. I should have left it alone—let B go. If I had moved on, I could have made a name for myself on another film. None of this would be happening. If I had been one of B's victims…none of this would be happening.

I could jump.

Everything would be over.

What if it doesn't work?

As I pace the roof, I glance below. It's empty again. I find my way to the ladder, taking the cold steel in my hand, and inching my way to the ground in a foggy spiral. My vision becomes dark multiple times, returning to the dingy colors of cement when my soles take the last step.

I…I…What is…

I spin and stumble into the chest of a man. His salt-and-pepper hair and extreme height are the first pieces that make sense.

"Hello, miss. How are you?" I look up at the bearded man sporting a cowboy hat. His navy shirt, dark blue jeans, and boots match most of the men inside. With gentle brown eyes, he appears kind, but don't they all?

"Hello…" My chest heats as I spot the pistol strapped to his side. *Death; it's the only thing I see. It's the only solution. It's my only way out of this. The only way to stop the cycle.* "Hello, handsome. How's your night going?" I ask, monotone.

"Better now." His eyes wander as he smiles.

I advance closer to him, running a finger across the collar of his shirt. "I could *really* use your help."

"I-I think I could manage," he stumbles over his words.

I bat my lashes slowly with each seducing proclamation. "I'm going to need something from you." I trail my finger down the center of his shirt. He's more muscular than he appeared, and my eyes lose focus.

Come on. I can do this. I'm a monster. I'm a zombie. Bennett said I can do *this*. I'm as capable as he and Shifter are.

Reaching for his belt, I hold onto the buckle. "I'm in desperate need of something fairly long and hard like this." My hand shakes, slipping my fingers over the gun and removing it from the holster. I tuck it into the back of my jeans, remaining steady. "You've been very helpful, sir, and now you feel really good, helping a pretty young woman, yes?" I nod.

He mimics my movement, and I bring my hands back to myself, disappearing into the dark.

I can't believe that worked.

As I glance over my shoulder, his eyes narrow with confusion. He has no idea what happened. It's as if for a second he forgets what he was doing, then he walks into the bar as I hide in the shadows.

I want to puke. That was horrible.

It's only going to get worse. No matter how much I keep trying...I won't win. I'll never get rid of the pain. If I'm not causing it, I'm engulfed in it. It consumes me completely. Nobody can save me. Only I can.

I know what I have to do.

I rush over to the ladder, repeating the same blurred steps. With each cold bar, I take the next one faster. My eyes search rapidly for an answer I can't see. At first, it's my vision that appears to be spinning. Then, it's clear that it's me. I'm spinning. I'm screaming at the stars—the burning balls of fire that are engulfed in pain like my heart.

There isn't another answer. This is the only way to stop it—the cycle, the pain, the heartbreak. This will take it all away.

I draw the gun from my back, removing the clip. It's full. I push it back in place and point it in the air, pulling the trigger. Nothing happens. My hands shake manically, caught somewhere between adrenaline and fear. I've never shot a gun before.

I flip it to the side, trying to regain focus.

It's the safety button.

I push it off, raising it back to the sky before I can think twice. My screams drown out the ringing, and my nails rip at my scalp.

Worthless! I'm worthless.

I keep screaming, becoming more and more irate in an uncontrollable mess. "No! I don't want to do this anymore. I can't do this anymore." Falling to my knees, I stare at the pistol through wet clouds of fog. *It could be over.*

I throw my hand back up, pulling the trigger for a second time. My screams turn into disgusting, ugly, weeping moans. I can't breathe. I can't slow the heaving of my chest. It rises and falls as my body shakes. I hold my ending in my hand, bringing it to my face, and I stare at my way out.

The opportunity is in my hand! It's right here! What am I waiting for? Am I going to stay here on my knees, hoping someone will do it for me?

No.

I lick the salty pills off my lips. "Baby girl, we are born fighters. We fight until we don't want to fight anymore," I weep.

As I point the tip to my temple, I press it until it's painful. With heavy lids, I close my eyes and exhale.

Take me anywhere without pain. Whether it's in beauty or in darkness...anywhere, I don't have to pretend.

"Cherry..."

Bennett.

I squeeze my eyes closed tighter.

"Cherry, please...Look at me." I blink through wet lashes, finding him kneeling in front of me. "I told you...if you die...I die. If this is what you want, if this is what you're doing, the second bullet is mine."

"You don't want this," I disagree uncontrollably.

"I want you." He reaches for me, but I turn my face from him.

"You told Shifter I'm dangerous!"

"We're all dangerous! Cherry, I killed almost thirty people! It's not our fault we're monsters."

"Yes, it is! We signed up for this." *I signed up for this.* I signed up to wake up every day knowing I have the potential to hurt someone.

"I didn't. I signed up for you and look where I'm at—waiting my turn to look down the barrel of a gun." Why is he so calm? I can't breathe.

"You only like that I'm broken—more broken than you. I make you feel better about yourself."

"You're wrong, darling. I like that you understand that part of me, but I don't enjoy talking you off ledges or covering up your messes. Why do you think I keep trying to get past this fucking barricade you put between us? *I don't want you to hurt.* I want you to be better than me. Please...please, I'm on my fucking knees, Cherry, please...put the gun down."

I can't. I can't do that, B.

Tears stream down my cheeks, layering the mess that already exists.

"I don't want to fight anymore. I can't save anyone," my voice cracks.

"You can save yourself!"

"I can't save myself! I'm tired of treading water, and I want to drown. I yearn for the water to swallow me whole, fill my lungs, and put an end to my agony. Bring me peace in the ways I've imagined far too many times. I came face-to-face with a nightmare, and I watched him bleed. I heard his pain. And it changed nothing. I. Can't. Save myself."

"Yes, you can. You are fucking worth it. Do you hear me?"

"Live for me! Live for me, B."

"I won't. I can't do that. You are the first piece of purpose I've found in years. Why would I let go of you? Why wouldn't I join you? There's nothing here without you."

"Tell me, B. What do you see? Tell me, so I can tell you how wrong you are."

"You're a shoebox shoved in the back of the closet filled with painful pho-tographs attached to strings from a lifetime ago. Cut the strings. Burn the photos. Stay with me. You are not the hero, Cherry! You shouldn't fucking care. You don't have to make some huge mark in the world for your life to be worth living."

"Says the man who is adored by millions."

"I feel like a fraud!" He yells, making me jump. "All the fucking time. Hun-dreds of thousands of people tell me I'm amazing and talented, and I don't fucking believe them. And you..." He sits back on his heels. "You're the closest thing to heaven I'll ever get. I'm terrified of losing you." He reaches out to me, then hesitates. "I don't care about anything—the fucking movies or the books or the life I once had. You are my home, not any place or anything will make me feel whole like you." His eyes well with tears, something I never imagined I'd witness. "I want you to stay for me, and it's fucking selfish, but I'm that guy. I'm a selfish asshole, and you're a broken unicorn. We'll comfort each other's dark, disturbed souls—just you and me until they burn us." I drift between his eyes. "Fucking stay with me. Don't make me beg. I'll fucking stay on my knees all night if I have to...please, baby...I'm here. I'm never leaving. Put it down."

"I'm beyond repair," I whisper.

"As long as your heart beats, there is hope."

"Hope?"

"Sunrises in Italy, sunsets in France, full moons in New York. Whatever you need to see, whatever will prove to you that beauty exists in this place. I'll give it to you...as long as you stay."

"I...I'm not good enough."

"That's not very characteristic of you."

"You don't know me, b. You only think you do."

"Fine. I don't fucking know you. Give me fucking gun." He pulls at my stiffened arm. "Give me the fucking gun, Cherry. I'll take the first bullet. If I don't know you, then I guess it won't bother you to see my brains fly across this roof. It won't bother you to see my useless, demonic body limp and crimson. It won't bother you when my flesh turns warm and I'm another casualty of a broken world. So give the fucking gun!" I jerk away, keeping the muzzle pointed at my head. "I'm not afraid to die. Death is inevitable. Where I'll end up is another story. That fucking scares me, Cherry, because no matter where my soul roams, if it's not entangled in yours, it must be hell." Tears roll down my cheeks, and it's as if I sense the sinking feeling turning his stomach. "I don't want to yell at you. Just please, please put it down."

I pull it from my temple and drop it the short distance to the floor, immediately falling into Bennett's arms. Without control, my breath turns to gasps and heavy inhales. His thumbs take my tears, pushing them into my hairline.

"Do I want to know where you got this?"

"Seduction." I exhale hard, letting a short laugh escape. It's not funny. It wasn't.

"My little exhibitionist." He brushes my hair back.

"I would...I..."

"Hey, look at me." He takes my jaw, letting his hand fall to my forearm. "One. Two. Three. Four. That's it. Five. Six." I shake, exhaling. "And if you ever decide to pull that trigger, put it in your mouth, not the temple." I don't know if he's serious or if it's a joke, and knowing B, he's not joking.

"Where did you learn that? The counting." I tug at my skin, wiping the mess from my face, and slide my hands over my jeans until they're dry.

"It's the dick jewelry story again." His laugh gets me every time. "Come here." He pushes the gun away and lies down, pulling me to his side. His hand takes my skin like a blanket, massaging over my arm. "I had anxiety attacks on repeat that first month after waking. When I stopped pretending it wasn't a problem, I found this shit on the internet about meditation. I had it before I died, too. I just didn't realize it. I'll be strong for you, darling. You have that in me, but that's not what you want. You want someone who understands, not pretends to. We only play pretend in front of the world, Cherry, not to each other. Now, tell me how you managed to exhibit that gun, sneaky girl."

"I didn't *exhibit* it." With an open hand, I smack him in the chest. "My name came from a tree." I sit up and look down at him. One hand stays tucked behind his head as he sees nothing beside me and the stars.

"Oh, yeah. I see. My *little Cherry blossom.* Fuck, that's too cute for you." He sits at my level, taking my chin between his finger and thumb. His gentle lips press to mine.

"I want you to read something and—" He slides around, yanking his phone from his pocket. "I wrote it on my phone this time."

"It was more convenient, wasn't it?" I wipe my eyes again. I'm tempted to say *I told you so*. He unlocks his phone and slides to the right, clicking on a notepad app.

"I don't plan on making it a habit."

I take the phone, reading over the document while he intently watches me.

Two people like us should never have climbed the ladder and tried to walk across the tightrope. I thought I knew my place in this life. I figured out where I belonged after I died. Then she opened my eyes. Chelsea broke everything inside of me. The mansion I built around me wasn't shatterproof. Her black magic haunted my thoughts. She blocked my outlets. And it turns out I was hers. Every time she wrapped her hands around my throat, I knew it. I had a new purpose. I wasn't devoted to my agenda anymore, nor was I devoting my life to her. I was embracing my dark angel. She was the part of the story I couldn't predict.

My face heats. "Am I Chelsea?"

"You're Chelsea...and my co-writer. I want you to write this chapter and put your stripper name underneath mine." My smile must take up my entire face because his eyes swallow me whole.

"I like to be on top." I rub my nose, wiping my misery away.

"No. It's not happening." He stands, holding his hand out.

"Fine." I take it and rise to my feet. "But I don't want it to say Cherry Kaas."

"You want a pen name?" His brows perk up and lower. Lacing my fingers between his, I slowly meet his eyes.

"I want it to say Cherry *Larson*."

"You're going to have to work for that."

"No, I'm not."

"Fine. If you want the name, you're going to have to dance with me." He dips forward, flicking his tongue up my neck. "Right here. Right now."

"I stole that guy's gun and then shot it. The cops are probably on their way."

"Fuck them," he asserts. "We do what we want, and right now I want to dance with you and later beat your ass for thinking you could leave me."

"Let me see your phone first," I mutter.

He clasps his hand around my wrist and puts his phone in my palm, curling my fingers closed over it. He takes a step back, surrendering.

I love you. These three words have the power to change your entire existence. They can heal you or hurt you. And up until recently, only one person in my life has said those words to me in my twenty-something years. That was until him.

Before him...well, welcome to my dark little fairytale. A zombie rescued me from putting a bullet in my head, and I think that's really where everything begins.

I hold my masterpiece up, waiting for his thoughts as he holds me tight.

The simple thoughts keyed to a digital notebook don't feel as good as they do when I press them to paper. I understand it.

Do I still want out of this life? Yes.

Am I willing to let Bennett Larson help me, and I mean really, fully, let him inside my head at my lowest points? I have to try. I want to try. I was begging him to rescue all along, wasn't I? For someone as stubborn-minded as me, I suppose I've been running from this for too long. As I held myself together, convinced I had to be strong, I've always wanted someone to take my pain, be my strength, and rip me from the edge when I finally broke...because we all break at some point.

"You're going to take my job." He plucks the phone from my hand, slips it into his pocket, and twirls me in circles. "Dance with me, Cherry bomb."

He holds me tight, taking all of my weight as I let my tears crash into him.

Bennett In Silence

*"T*ime to go. I want to get out of this state."

Shifter and I have come to an understanding by force. At the bar that night, we bonded over a cigarette—which Cherry caught us with—after Wes lost his temper. I won't lie, he's quite intimidating at his size when he gets riled up.

He has a weak spot for the presence of women, though. It wasn't until Cherry walked out and I allowed Feather to sit at the bar to order something to eat that he grabbed Shifter by the throat. A group of locals, younger than the rest of the crowd, enjoyed the show and offered to replace the beer that had crashed to the floor. Shifter stormed off with a bummed ego and a reality check. Wes is right. We can't be at each other's throats while a larger threat is endangering our plans.

My timing couldn't have been better. If I didn't go outside to talk to him, I wouldn't—I should have assumed Cherry found a way to the roof. The structure mimics that of Freedome. I might not have been concerned about the gunshots if I were inside—wrote them off as bottle shooting and my-dick-is-bigger-than-yours competitions.

Would you expect more of me—the biggest asshole you know and love?

I saw the ladder and had to follow her. Saving her life wasn't what I was expecting to do. Who knew I was capable of that?

You did. Shit, sometimes I hate your support.

So, Cherry...She actually thought she could give up? After everything I've gone out of my way to do? I'm not letting her leave without me. She's my suicide and I'm her life. If I'm living, so is she, and if she dies, so do I...and I'm not ready to die. Fuck that. I'm not ready to hash out that mystery.

Ah, there he is. Right? There's the big bad Bennett.

It's all about me.

If it benefits me, I'm in.

Some days I wish I had never met Cherry...because now I'm lying to myself. It's not about me, is it?

"Yes, boss." Shifter smirks and smacks Wes on the shoulder. "You good, man?"

"Yeah." He forces a smile. "What do you think, Cherry?"

She glances around and returns the same forced smile. "Another time, it could be fun."

"Another time," he agrees.

The SUV stays silent, four broken people and one scared for their life, all struggling to see the light in our dark existence. Eventually, they drop like flies, one after the other, falling asleep as I drive through the night.

The blood on my hands came with a price. I've done and seen enough to say the shock value has to be quite extensive in order to affect me. Tonight, she got me. The timeframe when my think space is busy—coordinating, driving, and analyzing this mission—it's as if it were like every other memory. Then, it gets quiet, and the images stick to me with pins. I try to wash them away in the mirror, but they remain. She's holding the gun, and I'm almost a second too late. Her finger is on the trigger, and I'm on the verge of being too late.

"Keep the change," I tell the tall skeletal man at the check-in desk. It wasn't even five dollars, but I have a feeling he doesn't hear that often. I plan to evade check-out. We'll only be here a few hours. Then, it's back to it like we originally agreed. After the events at that bar, it was necessary to take a break.

"Who's she staying with?" Shifter asks as I hand him the keycard to his room, noting the hostage in the back of the car. I pull out a stack of money, unwrap a fifty-dollar bill, and hand it to him.

I have to feed the henchmen.

This is the shittiest place we've stayed—a two-story motel that hasn't been updated since the seventies. I'm waiting for the place to get raided for hookers and drugs. It would be something to write about.

Glancing through the wall of glass, I easily spot Wes propped against the front bumper of the vehicle, checking his phone. Cherry walks around the rear with her navy duffel hanging from one shoulder. Once I'm finished dealing with everyone, I have to get a few thousand words into my laptop. My think space is overflowing.

"With us." The upward roll of his eyes doesn't go unnoticed. "Don't question me." His hands shoot over his head, and he backs away. "Wait." His sigh is enough to make me reconsider what I'm about to say. "The gunshots...It wasn't a local chasing a coyote away. Cherry..." Now I sigh. Why am I telling him this? I look past him, chewing at a fragment of skin on my lower lip. "I found her with a gun—" My eyes get lost on the ground as my jaw hangs. My mind is plastered with the image of her. Shit, I get it...the pictures that she can't delete, the things she has seen.

She can tell me about her demons, every fucked up thing that happened to her, and I only give her sympathy for the time frame, then move on with my life. She can't move on. She's constantly reminded, unable to heal.

I clear my throat. "She had it pressed to her head and was ready to pull the trigger. Saving her is completely selfish. I wouldn't save anyone else. I'd let them blow their fucking brains out in front of a crowd." I don't know if I'll ever regain a moral compass, and if it weren't for her, I wouldn't care. I would feel the need to talk to Shifter.

As our eyes connect, he's unreadable, wiping any reminiscence of shock or pain from his face. "Yeah, yeah, yeah," he nods. "You're not gonna fuck it up. I get it. Doc Feather is best under your watch." He turns away, holds the cash and keycard in the air, and walks toward Wes as the door falls closed. "Beer and board," he shouts.

I open it back up and call for Cherry. "Let's go, and her." I point.

She joins me, walking down the sidewalk to our shag-rug paradise. "She's coming with us?"

"Yeah."

"She's hot."

"What?" I do a double-take.

"She's hot. We should fuck her."

I glance over my shoulder to make sure she's following. "She's going to hear you."

"So, we did Shifter, why not her?"

A day can't pass without Cherry attempting to raise my blood pressure.

"First, *you* did Shifter. Not me. Second, she's not one of us. She's the opposite. Third, I know what you're doing."

"What?"

"Trying to even the playing field." I stop in front of our door. "We've both used people to get off. This isn't the right escape. It's over. Let's move on, and if you still think you need to make it up to me, *I do* miss those pigtails."

I push the door open as her beautiful smile rises to the apples of her cheeks. It's fucking groovy.

Bennett, It's The Climax

"I hate it," I grumble and push my laptop away.

"We literally kidnapped someone. Abduction, B. I think that's a high in your story. A plot thickener?"

"More like a low. Thin, darling."

Feather is rolled to her side, allowing as much distance as she can get between us on the twin bed parallel to ours. She's out cold, breathing shallow.

Our showers lasted five minutes each, enduring limited hot water and pressure that I'd classify as ass. Oh, how my pre-existing life meets my current. At one point, Cherry shut the bathroom door, and it got stuck. I thought I was going to have to break it down. After I shimmied it enough times, it popped loose.

"Our lives are unusual, B. It'll make a good book, and I shouldn't have to tell you—you're a good writer." She gazes up at me with her chin uncomfortably digging into my bare ribs. Her petite body rests between my legs. I tuck another pillow under my head and weave my fingers into her hair. *I almost didn't get to do this again.*

"Yeah, I'm fucking brilliant, right?" I chuckle. "It's just—it's not coming to me like Red Tape did. I wrote that book in two months. This, whatever the fuck it's going to be called, has been fucking me hard with no lube." I catch her eyes as her pointer rolls back and forth across my nipple. She adores the piercing...or at least finds it amusing. I swear she's replacing that fidget ring on her hand with my body.

"Stop trying to rush it. It'll come to you."

"Did you see the future?"

"I saw the future, a crazy, yet charming man promised me."

"Charming? Do I know this man?"

"You do, and he promised me a house overlooking the ocean...with a big fluffy cat rubbing against my leg and his white-eyes scanning an old ratty notebook as he sits fireside."

"Fluffy cat?" I'm going to have no choice but to buy a big fucking fluffy cat with some dramatic-ass name. Clifford Von Cinnamon Struddle Castle, The First.

"I'll name it after our book, if you pick a good title." She reads my mind.

"You end up with something more dramatic than whatever I conclude as my—our title."

"I like the name Georgia."

"Georgia Peaches & Cream Von Hickory Hell."

"Classy, especially the Hickory Hell part."

"Enough about the Hickory Hell cat. Can we go back to the white-eyed part of this vision?"

"The extra spicy version."

"Yeah, well, do you think I'd get to keep that after I take your cure?"

She leans onto her forearms, putting her weight on my lungs. "I don't care what color they are or what abilities you have, as long as you don't chop anyone up or strangle them or run them over."

"I can bury them alive, though, that's still on the table, right?"

"What did they do to deserve it?"

"Made fun of my girl's stripper name."

"Same old B. An asshole." She smacks me in the face and grabs my chin as I chuckle.

I snatch her wrists and hold her still below my neck. "*Your* asshole."

"You want to fuck me in my—" I kiss her mouth, shutting her up.

"With the complimentary travel-sized lotion this fucking *gorgeous* motel came with. Easy slip and release."

"It's probably as outdated as this place."

It was the closest, and after driving for two days, it seemed good enough. I didn't see any cameras either, which works out for us. Less liability. I have a reputation, as does Cherry now, besides being wanted rats.

"Oh, don't back out now." I tug her lips to mine, lowering my voice. "It's not the lotion you fear. It's how you won't be able to keep your mouth shut when I fuck you. Wouldn't want to wake the prisoner." I dip my head toward the neighboring bed.

"Want to play the quiet game?" She taunts. "It's a little more complicated than you're usual preference, in my opinion."

"Backdoor quiet games?"

"Front door, Romeo."

"Fine, no seventies lotion lube." I heavily sigh, tilting my head back until it hits the headboard. "Rain check?" I grasp her jaw and lean back in.

"Don't invite any visitors over when you buy this beach house. You owe me the best night of my life."

"Who the fuck would I invite, Shifter?" I draw her chin closer to my mouth, bending forward to kiss her lips.

"You like him."

"Don't go crazy on me. We have some common interests, but I don't *like* him."

"Whatever you say."

"Cherry," I growl.

"B," she sings.

I run my fingers through her hair, brushing it back into a ponytail. "Do you have anything you want to talk about tonight?"

"Not really."

"Are you sure?" I tug on my homemade handle.

"I'm not forcing you to take the cure, B."

"Wherever you go, I'm destined to follow."

"That's false poetry."

I fixate on the ceiling. "I can tell you what's going to ease your mind."

"I'm not holding a gun, B."

"I'm terrified."

"You don't have to take it. I promise you, I won't make that demand. I…" Her chin digs into my chest. "Benny will always be in there." She taps the space my heart beats. "Besides, you're the one who has to live with the side effects."

My brows raise, considering the pros. "Benny is a scared bitch."

"Bennett is a scary bitch."

I smirk. "You think I'm scary?"

"Nothing I can't handle."

"Do you know why I hate being Benny?"

"Why? I rather like him."

"All I've wanted for my entire life was to be heard. To be wanted. The man I was before would have crawled on hands and knees until the gushing red for the praise of his parents, peers…The man they turned me into *took it*."

"Someone found you when you were just Benny. They found Red Tape, and they loved it. They shared it and spoke of it and pushed it to more eyes. Now, nobody can shield their eyes. A man of monstrous capacity, you forced their hand to turn the page of your book."

"Now it's our book and I swear if you try to leave this world before we finish it, I'm going to climb the ladder to Heaven and drag your pierced nose, cute-ass self back home."

"I'm okay, B. Right now, I'm okay."

"Are you sure?"

"If I promise to put more expectations on myself and less on you, will you forgive me?"

"There's nothing to forgive."

Wrinkles take her forehead, and for a long distance, she remains silent. "Don't you wish you could turn it off?" She stares into my depths. "I don't want to feel anymore."

"You'd rather feel nothing, and I'd rather feel pain. Equally, we feel pleasure within each other, and that's why I need you to fight. If you don't, if you find a way to stop feeling, you won't feel me. Selfishly, I'll be alone again with only pain to comfort my existence. You'll be an angel, but this could be the last time you dig these nails into my skin." She takes the opportunity, leaving claw-like marks down my chest. "Anything else you need to get out of that thick think space?" I tap her temple.

"I'm okay."

I let her hair fall and dip to her mouth, taking her tongue with mine. Her waist pleads for my grip as I wrap my hands around her and pull her tight, sucking at her neck.

"Fuck, I want to throw you around." As I roll, tucking her body beneath mine, I pin her to the ugly floral blanket. I press my lips to her chest bone and laugh against her delicate skin. "That's right, eye stays on me. You know how much I love that." My fingers spread wide, feeling beneath her tank top, and I sink my teeth into the lowest exposed part of her side. Her body squirms below me, but she holds her tongue, not making a sound. "Okay, darling. I might take you up on that game."

Looping my fingers under the elastic of her shorts, I rip them down with her frilly underwear. My hands take her calves, catching the smooth curves as I lift one foot and pull her shorts off. I squeeze her ankles, pulling her to the end of the bed, and her squeals erupt as she smacks her hand over her mouth.

"Shh," I warn. Her normally smooth pussy is more bristly after not shaving for a few days and is ever so attractive. Every time I'm with her, it's as thrilling as that night in the woods. It's the little things, like the potential to get caught.

I grip her hips tight and flip her over. Her hands follow, slapping to the mattress.

"Shh," I repeat, shaking my head. "You're going to lose this game."

As her fingers clench the sheets, she looks back at me. "No, I'm not."

With two fingers curved between her legs, she holds back moans. It's like a fucking silent movie besides the sweet sound of her arousal. I want to whisper sweet words to her, but all I can think about is losing the game by saying something idiotic like *soak my dick*. She's not winning this one. I tug my shorts down and press the head of my cock to her opening. She arches her ass up higher, pushing to her tiptoes.

"Fuck, that's it, baby."

"Shh," she hushes me.

I drop my shorts in a rush, gliding through her slick, wet pussy lips, and drive into her, a quarter of a way before I decelerate and make her wait for the whole thing. She tries to stick her ass out farther, wanting more. I tease her as she shifts her hips, begging me to find that soft spot and grind into her.

"B," she whispers, falling from her toes. I dredge in fully, pumping in and out of her. She unravels, trying to muffle her cries into the comforter. The temptation to smack her ass until it's tomato red torments me. Why must it be the *fucking quiet game?*

I spread my legs wider, on the outside of hers, and drop my chest forward until it's against her back. Pulling the hair away from her neck, I chew on her earlobe. "This game sucks. I want to hear you." My hands border her head as I sink into her.

"This position is so hot," she whispers.

"Do you like this?" My hot breath trails from her ear to her neck, where I drag my teeth against her skin. She overextends, surrendering her artery to my lips.

"God, B." She pulls away, drilling her teeth into my wrist, and I jerk back from the pain.

"My little sadist," I mutter.

I pull out, taking a step back.

"Don't look at me like that." I keep my voice low and hold out my hand. It doesn't take her long to come crashing into my chest as I yank her up. As I steer her around until her shoulder blades hit the window blind, my mouth attacks her neck.

"Mhm," she moans, tipping her chin up. "B...No marks."

Her soft jaw settles in my palms, and she stares into my soul. "Your eyes are beautiful. I could fucking drown in them."

"You're not being quiet," she mouths with very little sound.

A breathy chuckle leaves my mouth. I glance down for a moment, then snatch the string to the blinds beside her head and pull, shoving her shoulders back and kicking her legs open. Her round ass deepens into the glass, and my knee takes her pussy, putting pressure on her clit. She rotates her hips, working it to her advantage.

"How's that feel, darling?"

"Shh."

I pull her thigh over mine, and she hooks around me as I enter her. "I know you want to moan. It's all over your face," I whisper. "The way your mouth hangs and you can't keep your head still, constantly switching directions and trying to launch forward." I constrict her air before she can reply and hold her in place.

"Scream, baby. Let me try to shut you up." She lets out a hard moan, and I hold tighter, sinking into her ocean eyes. She looks at me with passion and heat as I look at her in a way only described as wanting to eat her for breakfast, lunch, and dinner, spit her out, and destroy her within my teeth all over again. Her moans get louder, and I squeeze more. It takes her, turning her silent, and I know to let go. I'll never let her fade completely like she did that night at my house. She couldn't make me.

"Quiet."

"I can't," she coughs.

"Alright, fuck it." I pull out and grab the car key from the desk half a foot away, hitting the unlock button on the fob. Once I set her feet to the floor, I grab the door card. "Outside, now."

"Naked?" She yells in a whisper.

"I'm naked. You have a top on. It's dark." Her eyes narrow. "Do you want me to fuck an orgasm out of you or not?" I open the door, and after a few seconds more of hesitation, she agrees, peeking into the darkness. Nobody's out there, and only one of the building's exterior lights works. "Go."

She steps out onto the sidewalk, and I walk around her, taking her hand to lead her to the tailgate. She holds her hand in front of her, hiding her pussy for no reason other than the thought of being caught. I quickly turn the interior lights off after opening the hatch.

Is this risky for who I am...for who we are? The Hollywood couple that every tabloid and gossip website would love on their front page? Yeah, but doesn't that make it more exciting?

"Bend over."

"You're not serious."

I dip my head to the side, saying it once more. "Bend the fuck over."

"Fine." She gets saucy.

"Do you forfeit?"

"No!" She snaps.

"We'll see about that."

I grab a ponytail full of hair and wrap it around my hand. "Wider." She spreads her legs farther apart, and I ease back in. "Can you stay quiet, darling?" I tug her neck back as she braces her hands on the trunk carpeting. "You're enjoying this, aren't you?" She breathes heavier. "You like it when I parade you around. You'd like more if my cum was warming the inside of your sweet pussy."

"Oh," her moans escape. "Yes," she cries out. "Don't stop."

Fuck. "Are you mine, Cherry?"

"I'm yours, B."

"Fuck. Yes, you are."

She gasps, then holds her breath.

She does it two more times. Fuck, she's close.

I trace the contour of her waist and cup her breast, circling her hard nipple with my thumb. Pinching it between two fingers, she takes a deep breath in. It empties with a moan that drives me fucking insane. Her walls tighten around my dick.

"Hold on to it," I pant. "I know it feels good right there. Don't let it go, yet." I tower over her.

"I c—I can't." She exhales pulse. "I'm—"

"Come for me." She clings to her orgasm while waves squeeze around my cock. "You know, I love those sounds, but..." She relaxes, clawing at my hands, and I slowly pump long strokes in and back out. Her nails dig into the veins protruding across my hands. "I win."

"Fuck me," a voice calls out. "Why the fuck am I always running into you two like this?"

Cherry and I both lock onto Shifter. My eyes roll to the back of my head, and I remain buried in Cherry as he gets a clear view of my bare ass.

"Want tagged in?" I scowl, unamused.

"No. Fuck no." He switches his plastic bag from one hand to the other. "Sounds like she's already satisfied." He continues walking past us, toward his room.

"That's right."

"Sorry, Shift!" Cherry calls.

He flicks his free wrist, not looking back.

My signature laugh rumbles out of my throat. "I fucking love you, but *I did win.*"

"It was a tie," she argues. "You didn't shut either."

I lean into her with my mouth against her ear. "I won."

"Did you, though? Were you the one who got off?"

"Don't worry, darling. You can suck me off when we wake." I slide out of her, and she stands. I grab the keycard and close the trunk. "Let's go to bed." Hoisting her up by the thighs and over my shoulder, I cover her exposed skin with my hand as I run back to our room.

Bennett VS Plastic Monsters

"We're about forty-five minutes out," I announce, flexing my fingers on the steering wheel. "Are you ready to revisit the ever-loving shit-hole of East Grenton?"

"No," Cherry admits. "I don't have a choice. Do I?"

"There's always a choice."

"Yeah, one that will put us right back to where we began."

"That wasn't the worst place."

"Playing pretend? I thought I wasn't allowed to do it anymore?" She glares at me.

"With me. Not with the world."

"It's all...silicone and plastic. I can't go on that way, B." Her thumb flicks over her ring. "I don't want the fear following me around, always waiting for the monster within to reappear."

"I know." I press the tip of my tongue to my teeth. "You can't blame me for trying."

"It's a waste of your time."

"My time is quite sketchy. The days are uncertain, and talking to you, bullshit or truth, would be the best way to spend my last breath."

Wes peeks his head between our seats. "Aw, what a sweetheart."

As I narrow my eyes, Shifter's image appears in my mirror. His position has remained the same, as he continues to stare out the window, just like he was doing about an hour ago.

"I can't wait to get a real shower," Wes continues. "I'm gonna soak that water up for thirty-five to forty minutes, give or take."

Shifter awakens. "No, you won't," he retorts. "You won't last that long. It's one week too many days since you got it in."

"And too many days since you fucked your hand," Wes fires back.

"I have a doll for that. Her name's Candy."

"I bet she's classy."

"She's a one-man kinda girl." Shifter's gaze focuses on Cherry. "She doesn't talk. I'm pretty sure it's because she has *a thick southern draw.*"

"A down-home southern gal made of plastic? Never heard of it."

"We're all made of plastic," I interrupt.

"Maybe in that Hollywood world you're used to," Shifter replies.

"Past the implants and inserts, we live on a burning planet. Plastic particles consume us, whether you spend thousands on bigger tits and lips or you're simply existing."

"Yeah, yeah, yeah. We're all fucking dead." He returns to staring out the window as the car becomes silent again. "We're all fucking dead."

"Some of us are better off," I admit. "Zombies."

"Well damn, ya'll know how to kill a mood." Wes stretches his arms above his head. "How are you doin', Miss Feather?" He asks our golden ticket doctor. She's shrunken to the back of her seat between the two men, feeling small both physically and mentally.

"Okay."

"Are you sure? You're not hungry or anythin'?"

"No," she replies, likely lying.

"Our in-house chef will keep you filled," Wes insists. "Slow is surprisingly good in the kitchen."

"Slow?" She questioned.

"Solomon. His name is actually Solomon. When you've been together as much as we have, you utilize interestin' nicknames. You're not still afraid of us, are you?"

"No." Her lips say one thing and her eyes another, drifting to the back of my head.

She couldn't admit it if she wanted to. That would make her appear weak, and she wouldn't want that—Miss Independent. Tell me I'm not the only one who gets that vibe. You get it, right?

Timid words bring my attention to Cherry. "Do you remember any of us?" She asks.

"I...Faces. I remember all of your faces...and you, David, and *him*." Her unsteady glare returns to me. "All of you had visited my sector."

She piques Shifter's interest. "You had assigned areas?" He asks.

She nods. "As any job with a large staff would."

"What can you tell me about Ronald Hyderton?" I ask.

In her silence, she shakes her head from left to right.

"You can't tell us anything?" Shifter asks.

"I don't know anything. I've never met him."

"You want me to believe the gossip wasn't thick in your *sector*?" I scoff.

As she becomes tense, Wes decides to play up his good guy role. "Lay off. She doesn't know anythin'."

"I have to meet with this dickhead—who had a significant amount of play in creating this version of me—"

"A monster," Shifter interrupts.

"Takes one to know one, huh?"

"I think we've all established what's going on here," Cherry insists. "Shifter being a zombie should stay between us four until we agree it's a good time to tell everyone else."

"I agree," Wes says. "I'm still tryin' to wrap my head around it myself."

Shifter's gaze settles on Feather. "Right," he says. "I've avoided telling anyone this long for a reason."

"Cherry and I are going to the hotel. Am I dropping anyone off at the lab first, or are you both coming with us?"

"I'm staying with the doc," Shifter replies.

"I'll go with you. You know, I can take turns with Shifter, babysitting. No offense." Wes glances over at Feather.

"None taken." Her lips turn to something that resembles a smile. It's not one, and yet the closest to it since…It's been a long drive. "I understand my value. There's almost a comfort in it."

That's the most I've heard from her the entire drive as well. It's reassuring. She's not going to attempt to run, now, is she?

"Except me—you won't find comfort near me." My statement doubles as a question, neither met with a response.

"How far away are we?" Cherry asks.

"Not far." My words cue her gentle sigh. "Wes, once we get to the hotel, make a phone call and check on the details of this meeting. I don't want to walk into any surprises." *Honestly, we can't afford to.*

"Got it, boss."

As the car becomes quiet again, I debate my introduction. Should I congratulate Mr. Hyderton on his success in my creation, or should I slice his head clear off and continue on with my existence? The latter seems like the easiest solution. Yet, there's a part of me that wants answers. Was this experiment a colossal mishap or a few miscalculations they told themselves wouldn't be a problem? What do they want to do next? Will they attempt to replicate what's been done? Are they that fucking stupid? Or will they analyze and tweak, like every mutant evolved from a lab? Does he have others backing him? Will they come for us if he goes missing?

Fuck. The choice is made for me.

We report to the lab on time. I wouldn't show up any other way than dressed to the nines in another five-thousand-dollar suit. This is the first time I've been in this room. It reminds me of a conference room—commercial carpet, blank walls with a random painting, and a long rectangular table. I shouldn't be surprised by the corporate nightmare that exists within this building.

Mr. Hyderton extends his hand, receiving only my infernal glare in return. I refuse to stand up straight from the slouch I'm in, keeping my ass on the end of the table.

"Mr. Larson, call me Ron," he introduces himself. "May I call you Bennett?"

"I'm sure you never have before, why start now. Let's just cut to the chase. We all know who you are, and it's clear you know who we are."

"Indeed, Mr. Larson. That is true. I know all of your names. I know about each one of your families. I know your last job, what sports you played or didn't play in high school, and a few of you have a trail of ex-girlfriends."

"How many naps did you take while reading those files?" Wes interrupts.

"He didn't read them. His secretary gave him a summary," Shifter scoffs.

All the rats are scattered behind me, including Cherry. Shifter leans against the wall, crossing his legs at the ankle. Cherry isn't far from him, seated, followed by Charlie and Seth. Solomon, Wes, and Veronica are opposite of Shifter, with Dr. Feather, who is protected, positioned between the two guys. We don't feel safe. Neither does he.

Two bodyguards stand across from us, strapped. They should be inside the lab. The weapons they had and used on us before were specifically designed to stop monsters like us. It's probable that another laboratory exists and an armory. With how deep his pockets are, there is much more.

He looks at Wes in silence. A moment hangs, and then he opens his mouth. "Wesley Baker. Mother was killed by a driver under the influence at age seven. Lived with maternal grandmother until the age of sixteen, when she passed. Graduated high school by a thread and spent four years working for Fuller Carpentry. Fired after sleeping with the boss's daughter. Shannon was her name, correct?"

Wes remains standing, stoned over, and clenching his jaw.

The arrogant millionaire is trying to play God. He created something, and it's not of a sane mind. If he thinks he knows us, his ideals are words on paper. They lack true representation.

Shifter steps forward. "Ronald Hyderton. Fifty-three. Made all his money by cheating and embezzling. The poker king. It's not as brilliant as your front. You think you're in control, as if you have the upper hand."

"Those accusations were never proven." A condescending smile crosses his face.

"Yeah, yeah, yeah. I could go on, but I made my point. I know all about you, your wife, your ex-wife…your daughter."

"They call you *Shifter*, correct?"

"You can stick to David. You already know my government name, right?"

He nods, thinning his lips together. His suit, shoes, and haircut are expensive. As are mine, and I know the secrets that lie behind my eyes.

"I started this project ten years ago."

"Why?" I ask.

"For my daughter." He glances at Shifter, and my eyes follow. "She suffers from a slew of mental health conditions and instability. We sifted through a large number of candidates and picked out individuals who most likely had trauma and mental health conditions, determined by their background checks. Those that had not been previously addressed were the top priority. You are all different, and that makes your results of the trial vary widely." He clasps his hands together, poised to deliver the punchline. "This outcome wasn't ideal, though seven of you have signed contracts and I'd like you to continue to honor them."

"You want us to continue to be your lab rats and let you experiment on us without hesitation? You picked the wrong audience to cry about your sick kid."

"Not you, Mr. Larson. You never signed a contract, but I have a feeling you'll want to stick around anyway." He glances at Cherry. "I want to study the results. We will not be doing any more injectables at this time."

"What's stopping any of them from walking away? Small claims court?"

"This is past small claims. You pose a threat to national security. A few phone calls and all of your faces will be on every screen with a reward leading to capture."

"It wouldn't be too difficult for us to disappear. And we have your last doctor. I think we have the upper hand," I assert.

"I have all the research she needs to cure you. That's what you're after, correct? A cure? Some of you, anyway. I'm sure we can come to a deal. You're an intelligent man, Mr. Larson. Allow me to solicit six months. Six months of testing, and at the end of those six months, if we developed something to help your conditions, you will have access to it." He walks up to me, uncomfortably close. "You have my number. Discuss it and get back to me tomorrow. Let's stay twenty-four hours." He extends his hand again, and this time I reluctantly shake it. He confidently walks down the corridor and out the exit.

"No fucking way," Wes says, running his fingertips along his neck.

"I'm with Wes," Ronnie agrees. "He's a liar. We'll spend six months being poked with a needle and then they'll off us, quietly and all at once."

"I don't think we have many other options," I reply. "We need what he has to offer, and his threats can be proven. To be fair, we'll take a vote."

"I'll do it." Seth's green eyes stay on the floor. "I'll be their rat."

"Me too," Slow answers. After the stories I've heard about him, his decision-making tends to be rash and unpredictable. He still gets a vote.

"Two for no. Three for yes." I turn to the rat wearing a rimmed hat. "It's Charlie, right? I've heard you're opinionated, and you've yet to speak up. Is there anything going on under that fancy hat?"

Wes and Shifter trade glares and groans. That must've been the wrong question to ask him.

"Yeah." His hands jot to his hips, and he begins to pace. "I think this is going to be a shit show and blow up in our faces. It's all propaganda. I can guarantee he doesn't have a kid. And if he brings government officials into this, he'd have to confess to everything he's been doing in his private lab, including surrendering all of his research. Subsequently, he claims six months, and your freedom is granted. We all know how that's going to go."

"You can't *guarantee* it. He told the truth about the kid," Shifter cuts him off, unfazed.

I blankly stare at him. "Shifter likes to withhold information."

"I vote yes," Charlie announces. After complaining, he chooses to sign up for the six months. Now I understand the groans.

"Shifter?"

"Um, I'm gonna have to say no. It doesn't feel like the right path." He rubs his ear, and I hesitate. "There has to be another option."

He's wrong, and it's Cherry's turn. To feel the rain on her skin, she's going to have to endure the acid that pours down first. The pain, the unknown—in her case, it's a chance she should take.

"Cherry?"

"I…" She shakes her head in disbelief. "I can't believe you're going to trust them. How do any of you trust they'll help us?"

"What? I don't trust him. This is what you wanted, wasn't it—*an antidote?*"

My phone buzzes, vibrating my thigh. I close my eyes and hang my head before I pull it out to see the name. *Justin.* "I have to take this. It's Justin." I turn away, and Cherry's factory ringtone begins to play. As I tap the red circle to send Justin's call to voicemail, my glare settles heavily on Cherry. "Who's calling you?" Her agent is the only person who calls her, and I thought she was holding off on the job she was offered. She didn't want to commit to the role until she had her feet again.

"I don't know…Hello?" She answers it, and I instinctively want to hide when I hear the tone. "Yes, Mel," she loudly pronounces, glaring at me. "I am still dating Bennett…mhm, yeah…"

My phone rings for a second time, and I pick it up on the first string of notes. "Hello?"

"Mr. Larson, it's your assistant, Justin."

"I know who you fucking are, dumbass. When is the manuscript due?" I rub my temple, spinning leisurely on my heel.

"Oh, it's not about that. Post-production and Ms. Mills determined that the ending scene you discussed needs to be reshot. I'm forwarding her email to you now about lighting issues. Are you available next week?" Damn it. The screen director. I thought I had resolved that issue with my *particular talents*, but I was quite distracted.

My brows crease as Cherry mentions me. "Yes, he's talking to Justin now. Okay, I'll be ready for the call when the dates are set. It shouldn't expand past two days?" She nods. "Okay. Thanks, Mel." Cherry hangs up, and her bubbly persona shuts off with it.

"Mr. Larson?"

"I'll call you back tomorrow."

"But—"

"No. I need a day. I'll call you tomorrow," I repeat, knowing I'll ring him up around ten P.M. tonight, as I wind down.

I need a fucking cigarette.

I can't have a fucking cigarette.

"I could send you and stay here."

"You're not serious, are you?" She shakes her head. "I can't see you relinquishing control of a movie—your movie. What—I'm..."

"I chose everyone on my team because I know they're great at what they do. Nothing I've written and filmed would be possible without them," I admit.

"Hah." Shifter's stifled laugh takes my attention away from Cherry. "Would anything be possible if you weren't a lab rat? Why bother staying?"

"Because, unlike those people, who I'm certain will do their job as they have always intended, Hyderton won't. If I'm not here, what's stopping his team from taking everything? You don't fucking trust them. We'll neither do I, and that's the point, Shifter. If we don't control this narrative, come to an agreement on our terms, and hold him to it with a plan when it all goes south, we lose any hope of answers. And as much as I want to keep my abilities, I care about her." I point to Cherry. "She's the reason I'm here. And I know fucking well enough, if it came down to it, you'd do anything you had to do to find a way to calm her mind as I would."

"She said she's not on board."

"She's being fucking stupid."

"Excuse me," Cherry calls out. "*She* is in the room. I can make my own decisions, Bennett."

"She's scared," Wes says. "I'm scared."

"Now isn't the time to be a bunch of pussies," I declare, exchanging glances with each one of them. "We are what they fear. Each one of us who was constantly underestimated and sold short—we are the chosen."

In silence, an unyielding laugh comes from the wall Shifter has propped himself against. "Oh, the chosen ones. How's that novel coming?"

I'm going to knock that pretty smile from his lips.

"Would you like to speak outside?"

"I've said all I have to say." He straightens, stiffly passing me and walking through the doorway.

The room slowly disperses, and Cherry makes her way back to Shifter. I wait as she exchanges words with him, hugs Wes, and says her goodbyes to the rest of her *family.*

They remain here—their home—but I want to get the fuck away from this place. I need to leave for the night and return when we're able to come to a clear arrangement.

The pressure piles on my shoulders from all ends.

CHASING THE HIGH, BENNETT?

*V*iolence. It's my high of choice...or outlet. Once, it was video games. Then, it concluded lives and stretched the imagination of sexually deprived women. Now, it's the distance between Cherry's kiss and constricting palms. I don't get off on being hurt. You should know by now I'm more complex than that.

Bennett, you're mind is on sex again.

Darling, I must stress, this is my content state. Would you rather I go back to killing people? Look, we both know I don't cope in the healthiest manner. I won't judge you if you won't—I will judge you. Please, before you swipe your sugar daddy's platinum, reconsider the low-rise jeans and platform, chunky, fucked shoes. Was it the off-white ones you picked out? What do they fucking call them—sand? It's equivalent to naming makeup colors after coffee. Would Miss Vanilla Latte report to the front checkout to meet their party, Darling Cappuccino, and Ms. Caramel Nutmeg? Am I pissing you off? Good.

Stop giving me advice.

As I was saying, violence is my high, outlet, and all of the above. When Cherry challenges me to a cat-on-cat sword fight, the world melts away. The storm comes before the calm. And once the calm fades, we face reality hand in hand...throat in hand?

I will always choose violence.

"Fuck," I groan. "You can do better than that!"

Cherry pulls her hand back and swings it, connecting with my cheek. The slap heats the corner of my grin. With my wrists tied to the headboard of the king-size bed in our hotel suite, two of her shirts looped together kept me from evading. She rides my dick and my body is covered in her marks; red hand prints, scratches, teeth marks, and the amount of times she's choked me out has to be a record. Neither of us is okay. We're fighting for our lives in a place of desperate agony. She gives me her pain, and I laugh it off. Every deep chuckle that rolls through my throat admits it's fucked. That we're fucked. And I accept it. This is where we are. It's pointless to be frustrated with myself when a hundred other men deserve my spite.

"Are you going to do it?" She yells.

"Should I?"

"What's wrong with you? Should I? *Should I?* You're fucking Bennett Larson, the big bad zero-zero-one, the zombie of lab rats. Is that the man who's asking me what to do?" The skin-to-skin echo rises with the sting of her hand on my jaw. "You should be *the asshole.* Tell everyone who's in charge," she orders.

"You're fucking right." Hah. "You're my reminder, Cherry bomb."

"I'm you're crazy."

"You're my everything."

"Call Shifter."

"Right now?"

"Call him."

This isn't ideal. I wanted to focus on something other than this—fuck, anything else. She couldn't. We're operating on different levels, except if she tells me to create more violence, I'm signing my name on the dotted line. Part of me wonders how twisted the wires in her think space are. If she said "kill them" would I do it? Would I risk her resentment for a temporary high? It would be a damn good high.

She hangs off the side of the bed, suctions her legs tight to my sides, and reaches for her cropped hoodie on the floor. If she falls, it's going to hurt both of us...in ways you don't easily recover from.

"Don't fall. I'll go on a murdering spree if you break my dick."

"That's the threat you choose to go with?"

"Innocent housekeepers and front desk agents, darling."

"Can that actually happen?" She sits up, reaching into the pouch and pulling her phone out. "A man can break their penis?"

"Yeah, and I don't want to experience it. I don't know if a broken cock would be more brutal or if ripping my barbell out would."

"I forgot, you're well-versed in penis healing. I'll make note of ways to…further obligate a man."

She taps the call button on the screen, and Shifter answers on the second ring. "What's up, sweets?"

"You're on speaker. Bennett wants to talk to you," she replies, holding the phone between us.

"Tell that fucker to be at the lab in an hour. I know he'll make it happen."

"B!"

"What?" She grinds against my dick. "Fine. Two hours. Tell him to be there in two hours."

"What are you going to do?" He grumbles.

"Remind him who we are. I needed a reminder myself."

"I don't—"

"Your opinion isn't—"

"Yeah, it does fucking matter. Mine, Wes, Ronnie, Charlie, Solomon, and Seth. This isn't about you and Cherry. It affects all of us."

"You'll get your turn."

"There aren't many choices to make if the head honcho is drowning in his own fluids."

"I won't kill him."

Cherry's cheeks flush pink. "Bennett needs to go now, Shift. See ya soon." She tucks her hair to one side of her neck, letting it fall over her shoulder.

"Two hours?" I ask. "That's excessive."

"It gives me another fifteen minutes torturing you and at least half an hour soaking in the jet tub. We'll have plenty of time to drive back to East Grenton."

"Fifteen minutes isn't enough."

She trails her finger across my chest. "I'm not going anywhere."

"Yeah? You're never leaving?"

"Nope."

"Swear it. Not in two months, two years, or two lifetimes. Because I'm counting on you to match my devotion."

She savagely claims my mouth, sucking the corner of my lip in. "Thank you," she murmurs.

I sweep between her parted lips and her eyes, ravaging her hopeless gaze. "Don't look at me like that. You got me, darling."

Her eyes narrow before a smirk pulls at her cheek. She tries to wipe it off, covering her face in her palms as her hair hangs across her eyes.

"This isn't fair. I can't stop you from hiding when I'm locked up." I rattle my arms around.

Yeah, I'm still tied to the bed. I could easily pull free if I really wanted to, but I humor her do-it-yourself restraints.

"Hold on." She leans forward, her hard nipples drift against my chest, and her breasts spill over me. The farther she reaches, the less of my length stays within her. Her back curves, and the temptation to break free and run my hands down her, to squeeze that ass in my hands, becomes more difficult to resist.

She finds whatever she was searching for and slips back into her place. She clouds my vision with her full frontal display, tits bouncing vaguely. As I glance up, she's tightening a hairband to the side of her head.

"Fuck." My deep chuckle ripples through my chest. "You better untie me so I can pull on those pigtails, schoolgirl."

"This isn't for your pleasure."

"Whatever you want, tell me and I'll make it happen."

"From behind?" A glimmer of her playful nature returns. She looks up at me with a falsely innocent pout, twirling the ends of her strands.

"Behind, above, every way you can imagine. Do you want me to call Shifter back and tell him three hours?"

"No. Talk bloody to me."

"Bloody?" I flex my brows.

"I'd impale Hyderton with a blunt-edged shower rod," she says without a quake in her tone.

"Would you like me to deliver his head on a stick?"

"Only if there was torture involved."

"Don't keep it to yourself. Tell me your ideas, darling." *She needs this more than I do.*

As I rush into the lab, my chest held high and posture in check, Cherry's fingers remain laced between mine. We head toward the miserable conference room, stopping when I see Seth.

"They're in the dining room," he greets us.

"Who let him in there?" Cherry asks.

"Doesn't matter," I remind her as if she weren't the one to fill my head with masculine toxicity. I walk past Scooby-Seth, through the painfully bright hallway. Hyderton spots me entering the room and begins to stand. "Don't get up."

I spot the bottle of Jameson on the counter, leaving Cherry and making my way past the table. I circle behind the island, stretching a foot long. The industrial-sized kitchen busies my time. It takes a few shots to find which cabinet stores the glasses.

As I spot them, I snatch one, and less than gently, I place it on the counter. In silence, all eyes study me. I fill the stubby glass halfway, replace the top, and make my way to the freezer, searching for the ice. *I'll admit, I did that backwards. Someone else will clean that up later.*

I rejoin the table, sitting across from the billionaire. With the flex of my shoulders, I exemplify an ugly grimace.

"Have you come to a decision?" He asks.

The ice in my glass clicks against the side as I stick my finger in, stirring it. I suck the whiskey clean before picking the glass up and downing the double shot. As I plunge forward, the ice rattles once more, and I let go of it. Hyderton's beady eyes focus on me before he ensures the full attention of his bodyguards meets his direction.

"We—you and me—both have money, Mr. Hyderton. We have the freedom to do as we please. Do you agree?"

"Yes." He intently waits for the punchline.

"We're both bad guys trying to be good guys. You don't have to agree. It's the truth, but the thing is, you're a guy who gives ultimatums and threats...and I'm more of the...take what I want and *never* ask for forgiveness kind of guy." I straighten and flip the charcoal cuff along my wrist until it reaches the top of my forearm. As I glance up in amusement, he tugs his lips inward. He's not holding it together as well as he thinks. Each little movement, like the hard gulp that moves his Adam's apple in a bob to the heat building moisture on his skin, proves I have the power. How could I forget that?

"You want to save the world and get all the credit. There's selfishness in that statement, Mr. Hyderton." A fuzzy heat runs through my chest. Cherry watches closely, soaking in the transition happening in front of her—the light eyes of humanity fade as the colorless monster seamlessly forces their way out. "You can have all the credit and the glory. I have no problem with your lies. The thing is, though...the only way to do that is to *walk away*. You have to walk away and let your team of doctors do their job. You're the big man. You shouldn't have to waste time here. You need to go golfing with potential investors. Your discovery is going to make millions. You don't want to waste time here," I repeat. "Your discovery needs heavy-lifting investors." I'm on a different playing field today. I'm not telling a woman she deserves a good time. I'm not easing her worries and reassuring her that I can make her feel amazing. I'm not making an employee think they're blessed for the extra hours of pay. I'm not fighting every particle of dark-being as I convince a doctor to remain calm. This is the old version of me twisted with the new, passionate about a girl, and stronger than anyone who gets in my way. "All you need to do is hand over *all and any* research, including patient profiles, to your head doctor, Ms. Feather Romberg. She is going to do all the work for you. You get to go home and forget the names, the formulas, and the bloodshed that happened in this laboratory. All you will remember is you're about to make millions on a life-changing medication for people like your daughter, and you need to focus on investors to back it."

I lean back, stretching against the chair. "It's that simple, Mr. Hyderton. Tell me you agree."

"I'll call my secretary now to box all the documents up after she deletes the files from my server. Tell Dr. Romberg that I expect to receive trial statistics in six months. In six months, my investors will be expecting a detailed meeting with documents to back up my discovery."

Fuck, yes. Do you see how it's done, darling?

As I rise from the table, a smirk Cherry would classify as arrogant tugs at my lips. "Excellent. We're done here then. I'll see you out."

I lean into Shifter's shoulder as I round the table. "Mind fuck them." I nudge toward the two bodyguards. "We're in charge."

Once they leave, I take Cherry's hands and pull her to my chest. She wraps her arms around my neck, presses to her tiptoes in those fucking hideous sneakers, and lets her lips touch mine.

"You're my hero, B."

"That's what I'm going to call it, *our* book." I lean closer with a whisper. "*I'm Not The Hero.*"

Her lips purse.

Why does she make me nervous like this?

"That begs the question, do I name my fluffy cat Hero...or do I name him Villain?"

The rumble of my faint chuckle pours down her neck. "Baby, I'll buy you two."

Her lips devour mine with every nibble and suck, as if we're star-crossed lovers who made it over the mountain of destruction. We've barely started to climb.

My gaze falls as I let go of her. She rejoins her friends, easily finding her way back into the conversation. Shifter separates from them, and I find his still frame beside me. His arms are tucked across his chest. "You made it happen," he calmly admits.

"It's far from over," I reply, monotone. "Now the doctor needs to work her magic before we have a repeat of...that night."

"She seems happy." He studies Cherry as she laughs with Wes, attempting to style Charlie's messy hair. "She really had a gun to her head?" He looks at me, and I'm unable to leave his framed eyes.

"I wasn't lying when I said I'm afraid of what she'll do. Strong will isn't always her superpower. She won't live a life she can't bear." I glance back at her. "She needs medication or a miracle. This shit they tried to do only made our mental health worse."

"They chemically alter our brains, but how many of us were stupid enough to sign the paperwork without reading every detail?"

"Exactly, Shifter. Exactly. Now you get to be the hero. Feather, better be able to fix this, and I need you to see to it."

"Me?" He digs two fingers into his chest.

"You're the alpha again. I have to go back to Nevada for reshoots. I don't want to be fixed. They do...Cherry does. I'll keep her safe in the meantime. You have two weeks to come up with something. Do whatever you have to do. Convince her." I face him directly, uncrossing my arms. "Cherry is going to do it again, and there's a slight chance I might not be around when it happens. Let that be your motivation. You love her, and you care about these rats. Make it fucking happen." He nods when I give him a shoulder pat.

"Two weeks is cutting it tight."

"She's smarter than leads on."

"Still, two weeks?"

"Save Cherry. Make it fucking happen."

As my eyes leave him, Charlie walks up to me. "How did you do it?" He's loud and draws everyone's attention.

"Mind persuasion is my expertise," I answer bluntly. "If you try hard enough, maybe you'll be able to do it too." *No, he fucking won't.* "For a few weeks anyway, until Dr. Romberg figures this shit out. Half of you already agreed to be test subjects for Big Ron. I don't let the new circumstances change your mind now."

He shakes it off, clearly wanting to say something more, and turns away. Just as quickly, he faces me again. "How?"

I lean in. "Aren't you one of the people who refer to me as a zombie? You have to die if you want to be like me. Maybe they'll let you keep your hat in Hell."

"Hell. You've seen Hell? I call bullshit."

"You're right. I don't know if I believe in that shit, but I can tell you what being dead was like for me." I pause. "It was black emptiness, followed by dirt in my lungs. Can anyone tell me how I was buried? Was I buried twice?" *Maybe the doc knows.* "I wouldn't suggest the death route unless you trust whoever is supposed to bring you back." His lip twitches and his eyes fall.

"Anyone else?" I ask. "Alright, good. Cherry and I have to leave for a few weeks. I'm still Bennett Larson, and I have appearances to make. Shifter will be monitoring Dr. Romberg closely. Nobody does a fucking thing without consulting him. Everyone needs to be on the same page."

Wes's teeth cut into his lower lip, and he side-eyes Shifter. He's better off telling everyone now that he's a zombie too, but from his response, he's not going to do it. His expression is as stiff as his unusual posture.

"Looks like everyone is in agreement," I add. "Okay, business calls. I'll meet you outside when you're ready, darling." Cherry scans my body, and a hint of a smile reassures me before she begins telling Wes and Seth about the Nevada set in the middle of nowhere. "And hey, Shifter...one more thing. Get me all the information you can on those darts. I don't think we'll have to worry about them. Either way, it's good to know as much as we can. No secrets." He nods, and I walk away.

Let me catch you up while I have a minute to breathe. I set the shoots up with Justin after he called with such urgency. As expected, he got to work fast, clearing the cast and crew we need. I can't wait to get the fuck out of this town. Unfortunately, in two weeks we'll be back in East Grenton again, only with different expectations. More.

I wish I had the words for a recap. Exhaustion is taking its toll on my think space. I can't wait to get a solid night's sleep in the empty quiet of my trailer.

REVISE & VERIFY, BENNETT

"Hey, flower." Not this joker, Ames Heart. Fucking wonderful. "I thought you'd be on set for that role you got."

The pretty boy doesn't seem to remember what happened between us.

Yes, darling. I'm talking about the night I beat him to oblivion. Is it recap time already, or should I share a life lesson? Both are the same. If you kill a guy and bring him back to life, be prepared to have the witness hold it over your head for the rest of their existence. Yes, I'm talking about Cherry. She may be my home, but she's Cherry—divine beauty, set to make all evil acts whole. As if redeeming our horrific qualities would somehow save our souls? Yes, I'm once again boarding the pity train, where I complain about seeing nothing besides black emptiness instead of my angelic sister when I died. If Annie knew I was stuck on this endless path of resentment, she would kick my ass.

Note to self: Triple-check that all Annie's have been swapped out with her artificial alias before sending to editing. Do not fucking forget.

That night I knocked Ames's face in, and I discovered I could restart hearts, it panned out in my favor. If you want to say everything happens for a reason, my entire existence makes sense.

Ames is suited up in Jensen's attire—*my imported character from Sold Se-crets*—sporting each iconic piece from the navy blazer down to his glossy shoes. Cherry looks as sexy as ever in Samantha's high-neck, curve-hugging black dress. Her hourglass figure is perfectly accentuated by the cut that falls just below the knee. A show-stopping necklace, matching the rest of her jewelry, embodies Samantha. *My characters come alive before me like they had previously. Their story bleeds me dry with every scripted word they speak. That sounds brutal, doesn't it? I suppose it is. And somehow...freeing. Cherry took out her nose ring before I could complain. Her lipstick is perfectly lined. There's a temptation to mess it up. Fuck—the temptation is to mess her up, to tear that dress to pieces, and to let her be the pain that brings me pleasure. I know you'd be disappointed if I did that and had to scrap a movie over a fucked ending. You're dying to see the characters you fell in love with on a screen, delivering lines you have inked on your skin, and deep kisses that make you swoon, right before Samantha tramples Jensen's heart in the gravel.*

"Hi, Ames," she politely replies. "Look at you, Samantha's perfect match." She avoids his question as I continue stalking in the shadows.

"Yeah, luckily this isn't the scene when she leaves him on his knees," he laughs.

"That hurts the ego, doesn't it?" She laughs. "I know we nailed that one in the first take. They had all the angles they could've wanted," she flirts. "Too bad we had to reshoot the final scene."

"Is it? I'm glad to see you again."

"You could say everything has an upside."

"This isn't interfering with your other job, is it? I know how Bennett Larson can be demanding—easily lose an opportunity because of him."

"No. I made it work." She smiles.

"Are you two still together? Tabloids have been recycling the same garbage when I catch them."

"Yep. I'm seeing him." Her replies are short and to the point, giving him less than what he desires.

"I know my opinion may not matter, but I think you deserve more than that guy."

"*That guy.*" She pinches her lips together. "What do you mean?"

"He's a prick. He thinks he owns everyone, and you're not the type of girl he can own."

"You're right. I'm not the type of girl he can own. I own him."

Air slips between his teeth as he laughs and shakes his head. As his unsteady gaze meets hers, he becomes cold. "You're serious?"

"I have the big bad Bennett Larson wrapped around my finger, Ames. And he's actually quite sweet when you get to know him."

"Sweet?" He tucks his chin. "Does he have you brainwashed, flower? Blink once for yes."

"Come on, Ames. He exhausts all of his demanding energy on set. After hours, he's all cuddles and reading romantic poems under the stars."

"Now I know you're lying."

She giggles. "I guess you'll never see what I see because—" She clenches her teeth together. "He's not into men."

"Not even well-educated men with six packs?" His cheesy smile tugs upward.

"Hello, Ames," I approach them with my coffee in hand. "On occasion, I might find myself in a threesome with a four-eyed dark-haired dream boat, as long as he's a good boy and follows directions."

"Mr. Larson, I was um—"

"Yeah, you were *um*." The busy set crawls with those necessary for the reshoot. Ames hasn't changed. It's good to know my...*alterations* left him unharmed. The coward is intact, tail between his legs included.

"How are you?" He asks.

I came in early to review the concerns of my assistant director and director of photography. Mel saved me with this one. With everything that's been going on, I couldn't have utilized these people more, especially with my unrealistic timelines. They made it happen, and I'm here to dot the I's and cross the T's. Pressing Ames Heart is only a bonus.

"Well, I haven't killed anyone lately."

Oh, Bennett, you didn't have to say that so dryly.

I don't have to do a lot of things. You understand me at this point, right? We're on the same page? Then, you see why I can't simply let Ames flirt with my girl and shit-talk me without scaring him a little bit, maybe sparking a hint of a memory?

It would be a true testament to my abilities. My weakness in controlling Feather told me enough. What's that saying? If you snooze, you lose. No. Uh, shit...oh! *If you don't use it, you lose it. It's either that or stress affects zombies the same way it affects humans. It fucks you over both mentally and physically.*

His anxious laugh is quite hideous. "Right," he says.

"Or...punched anyone. How about you?" Oh, settle down, Cherry, my love. You can leave that little demonic glare in the trailer. I just want to see if he remembers anything.

"Can't say I have," he says through his teeth.

"Good to know. I heard you partake in boxing or MMA shit."

"I've been in the ring. If you're interested, you could join me sometime."

"I'm more of a street brawler," I admit.

"That seems accurate." He nods.

"I'm not as...broad as you. I bet the women can't wait to scrub those washboard abs."

"That's how I got the role, isn't it?"

"It wasn't my choice, but since you're making a point of it, maybe you're right. I should make sure the next high-paying lead is a skinny, broke kid. I wonder if Justin has considered acting."

"Good luck with that."

"Oh, I don't need luck. I'm Bennett Larson. Everything I touch turns platinum...or decays, never to see the light of day again. I wouldn't want my name on something that reeks of death." And cue awkward silence. "It was nice catching up. I'll see you soon."

I lift Cherry's chin with two fingers, placing a soft kiss on her lips. "You okay? Seems a little off." There's one thing Ames will never forget. Cherry will always be mine.

"I'm fine." Her words are soft spoken. "A little dizzy. Don't worry about it." She smiles, looking away. "I'll be fine."

"Remember who you're talking to, okay?" I fucking hate when she hides. "B."

I get it. She's managed with these side effects this far by herself. "Sorry." I take her lower back.

"We'll talk about it later."

As my fingers leave her, I move towards the monitor setup, keeping myself busy while everyone gets their shit together.

"It's good. The shots are fucking perfect."

"I agree," another producer quietly says.

With his head buried in his device, Justin returns to me. "Did you check your email today?" He asks. "I starred the email from Emma Newbler...your editor."

"I know who Emma is." I'd know it when I read the email anyway. "I'll send her the file tonight."

"Did you finish it?" His curiosity overpowers his insecurities. I have to give him credit every time he opens his mouth. And fuck it, I'll tell him.

"I have a few more chapters to write."

"Oh." He rocks on the balls of his feet.

"What?"

"I thought you would have told me it's none of my business." I deadpan, regretting telling him anything. "Cherry is rubbing off on you. She's good for you."

"Don't get ahead of yourself...She is good for me," I mutter. She is gradually repairing parts of me that I thought weren't redeemable, and I'm not the only one noticing. Her hair flows back as she smiles and nods, talking to a group of people that I can't place. "Don't get any ideas of slacking off or thinking we're going to be friends. Also—" I snap. "I'm considering taking some time off." His brows furrow. "A few weeks. I don't intend to stop writing."

"Oh, okay, do you want—"

"I won't be adhering to a timeline."

"Can you give me dates?"

"Once I've decided, you'll have them."

"Will I need to push anything scheduled further out back?"

"Not right now."

"Okay." He starts walking away when I call out to him.

"And Justin, I hope you didn't waste your bonus on some girl...or guy." He freezes. "Cash goes farther at a strip club."

I may have brushed off that scandal involving him after Cherry tried to get a rise out of me with it. Something along the lines of fucking someone's husband. Let this be the scold he needed for getting involved in drama on my set. Sling dick somewhere else.

But Bennett, you're fucking your co-worker. Ah, ah, no. That's not the same, and you damn well know it.

Cherry's make-up friend—what's her name—had a prior engagement and was unable to make the reshoot. It doesn't matter to me. Makeup artists are a dime a dozen. It seemed to bum her out, though. I'm considering surprising her by inviting this woman and her husband over after we move into our paradise. The timeline is hairy. I'll figure something out. She'd love that, especially the part where I try to be socially normal. How entertaining would that be for you? Am I capable of having small talk, grilling burgers, and sharing beer?

Baby steps, B. I don't need the reminder. I'm constantly fighting the two worlds in my head, trying to balance them while raw dogging zombie mode. If this doctor can perform miracles, should I take it? The miracle pill?

How am I supposed to go back to being another normal guy? It's not like I'll suddenly be Benny. My name won't leave the extensive work I've put out. I'm not going to be that guy.

Then there's telepathy and photokinesis. I haven't reached my full potential. Am I willing to give it up before I know what I'm capable of?

Fuck. Why is this so hard?

Bennett Beyond Rooftops

"Why didn't you tell me you were coming up here?" I step over the top of the ladder onto the Freedome roof. As I close the distance, I tuck my hands in my pockets, while the wind whips the tail of my ebony sports jacket. As I look down, standing above her head, she types on her phone. Her knees stay bent while she flexes at the curve of her back.

"I knew you would find me." She pats the floor beside her. "Come on. Trauma licorice me, B."

"Oh," I sigh. "It's been a long day. A long month."

"I know."

"Are you writing?" I walk around her and drop down to her left side. My leg brushes hers, and she shifts a hair closer. As I drape my arm over her knees, the quirk in her lip falls.

"Yep."

"Good. You're better at this than you think. I sent my editor the chapter you wrote last night with the rest of my manuscript."

In a sudden rush, she sits up and drops her hand to my forearm. "I'm nervous."

"Why? It doesn't matter what she thinks. It's about you and your voice, your craft, and creativity."

Look who's talking. Fuck, I've been in such a grey space lately, I've questioned my greatest work of art, and now I tell her to live authentically and don't give a fuck.

"Actually, no. I'm not going to do this with you. I'm not going to tell you to hold your head high and share your tears with someone to dissect. I won't lie to you. I've fucking hated my voice lately. Getting words to form on paper has been a job, and what do you do when you hate a job and have to do it? You half-ass it. You push out whatever you can and say here it is." A heavy sigh escapes my lungs. "It's okay to be afraid. It doesn't make you weak."

"It makes me human," she says. "It makes us human."

"Sometimes it's nice to know we're not complete monsters. We can feel."

She shivers, cuddling under my arm.

"Why do you insist on these fucking cropped shirts? You wore a normal hoodie last week."

"They're comfortable, and I wore *your* hoodies last week, if you didn't notice, because I needed your comfort, not mine." She burrows into my ribs, taking in my scent.

I can't imagine I smell better than black coffee and... "Do I smell good?"

"Yeah, like...burning wood or um, a campfire, and I don't know, stale coffee."

I look at her sideways. "Stale coffee? What the fuck does stale coffee even smell like?"

"I don't know," she laughs. "Earthy. Bitter?"

"Oh, darling. What's on your mind?"

She smiles, letting out a long, quiet exhale as it falls. "I've seen a lot, B, and it makes me wonder why I'm here. I keep questioning it." Her brows wrinkle. "I feel like a burden talking about it."

Her imperfections pulled me in because I can relate.

She's past *trauma licorice.*

"You can talk to me about anything. Fuck, let's discuss taxes on feminine products." Her giggles give me goosebumps.

Her laugh kept me because it's home.

"It's a shame. It's not like I have a choice in bleeding out every twenty-eight days."

"Your feelings are valid. Tell me more."

Yeah, baby, keep laughing. Keep smiling. I love that fucking smile.

"Have you thought about seeing your parents again?"

"When did we start talking about me?" Her glare steadies on me. "It's been too long, darling. They've moved on," I insist. "Do you miss your family?"

"My mom. Sometimes."

"That's hard."

"You're lucky your mom is alive."

"My mom grieved more when she lost Annie."

"How do you know that?"

"She...They always loved her more."

"I think you're wrong."

"It doesn't matter if I am. That life is over."

"All I'm saying is, if you can try, you should. Go see them before you regret giving up." Her fingers widen, exploring my leg.

"I lost a lot of time. It's been so long..." The stars are bright already. Even with the sky only partially darkened, they remind me how big this galaxy is. On a planet that seems doomed, millions of lives exist, and I'm left questioning what I do while I remain here. "What if they don't remember me?" *Is it worth it? Is any of this worth it?*

"Then...at least you know." She shrugs. "You wonder about them, don't you?"

I shake my head, twisting my fingers around hers. "Why are you always right?"

"I was born to defy the odds." She frames her face with her hands.

"Would you want to meet them?"

Her blue eyes fall on me, unable to settle her gaze. "If you want me to go with you, I'll be there. Is that what you mean?"

"I don't know." A short laugh erases the subject.

"That wasn't a no."

"You are all I need." I close my arms around her waist, rolling her to the cold surface. Her contagious laugh pulls me closer, and I kiss her nose. "Do you think about your mom a lot? Is that what's bothering you?"

"Maybe...not all the time, but sometimes."

"What was it like...finding her? Hold on. Let me rephrase that. Not...what you saw. I don't want to push you to relive that, um...When you happened across her, were you alone?"

"I was. I get it, B. You can't help but want to know how she did it. What was it like finding her? It was...ghastly. Not a gruesome scene, though. You're picturing worse." Her soft smile curves and immediately fades. "I found her in bed and tried to wake her up. I shook her...and shook her. I screamed and held her and..." Her lips pinch together. "She OD'd with prescription pills. For a while, I would replay the whole scene quite often in my head like a movie. One of those rolling clips that live rent-free. I got up that morning; we shared a room. I put the filter in the coffee maker, filled it with water, and turned it on. While that was running, I made toast and painted it with peach spread that we made a few weeks prior from scratch. I was using it sparingly because it was the first time we had done anything like it. I wanted it to last. Eventually, she got out of bed and sat down at the kitchen table with me. We talked about the jam and the forecast. I had an eval at work I was worried about. She insisted I would do great. I was consistent. I always arrived on time for my shift, always gave one hundred percent, and the customers liked me. I kissed her on the forehead and told her I would see her after work. After work..." She swallows and looks past me into the deepening sky. "I unlocked the door, set my bag down, dropped my keys in the bowl on the counter, and called for her. For months, I could hear myself calling her more than I remember the tone of her voice." Tears silently skate over her cheeks.

"Shit, I didn't want to make you cry." I hug her tighter. "That shouldn't have happened to you."

"It was her choice."

"No." I pull her face from my chest, holding her jaw in one hand. "That's not a choice. That's a person who didn't get the help they needed in time. The system is flawed. Nobody wants—"

"It's a choice." She frowns. "If I don't want to stay in misery, why should I be forced to?"

"That's it. You want to end the misery. There are other ways to do that."

"Like strangling my boyfriend?" Her hand meets my neck, delicately stroking her thumb down the center as I swallow.

"That's not one of the traditional methods. We're not exactly normal people, either."

A filter cloaks her face, and she dips her chest back down to mine. "The world is so ugly, B. It's hard to exist."

I dip forward, whispering. "Fuck the world." My lips meet hers. "It can't control us." I tilt her chin up with a single finger. "You're not the only one that...I've seen you jump...You're making me stumble over my words, darling." A light exhale escapes my throat. "Cherry, I've noticed more than you think. Sometimes when someone—me—raises a hand, you jump. It's weird. When we're intimate, we love that shit; you love my hands swinging. Then there's time outside of that, where a movement or a sound fucks you up. It fucks *me* up. I experience something similar."

"Like the car backfiring? You freaked."

"How did you—oh, you were on the roof listening to what I told Shifter. He insists it's PTSD. I don't know."

She nods and closes her eyes, forcing her way under my neck. "What do we do?"

"Take one step at a time. Wait for a cure. Fuck like animals." I earn another smile. I don't need to see it. I can feel it. "Do you have any clue why you like it when I'm rough in the bedroom?" If Shifter is right about this PTSD shit, and Cherry has endured violent men, I'm curious if she has any insight. Are we both fucked in the head, or...what does it mean?

"I think it's about control. You'll stop if I'm fading. You do what I want you to. And I trust you. I push you, and you push me. I never feel afraid with you. You're always reassuring me." The movement of her cheekbones tickles my jaw. "And you make me talk it out, tell you how I'm feeling. You have a way that makes me feel good about it. I'm not afraid or ashamed."

"You've been ashamed?"

"Yeah…You'd be surprised how many men think you're a liability, a crazy bitch if you will, when you tell them they're not squeezing tight enough, they're not fighting hard enough, and they're not making you're heart rate spike to where it feels like you're about to have a heart attack. And B, you noticed the reaction that I barely realize is happening. I don't really believe I do that—jump, pull away, whatever."

"Do you think it was the *before* you?"

"*Before me*—like Benny is to *the Bennett Larson*?" A vibration shakes my throat.

"Yeah. It's a tick that stuck with you, and acknowledging it would mean you've experienced a positive change from being a lab rat. Imagining returning to something negative might put a damper on your will to be poked with another needle."

The air becomes unequally stale in silence.

"You'll always have a safe place in my arms." I draw an *x* over my heart, and she pulls away, scrunching her nose. "Cross my heart and hope to die. I'll never let you fall." Holding my arms wide, I wait for her to dive back into me. "You know my sister, Annie?" I rub the permanent reminder of her on my skin. "She made me feel important…And I couldn't get past nobody else making me feel that way. It was the heartbreak and depression gnawing at me, ever-so fucking quietly. She loved me from the day I was born and we met. You hated me before you even said my full name. And I didn't push you out like everyone else. I wanted to watch you burn at my feet or rise to respect me because I was making you famous. I was giving you the opportunity to live your dream. I was wrong. It was you who gave me an opportunity. Now look where we are, darling."

Her fingers dance over my skin. "I'm permanent, B. When are you getting a tattoo for me?"

"What should I get?" I hold up my arm, bending my elbow. "My shoulder is free."

"I don't care." Her lips begin to form a smile, hesitating. She cares. "It can just be a thing between you and Annie. I don't need to be there, too. You'll always be reminded of me because you're stuck with me forever."

"Forever ends, darling. It's not supposed to, but it does."

"Maybe on this plane."

"See, now you're tripping me out with the unknown again. Not tonight, my love. We'll say forever is a long time and leave it at that. Plus, I could use one more tattoo. You must have an idea in that beautiful, big brain of yours." I tuck her hair back, waiting for her to fling it loose again.

"Well...one. You're going to love it."

"Oh, will I?" I glance at her lips. "What is it?"

"A turtle."

"A fucking turtle?" A harsh, short laugh evades me.

"Yeah, a freaking purple turtle. *X* out the eyes and give it a long, crazy tongue, maybe snake-like with a softness to it."

"It's so stupid that it's brilliant. Have you been thinking about this for a while, or are you that good that you pulled it out of your gorgeous think space on the spot?"

She wraps her arms over my shoulders, sinking into my chest.

"My brain never stops, B," she admits.

"That makes two of us, and no cure can change that."

I'm not dancing with her up here tonight. I hold onto her, pulling her sliding body back on top of me, and pretending her hair against my jaw doesn't drive me crazy, while she nuzzles into my neck, and her heart beats against mine. That's all I want—to feel her presence, soak in her scent, and live in her ecstasy.

Whether it's been two weeks or three years, returning to the hell I hate to name—East Grenton—always sucks odorous ass. Fourteen minutes after ten, it's a morning I will eternally remember as sending my stomach into knots. In front of Cherry and her friends, I act like it doesn't bother me. It's for everyone's own good—thinking Bennett Larson is bulletproof. Cherry can know in private when I'm in need of trauma licorice. It's how she's been strong lately. Our heart-to-hearts travel deeper than sex right now. I'm okay with it.

I've stumbled upon this balance of acceptance. Some of my qualities I tried to leave behind have returned. I wanted to bury them again. It makes more sense every day why they've returned and why I need to allow them to remain. In the direct foreseeable future, my compassion won't extend farther than the people in this facility.

"What's been going on? Cherry said you wanted to tell me in person." I lean against the building next to Shifter. Despite the wind chill being nonexistent, it's a little bitter out. No matter how many times the sun peeks out from the clouds, I'd rather be inside having this discussion.

"She got it." He takes a swig of his energy drink.

"She got it?" Hyderton estimated it would take six months to come up with something viable, and she did it in two weeks. Shifter came through. "Are you sure? This isn't a bullshit attempt that she's throwing out to get you off her ass?"

"No, yeah. This morning, with complete confidence, she explained everything to me. I didn't understand half of it, but I believe she believes it'll work." He downs the rest of his can, shaking it to ensure it's empty. "Are you ready for this?"

"Are you?" I chuckle. "I'm past the point of the *what-ifs.*"

"I don't know." His brows sink together. "It's risky."

"I bet the girlfriend you had—the angel—she's worth the risk."

Don't look at me like that. He needs motivation. Yeah, it's a toss-up. Love, lust, and pussy make you go to great lengths. How much has he been willing to do for Cherry? Now, a girl he said was an angel—that will ensure you sign up to donate blood, plasma, and skin cells. I need him to be confident when we walk inside. They need reassurance, too.

"She won't take me back." Flicking the bottom of his lens, he pushes his glasses up.

"Why do you do that?"

"What?" He lifts the can to his mouth, realizing it's empty before he actually attempts to drink.

"Put yourself down like a coward. You're not, Shifter. That's why you stay here. Not for them, even if you care. It's easier than facing your family or fucking what is it..." I snap my fingers. "The pottery thing or painting, whatever you're into. You won't feel pain if you avoid it. What happened to the dickhead I met a few weeks ago? I wouldn't have pinned him as a little bitch."

"Sounds an awful lot like *you* care, Bennett." His lips part as if he's chewing invisible gum.

"Fuck off. You need to have the same confidence going into this as you had getting your shrimp dick out in my presence."

He lets out a sardonic laugh. "Now you got the jokes. Did you lose a bet, or was it a woman with that fucking cock ring?"

"That was all me spiraling out of control. I've never had any complaints."

"They were too busy being love drunk from the hypnotic voice."

"It's the eyes." I chuckle, swaying from one leg to the other, where I rest my weight and continue leaning against the wall.

"Right." His eyes travel across the pavement. "She won't take me back."

"You don't know that." I straighten, walking the foot's length to the door. As I grasp the handle, he looks up at me. "You don't know that."

A tightness takes his jaw. I choose to ignore it and pull the door open. "Are you coming in? It's warmer in here."

He stays glued to the wall. "Yeah, yeah. I don't mind the cold. Give me another minute."

"Suit yourself," I nod to the side. "I'm going to have a look at Dr. Romberg's work."

"Good luck understanding any of it."

"I'm going to use my particular set of skills while I have them."

"You'd take the cure for her?"

I shrug. "She wouldn't ask me to."

Smoke One, Shifter

*F*uuuck, I'm nervous. I thought I saw the worst, but this could go very wrong. It could go wrong, wrong, so fucking wrong.

"Hey, Shift."

Damn it. Cherry? Not now.

"B said you might want to talk?" She swings the door open, letting it slowly close as she stands beside me. There's that glow on her cheeks again...finally. Too bad the instant thought of her making me her sex toy, using my dick as her personal pogo stick, is never going to leave my brain. That was a mistake.

I love her. I'm jealous of what they have. They're fucking insane.

They're made for each other.

"I, uh..." As I clear my throat, she cups her hand around mine. "What are we going to do when she fixes us?" I shrug. "Go back to a world we haven't seen in years? I mean, you've been doing your thing. The rest of us haven't left this shitty town. We've built a weird sci-fi village, an escape for our daily glances at society, and then lock the door. Cherry, what if she doesn't fix us? What if she makes us worse? What if we're good for a few weeks and then drop dead?"

I'm tempted to dig my hidden box of cigarettes out of my stashing spot behind the camera above the door. If I do, she'll beat the shit out of me. If I were a dead man walking, she'd string me up before I could touch one last high. After quitting for the second time about a year ago, I was stoked to have moved on from being a slave to a little blue box. Sweets never needed to convince me how bad it is. I know. Everyone knows. Not everyone has something that makes them care enough to endure the cosmic mountain climb to free the addict. Is that what I am? What I was? Is a smoker an addict? My damn, it feels good when I can't find another way to cope.

I'm a sick puppy when it comes to these bold, smart women. Cherry was no exception.

These seasons that control my life—when I hit season five, depression of a thousand broken hearts, I hated myself for never telling her how I felt. Why ruin a good thing?

It was a dry hike to season six. Season six? Fuck, am I in seven now? Raven happened to be at the first art gallery I'd been to in years. I'm glad that Ronnie convinced me to go. I hate her for it, too. Letting Raven go was terrible.

What's that saying? It's better to have loved and lost than never loved at all?

Season seven? I can't even comprehend it yet. I thought I had surpassed the wildest days I would see. I fucked Cherry...*like, what*? That's crazy. I fucked her with her famous, monstrous boyfriend. Then, I finally confessed my love. Predictable, but this time...I'm okay. I don't want to push her away. I'm okay, and I can't *not* be. Her friendship is more important to me than a love story that won't last.

"I want the symptoms to stop, Shifter. I can't become *that* anymore. I don't want to lose control and kill—"

"Yeah, I get that." I draw her hand upward, kiss it, and hold it against my chest, my palm over hers. A beautiful blonde head falls to my shoulder, and she hums.

I've killed too.

She's going to hate me when I tell her. It's not a little secret or a white lie. "Sweets, there's something I have to tell you." Fuck. She's crying. Was it something I said? Does she already know? "Hey, hey, hey." She lifts her head with water-filled eyes, starving for something that I don't know how to feed. So

I tell her the only thing that might make it stop, that might soothe her aching heart. "I love you."

"Please don't say that."

Was I wrong? Shit, no. It's what she needs to hear, and I need to say it.

"It's okay. You can love more than one person. You can love them and not be with them. Love is infinite, but it's ugly and complicated, and I sound like I've been watching too much daytime TV. That's your bread and butter, isn't it? It was, anyway." Her feminine laugh complements the depth in mine. "That's my spiel. I'm not mad at you—for anything. Give me a hug, find that happy chick that walked outside a minute ago, and go to your man...because who knows what's going to happen, sweets. Don't waste time." I tip my head back, rubbing my hair against the wall. "*Oooh, Beee,*" I moan.

What the fuck?

I can't stop laughing.

Why did I do that? *Fucking Wes.*

I shake it off as her arms wrap around my neck, and I hug her back with one arm.

"I thought you would give me the details on what you've gotten out of Feather."

"Bennett didn't tell you?"

"Nope. Not yet."

"I'll leave that to him."

"Is it bad news?" She frowns.

"You'll find out soon."

She takes a step back, planning on walking toward the door. "Oh, didn't you want to tell me something, though?"

"Uh, don't tell Bennett my French is terrible. He still thinks I'm well-versed."

"I got your back." She smirks.

I'm tired of the secrets. I have to tell her. Soon. I'll do it soon.

"She didn't test it out! We're just supposed to hope it works?"

It sounds like I walked into an argument that I knew was coming. It's Mr. Keep-It-Clean, and he isn't just anal about the kitchen and dusting. He's an opinionated pain in the ass. I could hear Charlie's mouth a mile away.

"I'm not trying to be another test subject," he argues, posh with his hands on his hips. "Look what happened the first time," he complains, spinning his finger in front of Bennett's face. The lights dim, suddenly shutting off and quickly returning.

"It's like the clapper," Seth drums on his thighs.

"It's a fucking lab rat," I interrupt. "First off, we *are* the fucking trial, unless you want her to inject an actual rat, for months, and then try to treat it with her fix. Second, I swear you were signing up for this when Ronald Hyderton was the ringleader. Third, we all know what you can do. Stop turning the lights on and off."

"I'm not doing it." Charlie glares.

Ronnie marches between the two. "I'll do it then. You guys are pussies. What are the potential side effects?"

For the past two weeks, I have spent every two weeks in this lab watching Feather, pushing her, and motivating her whenever I could see the frustration setting in. Her intelligence is more than all of ours combined. Like every other normie I've encountered, she's not immune to the abilities of a lab rat.

It sucks that I have to tap into that part of me. Unlike Bennett, I don't use it often, only when I have to. The way it feels when I do is enough to make me do it again. It's a strong wave of emotional bliss. Yet, something about manipulating people makes me feel dirty. Then there's the fear sowing in my mind when it comes to that vial she wants to inject in us. Will it do the opposite of what she expects, and I won't be able to control my sense of restraint?

Bennett doesn't care like I do. If he does, it's hidden deep beneath layers of arrogance. If anything happened to Ronnie, to Seth, to Charlie...Wes or Cherry...Slow—wait, where the fuck is Slow? Did anyone bother to tell him we were meeting?

I can't fathom...If anything happened because I lost control, I don't know what I'd do.

I lost control once. I want to tell someone about it. I wanted to tell Cherry. She might hate me. I hate me.

If she knew that it was the same day Bennett woke in his psychotic rage, if she knew I was in Lab One, where he stayed, when it happened, and I didn't say anything...I could have told her while we were stuck in a car for hours together.

The typical patient under monitoring wasn't allowed in any of the lab rooms without strict reasoning, especially not Lab One. We knew the original test subject was in there, though. They never told us a lot about him. Rumors floated around. It didn't look like he was in a coma from an allergic reaction to me.

He sat straight up and looked me square in the face. His eyes were narrowed and empty, completely white, and this sinister smirk tore across his face as his soulless glare burned into the back of a female tech in front of him.

He threw the monitor into the wall, pulled the connections with it, and walked right past me as if I were invisible. I was nothing—a ghost in the wind.

The only reason I was in that room, to begin with, was because they killed me three days prior. That's how I died. It was their fault. Was it an accident? I wouldn't believe it. They had me on close monitoring. I was never left unattended. Nobody else was ever admitted to Lab One. That was the information I needed to prove my theory: he died first.

The night I realized where I was and who I was with, I mentioned it to Charlie. When I gained phone privileges, Charlie was the only person I could reach, and he was quick to let everyone know. The facts tend to blur when the story is told from different mouths.

As the tech in Bennett's way screamed, the woman taking my vitals ran for the exit. A security code locked the room. I understood that if I didn't stop the door before it relocked, I would find myself trapped inside with him. Her intention was to shut the automatic locking door behind her. She failed because she didn't account for me. I caught it in time.

And then...*I let the white-eyed monster out.*

I'm the reason the techs and scientists lost their lives.

I'm the reason why Cherry had disappeared.

"Uncontrollable emotions," Feather replies, answering Ronnie's question about side effects. She turns from the countertop, and with latex gloves covering her hands, she holds several tubes slightly tinted with an almost purple-colored liquid. "Headaches, mood swings, lightheadedness, maybe drowsiness."

"Nothing new," Bennett speaks up. "In the worst-case scenario, what would happen?" His stony face is more complacent than usual.

"Well, there is always a possibility of death."

"No way," Charlie interrupts. "I can manage like this. I have been dealing with for—"

A slow, heavy fist beats on the door's window. With the imprint of a nose against the glass, Charlie's rant ends. Ladies and gentle-monsters, Solomon Rife has arrived.

"Fuckin' Slow." Wes laughs, taunting him through the window. "Whoa, whoa," he teases, pulling the handle of the door for it to unlatch and letting go of it as it quickly re-latches.

"I vote Slow for the first test dummy," Charlie suddenly changes his tune.

As Wes finally lets him in, he waves his hands outward. "What the fuck, guys? Nobody said we were meeting in Lab One."

"Why would we meet anywhere else?" Charlie replies, cross-armed. "She's been in this lab for two weeks, moron."

"Your opinion almost matters to me."

Face to palm. What the fuck, Slow?

"That's not my opinion. It's a fact." His jaw hangs. "She *has* been in this lab for two weeks. *Fact.* It's a fact, Solomon."

"You're such an asshole, Charlie," Slow grumbles. Charlie balls his hand into a fist. "You wanna punch me?: Slow continues. "Come on, do it." He reaches into his pocket and pulls out a small, folded knife, flicking it in and out.

"*Holy shit,*" Charlie exaggerates. "You brought a knife this time instead of a water gun."

They charge each other, standing nose to nose. "Fuck you, Charlie. I was a kid."

"You're an adult now, but your brain never grew."

"At least my dick did. I've never had a complaint from a woman."

Oh, shit. Where's the popcorn?

"Watch your mouth." Charlie wags his finger again. "She never complained to me."

"Was she screaming *it's the best she's ever had* while you rail her from behind?"

"You fucking asshole." He lunges forward, shoving Slow back.

"I did that too." Slow darts around him, holding his fists in front of his face.

Fuck me. The show's over. Looks like I'm the lucky winner who gets to end the battle of the buttheads since nobody else has moved.

"Calm down!" I cut between them. "You," I point at Solomon. "Get the fuck over there." The smile sticks to his face as he walks to the other side of the room, past the double row of black marbled counters, lifting himself up next to the sink.

Yeah, yeah, Charlie dated that chick for two or three months, who ended up breaking up with him and then hooking up with Slow. Didn't this all go down months ago? Hoes came before bros, and they haven't settled the dust, have they?

Solomon, my guy. He falls into the reputation of a dumb, airheaded blond. He's not. It's the common sense he lacks, and by a landslide. He's troubled and pushes the limits. There's a runt in every litter, and that's why he gets away with so much shit. The young blood gets the benefit of the doubt, and the women follow because he looks like he just broke up with his boy band to go solo. I could pinch his cheeks and coo.

"As I said, I'll do it. Get out of my way." Ronnie rolls her eyes. "Which arm?" She slowly folds both sleeves of her sweater.

"No." Wes steps in front of her. "Let me do it."

"I got this." She continues adjusting her sleeves.

"Somethin' could happen to you."

"I know," she insists.

"If somethin' happens to you, I'd hurt her." His jaw clenches, flexing as he glances at the doctor.

Ronnie's forehead creases with two long lines. "Why would you do that? That makes no sense."

"No, that's the obsession."

What? Did he say the obsession?

"Obsession? Like...the obsession?"

"Yeah, ma'am."

Holy shit. I weave my fingers through my hair to my scalp, looking around the room to find almost everyone as mind-blown as I am. Not Cherry...nor Seth.

He's not only into her. He's been bitten by the bug that drives you to stupidity and violence. "You, Ronnie. Don't you ever wonder why you can't keep a guy around very long? I want you because I love you."

This feels like a private moment. I shouldn't be standing this close to them.

I take a few steps back, undetected.

"You...You were the reason I kept getting stood up and ghosted!" She smacks him on the bicep, and the sound echoes with brutality. "What the hell!"

I look between Cherry and Bennett. Cherry's lips tighten and her eyes become wide, communicating with me from a few feet away.

"None of them would have been good enough for you," Wes argues.

"That's not your decision. You know how much I hate that—those expectations. *You have to do it this way, Veronica!* The boyfriend I had in high school that my parents humiliated me in front of to get their point across, oh, how I would never have a future with a man who didn't come from a name, power, or money." She shoves her palms against his chest. "The boys below me aren't good enough, and the ones above me only want one night. Is that how I'm supposed to live what's left of my bizarre life? I leave my parents only to find a man who wants to control me."

"I'm sorry. That's not what I wanted to do. Please, let me do this. Let me make it up to you. Sugar, let me go first."

"Don't *sugar* me." She cocks her head. "We've never been that serious."

What in the actual fuck is happening? I knew he had a thing for her, but *what?*

My jaw is stuck on the floor, gawking at...What exactly is it that's going on?

As I collect myself before they decide which one is going first, Seth sports a big, goofy smile. He knew this whole time.

"I don't need you to shelter me, Casanova." Her head bobs in her usual vain nature. "I'm a Brili."

"Everyone knows you're a badass," he agrees. "The Brili name never did you justice. You don't take shit from anyone, and you do what you want. You're amazin', and I know everything about you. Don't you remember, you told me I was your best friend? Why wouldn't I be more than that to you?"

His balls are the size of coconuts! He's confessing his *love* in front of everyone. He's not Casanova, he's Prince Charming. Fuck yeah, do your thing, buddy.

"Wes…" She exhales from her nose.

"Okay. Well." He shrugs. "Regardless, I'm taking the first hit. I'm taking it before you." He lifts his arm flat, holding it in front of Feather. She glances around, awaiting a protest. When nobody moves, she clears her throat.

"Patient zero-zero-seven is first. Correct?"

"He's not a fucking number," Ronnie shrieks. "Wesley Jon Baker. His name is Wesley Jon Baker."

The smiles between Ronnie and Wes mean something. Her outburst gave them another ten-second interval where nobody else existed, and they spoke a secret language that only mattered between their souls.

I have watched too many of those blubbery movies.

When it disappears, Ronnie pulls at her sleeves and avoids looking at the rest of us.

She's into him, too!

Feather nervously eyes Wes' arm. "Do you want to take a seat?"

Man, this sucks for her. She's anxious and overwhelmed. I've been doing everything I can to keep it at bay. I want to show mercy on her, and I'm not sure how. She's a good person. She wanted to help people. When Trustinex originally offered her the position, she almost didn't take it.

I didn't want to learn this much about her. These last two weeks have been trying.

When you use your ability to make someone feel comfortable with you, they tend to cling to that comfort and share every little thought and idea. I picked her brain. Feather knew about those darts. Unfortunately, not a lot. She didn't have time to dig into the documents Hyderton sent over on the matter when she was busy trying to create a fix-all in six months to two weeks. Bennett now knows as much as I do. They don't leave lasting effects other than the pain from the bruising and lacerations that may occur. They wanted to heal the brain. They came up with something similar—quick-acting cell regeneration.

Wes and his tough-guy exterior—he doesn't bother to sit, squeezing his hand into a fist. "No. Jab me."

Feather's soft brown eyes search his charming baby blues, and before she inches toward him, Cherry runs over, wrapping her petite arms around his bulky shoulders. She hugs him as if it may be the last. My vacant daze shadows Bennett's. "It's going to work out, Cherry. I'm proud of you for pushing us this far. We wouldn't have tried without you."

Everyone has to feel those words. *I'm proud of you.* Words so many of us had longed to hear for years. *We wouldn't have tried without you.* She hugs him once more and walks back to Bennett. He tucks an arm around his waist as her soft smile encourages me to breathe. I exhale, letting it faultlessly shake out of me.

"Are you ready?" The syringe is filled, pinched between her fingers, inches from the vein, traveling the crease of his arm.

"Wait!" Ronnie yells. She attacks Wes, jumping into his arms. He holds her thighs and nuzzles into her neck. "I love you, too," she whispers.

We all heard it.

We all felt it.

A love story unfolds around us in the most beautiful and ass-sucking way. I don't want to be stuck with the three bachelors forever! I want what they have and what Cherry and Bennett have. Maybe what Cherry and Bennett have. I want the epic love.

So, no. Nobody is going to die. We're going to do this, and I'm going to beg Raven until she gives me another chance. Yeah, yeah, yeah. That's what I'm gonna do. Everything is going to work out. Everything.

Count Your Blessings, Cherry

I 'm at a loss for words. A thick mist coats my lungs, and I should exhale, but I hold it in. I don't know what's going to happen. We're all preparing for the end when we should be excited about a new chapter. That's how we've been designed, hasn't it? Always waiting for the worst?

"Cherry." I drift to the voice calling me. *Seth.* "Are you okay?" I nod, mindlessly. He holds out a blunt, and I'm tempted to take it. My arms shake. One. Two. Three. Four. Five. Six.

I didn't want it to be like this, and somehow that's what it turned into—saying our goodbyes. Except Charlie and Solomon. If we happened into an end-of-the-world battle, they would be insulting each other as they both became impaled with swords. Certainly, swords would be the choice of weapon. Picture this: a ship of pirates vs. an empire. We would be the pirates, naturally, and I would require a leather hat.

Dr. Romberg rested the needle against Wes's skin. The motion was slowed through my eyes. She held a cotton ball over the injection site, applying pressure. My heart became weighted, sinking me to the bottom of the floor. A metaphor.

I wasn't the one on the floor. Wes was. The kind teddy bear who volunteered to go first was a sack of limp flesh. He shook and jerked at her feet.

Everyone rushed to him with unrealistic, blurred speed. And I struggled to breathe. Ronnie caught his head, pillowing it along her thighs. What happened next? Think. Slow jumped over a lab counter. They were all surrounding him, and I was standing farther away, gawking.

As I remained a shell of a human, I questioned why my feet were cemented down and I wasn't doing a thing to help. I couldn't breathe. My heartbeat was pounding through my back with every heavy breath that blurred my vision. A foggy tunnel wrapped around me in a similar way as it had four weeks ago.

My exhale turns into frantic panicking. "What's happening?" I yell, awakened.

"Get him up," Feather orders.

It takes all four men to lift him onto the counter. Ronnie pulls off her sweater, tucking it under his head, and I stand next to her, wildly spiraling from face to face.

"He's in shock." She tugs his eyes open, one at a time, flashing a light over them. "The dosage must have been too high."

"What do you fucking mean, it must have been too high?" I scream. "Fucking fix it! Fix him!"

Feather pulls her stethoscope to her ears and holds the bell to his chest.

"His heartbeat is rapid. We need to slow it down." She starts attaching wires to him. "I need ice."

"Charlie!" Bennett yells. "Go get ice." Everyone gets louder. It doesn't matter if we're next to one another. One person yells, and then another yells over the top of the first. Nobody would expect us to be calm in this situation. Why would any of us react differently?

I walk away, pacing in a straight line while I press my fingers to my temples and rub until the pain becomes numb. I push past Charlie as he runs out the door, shoving Ronnie and barreling through Slow like I can do something they can't.

"Cherry," Bennett scolds me, grabbing my shoulders. "Calm the fuck down." I fight him, manic, and somehow manage to find his face. His eyes...they're white. Why are his eyes white?

"B..."

"I know." His sight goes to Shifter, across from him. His eyes are identical. "Don't say it." He's calm and focused, waiting and watching. "Look here," he softly demands my attention. "Count with me, okay?" I nod. "One. Two. Three. Four..." What's that noise?

My eyes dart away from Bennett to the high-pitched noise that destroys my path to calm.

Delayed words slip from B's lips. "What does that mean?"

"He's flat-lining," Feather admits.

"No!" Screeches pour from Ronnie's lungs as she slams her hands on the table. Seth scoops his arms around her midsection, reeling her back as she dips forward. Her chest heaves like a panting animal, baring her teeth.

Charlie runs through the doorway. His quick thinking gave us the upper hand. He blocked the door with a trash bin to prevent the door from closing fully and locking. "I have the ice," Charlie calls. He stands next to Shifter, holding the bucket out for Feather, beside him.

"It doesn't matter now. His heart stopped."

"So, do something," I yell. I'm about an inch away from smacking her head off the counter.

"Fuck this. If you want to live to try again, I suggest you stand clear," B orders Feather.

"What are you going to do?" She asks.

A softness takes my eyes in a suddenly heavy manner. "B." I'm scared. For him. For Wes.

"Count for me, darling." He holds his hand over Wes' chest. This is why his eyes are white. He was prepared for this. Everyone else was afraid, and I told them it would work out. Now Wes is dead. He's dead. And Bennett has to reveal another part of himself to save someone I want him to save.

He blinks and eyes Shifter. I frantically drift back and forth between them, trying to decipher the unspoken code.

"What's going on?" Silence. "B! What is it?"

"It's not working." His gentle words stab me in the chest with the force of a high-pitched scream. My scream.

"What! What can we do? What can I do? Tell me!" I latch onto his forearm, not aware of how childish it appears until I pull away.

"Cherry...baby." He sighs.

"No!" I bark. "Try again!"

"Cherr—"

"B! Please!"

His rough exhale isn't reassuring, but he holds his hands back over Wes. "Count for me. Out loud."

I wish I could understand what he's feeling, how it feels when he does this. Am I pushing him too far? "One, two, three, four, five."

He drops his hands. The movement pisses me off to the extent that I shove him.

"Cherry," he growls.

"No, B! This isn't right. You're supposed to be able to save him!"

"I'm not a hero! I tried." He presses back.

"Fuck!" Shifter yells. "I'll do it too." He tosses his hands up and fans them back. "I'll do it."

No. My head moves back and forth uncontrollably. Everyone will know. This isn't the way you tell them.

I glance at Charlie and Ronnie, hushing my voice. "Are you sure?"

"Everything has a way of coming out." Even through the white of his iris, I see the agony.

"Okay, let's do it. We're running out of time." Bennett holds his hands above Wes again, and Shifter follows. "Feel it, that grip that pulls every time you use it. The static, the seduction—let it take you and focus on what you want. Find the rhythm."

Ronnie holds herself, tearing at her skin. Charlie looks horrified and astounded, as I imagine trying to understand how this is possible.

The gasp for oxygen shoots B and Shifter back. They stare between each other and Wes.

"That fuckin' sucked," he groans through a harsh cough. "Thanks for the save...I need water." He looks around at the bodies surrounding him and then straight up at Ronnie, who stands above his head. "And a blow job."

A smirk lights B's face as he turns to me.

"How the hell did you do that?" Charlie questions Shifter.

"It's a long story."

"No, I want to hear it. All of it. Now."

"Uh, Charlie...Seth, Slow, Ronnie...I know this sucks to hear, but I've been keeping it from you guys. Bennett's not the only zombie."

Charlie crosses his arms sternly. "Explain."

"Do you remember the week before...the event? I was separated from everyone."

"Yeah, man. They put you in Lab One." I glance back at Seth as he speaks. He's still holding his joint between his thumb and pointer.

"Yeah, yeah, yeah. That's right." The warmth of his smile takes over his face, falling immediately after. "They took me to Lab One and gave me an extra vial and said I had to stay for observation. I don't remember much after that. Waking up, it was hazy. A woman came over, checked my vitals, and wrapped one of those cuff things around my arm to take my blood pressure. Then, I saw Bennett." Their eyes lock with another hidden message. "The woman didn't notice him till he threw the machine he was hooked up to, but when she did, she took off. I followed her. I wasn't sticking around, but...I didn't shut the door in time."

Charlie paces with wrinkles of frustration taking his forehead. "Wait, let me get this right. They took you in there to test another vial. It killed you and...what they brought you back?"

"A zombie. The living dead," Seth says.

Shifter's chest lifts, exhaling a deep breath. "Yeah, that's about right."

"And then he woke up mysteriously? Not a coincidence at all." Charlie deadpans.

"It was a few days after they killed me."

Ronnie rubs her reddened face and drops her hands. "You let him out of the locked lab. You let him out of the lab?"

"Yeah." He looks down at Wes and back to her, swallowing hard.

"How could you be so stupid?" She scolds him as she weaves her fingers into her hairline.

"I didn't know that was going to happen. She freaked, and it set an alarm off inside of me, like it would anyone else, to get the fuck out of there. He snatched the door before I could shut it."

"For years we lived side-by-side and all along you…you're just like him." Her glare could ignite a flame.

"He's been nothing but helpful to all of you," I argue.

"Shut up, Cherry. You hop on the enemy's dick and want to act like he isn't a monster."

"This isn't about me or Bennett. It's about Shifter being a good friend to all of you while you throw him under the bus because he's been harboring something painful that he wasn't ready to share."

He let B out.

I won't say my gut doesn't sink. It wasn't intentional. He would have found a way somehow. The obsession is hard enough to beat now, let alone when he first woke. We all understand it. We have to understand it…or we'll lose each other when we need to remain together more than ever.

Charlie's hands stiffen into fists. "I thought you were my friend. You lied."

"Charlie." He takes off toward the door. "Charlie! We all fucking lie." Holding his hands wide, he exposes his chest to his attackers. It's enough to stop Charlie from leaving. "Ronnie, you refused to admit you have feelings for Wes until he risked his life. Charlie, you act like you're the confident big man, but you're insecure. Slow isn't that fucking stupid, but he plays into it to lessen his responsibility around here, and Seth…You don't even care right now, do you? You're stoned out of your mind." Seth raises his arm, giving a thumbs-up.

"You lied about something huge! It doesn't compare," Ronnie contends.

"What doesn't compare is how I fucking killed someone and have to live with it every mother fucking day while you parade on your high horse like we're gods. We shouldn't have these abilities, especially when we can't control them. That's why she's here." He points to Dr. Romberg in animosity. "We need to be able to control them, or we're no better than monsters. Any one of us could snap. I don't want to fucking do this anymore than any of you and…yeah, it's more likely that I'll do it again or Bennett because we're these fucked-up zombies, but none of you are immune. Right, Cherry?"

"What did you say?" The most distant, cold words to be said come from Solomon. "What, did, you say?" He repeats.

"It's not what you think." Shifter backs away from him.

"Who did you kill?" He edges closer.

"It wasn't the girl. I swear, her disappearance wasn't on me."

He pins Shifter against the wall. "Who the fuck was it then?"

Slow thinks Shifter killed someone he knew or was friends with? Who did he kill? No, it doesn't matter. I mean, it does. A life is a life. It wasn't his intention. I can forgive him. We can all forgive him.

"It wasn't her! I swear!" He yells, shoving him back.

"Who the fuck was it, Shift?" Slow pushes him into the wall. He flinches, shoving him back again.

"It was Malondo! That fucking pig! Dr. Jack Malondo," he growls. They stare at each other, and my lungs collapse. Every breath within my body is stricken. The room spins, and everyone is a blur of white and black and blue.

No. No. No!

The weight of a thousand elephants crashes onto my stomach, and I see myself six feet under, the loose pieces of dirt flying over top of me to hide my corpse deep beneath.

"How could you?" I gasp. "How could you!" I repeat.

"Cherry." That slight tilt—don't you dare look at me like that. Don't you dare!

"No! You let me believe it was Bennett! I can forgive you for so much, so damn much, David! But I—I wasted all that time trying to get my revenge on him. Years of obsession focused on making him pay. Years, I didn't even realize how strong the obsession was."

"You took off! I thought you died, and I just got you back. I wasn't ready to tell you, and then I heard you tried to kill Bennett." His eyes swallow me. I step back with each inch he takes closer to me. "I was going to tell you. Sweet, I swear."

"When! On my deathbed?" He reaches out. "No! Don't you touch me." I wrap my arms around my body.

"I didn't make you do anything, Cherry. You made your own choices. Stop acting as if you've never done anything wrong."

"I didn't mean to kill her!" *Oh no.*

I close my eyes, hoping that when I open them, those words never came out of my mouth. It's hopeless. The words still exist. All of their faces. One by one. They won't look at me.

"I said it," I admit. "All of us are capable of killing, whether we want to do it or not. If we like it or not. It will happen. It happened. I lost control."

"Who?" Solomon asks.

"You don't know them."

"Them?" Ronnie's brows draw tight. "Plural? First, it was a *her*. What else are you keeping from us? When is everyone going to tell the truth?"

"The doc needs to get back to work," B says. "Everyone got their bitching out. We're done here." He attempts to shut the scene down.

"No. Spill your fucking secrets, Cherry," Ronnie demands.

"She doesn't owe you anything," Shifter says, stepping forward.

"Don't defend me."

"Everyone has fucked up. There's nothing more to tell," Bennett snaps. "If you're at each other's throats, none of this is going to end well."

"Fine," she agrees. "As soon as this is over, I'm leaving, and I don't want to hear from any of you again."

"Ronnie," Wes pleads, reaching for her wrist. "Come on." She storms out, leaving it at that. "She'll come around." His weak smile isn't promising.

Charlie hangs his head, following behind her. Then, Slow, speechless, exits. Wes's legs shake under his body as he stands.

"You can stay." It sounds like an option, but Bennett means it. Wes isn't leaving the room for a while.

"No. I want to go to my room." His hands comfort my shoulders as he hobbles past. Seth ducks under his bulky arm as if he could be a crutch at half a foot taller and three times as lean.

I reach for Bennett's hand, stopping him from doing anything further. "Let them go."

"Cherry—"

"No. I can't talk to you." I push past Shifter, leaving Bennett and him with the doctor.

I barely glance up as two knocks on the door preface Bennett's voice. "Darling."

"How could he do that to me?" B's shadow kisses the carpet as it cascades across the room.

"Let's go."

"Where?"

"Back to the hotel. You need to get out of here."

"This used to be my home. This was my room." He meets my pace, pulling me close as his hands take my lower back. "I was a part of something, I had a family and a caring man...It was all a lie." Neither the gentle stroke of my jaw nor the ocean in his eyes can settle the crawling beneath my skin. "I built my existence on false pretenses, and it's what my life became."

"We're real, Cherry." His fingers softly necklace my throat. "This is real life. It's not a nightmare you can wake up from. The lies are sewn into the stitches that lace our wounds. Accept them and exhale."

I didn't say anything. I got in the car in silence. We drove in silence. I got out and walked into the elevator in silence. My head was overwhelmed with sound, and none of them translated to acceptance or freedom. There wasn't any exhaling. I was holding my breath, buried in waves, spinning a piece of metal around my finger, awaiting a cure to the madness.

I hug my legs, sitting on the bed in the dark of our hotel room. "What are you doing?"

Bennett's beautiful, lean, tattooed, and scorned body is shaded in grey and black, leaving very little for my sight. A towel dangles from his hips below the cuts of his Adonis belt as she stares out the window. "Looking for the stars. Come join me."

"I'm naked."

"It's dark." My eyes sail in circles. "It's almost one in the morning. If anyone can see us four stories high in the dark at this hour, they should play the lottery. They're winning."

"You're too much." I find the floor and make my way out of bed. My cheek presses to the heated ridges of his back. "I love you." My fingers trail his lower abdomen.

"What is it?" He strokes the tops of my hands and conveys up my arms. "Talk to me."

"I'm having these thoughts again."

"I've had them too."

"You have?"

"Come here." He pulls me around, wrapping me into his chest. I attempt to gaze at the stars. It's not much to look at. A few here and there exist between flashing markers for airplanes. "What did you feel when you held the, um." A hot emanation of air hits my face as I glance up at him. His jaw teases between tightening and relaxing. "What did you feel when you held the gun to your head?"

"Scared," I mutter. "Lost. Hopeless...In control." Pressing my cheek to his chest once more, I reach up and circle his piercing. "It would make everything stop. That past, the present, a future without relief, and I had the power to do that."

"I think about the now—right now—ninety-eight percent of the time. The other two percent, I can't find a fix to my problems, and the way out is obvious. I don't have to struggle to escape the bullshit."

"But you've never put a loaded barrel to your temple."

"I've considered compelling someone to do it for me."

"That's a higher level of control." I find his eyes. "You smell good."

"I smell like sex."

"Like I said, you smell good."

His dark chuckle rumbles through his chest, vibrating my face. "I love your laugh."

"When I contemplate death now, I think about you. I don't know if I'll get to hear your voice in the afterlife. A voice of dark, disturbed humor and dirty little words, high-pitched squeals, and breathless moans." His fingers stroke down my back until he makes it to my butt, squeezing.

"I want to stay with you, B. I want this cure...But I can't face him. I trusted him, and he kept things from me. He let me believe you killed Jack. He ratted out Ronnie for hooking up with Jack. He let you take the fall for his death after he released you, and he thinks it's okay because we all have done stupid...horrible things."

"He doesn't think it's okay. Cherry, he left the girl he loved because of who he is. He's not proud by any shot."

"How am I going to forgive him?"

"You'll find a way to move forward because you're a good girl, darling. You're a good fucking woman—a good person. You're better than him and me."

"I'm going to forgive him because I'm a fixer, and if I see a glimmer of hope, I want to help. I don't think it's because I'm a good person. My happiness depends is influenced by the happiness of the people I fix." It's true. That's who I am. For some reason, I can't figure it out. Maybe it has to do with Mom.

"Every selfless act can appear selfish when you twist it enough times."

"His hope is gone, B."

"You're angry. I should be happy. Shifter isn't my favorite person." His finger caresses my jaw, tilting my chin up. "He's not the enemy, Cherry bomb, and in time you'll see that."

"I'm cold," I change the subject. "Can we get back in bed?"

He hoists me over his shoulder and tosses me on the bed, where I hurry to pull the covers over my goose-bumped skin.

Bennett is my shield. He separates me from the oncoming war in my head. He slows everything down and consoles my hurting heart. I should be able to do that myself. I used to think I did that for myself. Now, I'm realizing...I haven't been coping as well as I thought I had.

Bennett's Performance

*H*oly fucking shit. Did you get every word of that shitshow yesterday? Cherry told you, right?

Quick recap: Shit hit the fan. Shifter killed Cherry's ex or wannabe ex, Shifter allowed me to get free to kill everyone else, and I think some chick was killed too, but I'm a little fuzzy on that part. Slow was pretty unamused by the possibility. Leave it to eight fucked-up lab rats and a mentally influenced doctor to kill a guy, bring him back, and hash out a whole rampage of drama within a few hours of me and Cherry getting back in town.

Life lesson: Be the one who remains calm when chaos breaks out. You'll have the upper hand in decision-making.

Everything revolves around a secret. My secret. Cherry's secret. Shifter's secret. We all keep something hidden, and we're all searching for something else to bury it beneath. That's what this life has led us to. The motherfucking blame game. Don't worry, I'm not in the business of writing unhappy endings. I'm fighting for my own more than any that I've written for someone else.

Since the first trial didn't go as expected, we had to regroup.

Cherry's arms take my neck from behind me. Her lips nibble the shell of my ear. "Good morning, darling."

"How many words did you get in this morning?" I pivot from the desk, the illumination from my laptop screen fading. I've been up for hours writing. She must see the darkness deepening the skin below my eyes.

I find her lips, sucking her into my mouth, and tangling my tongue around hers. "A few thousand. Guess what?"

"Oh, tell me," the excitement engulfs her voice.

I reach for her hand and pull her to my lap. She gasps and giggles—pure joy in the simplicity. Her legs dangle from the side, and her arms never relinquish my neck. "My editor had very little feedback for your chapters. She loves your part of the story."

A smile slides across her lips. "It's kind of a messed-up thing to like. I guess if you think it's fiction, it's not as bad. It makes it less painful. A little."

I tap the keyboard, waking my laptop, and begin reading a section out loud. She hides her face with her hands, her robe-cloaked body deepening into my chest. Her hair flies over my chin enough that I have to brush it down before continuing.

Love means pain. It doesn't mean a prince charming will sweep you off your feet and make every problem in your life drift away. I'm sorry, darling, but this isn't a fairy tale. When you've been through heartbreak from the people you loved with your whole heart, unconditionally, it takes time to change the habits you put in place to keep yourself safe. I don't let my walls down, ever. My trust is earned, never gifted. I can love someone and still hide the raw parts of me that I'm afraid to share.

"Don't read that out loud. It makes me cringe."

"Since when are you self-conscious? It's fucking perfection." She kisses my jaw, falling into me with dreamy eyes as if she sees utopia in my face. "You're perfection." I kiss the tip of her button nose. "A fucked up little ball of perfection."

Awe, B. You sap.

Shut up. I know.

I'm fucking whipped cream, and that's my cherry on top.

Don't laugh. It's not fucking funny.

And you know what? I wouldn't have it any other way.

"Are you sure you like it?"

"I am."

"Good. I like it too."

"Can I be the vigilante, breaking every rule to keep you demons at bay?"

"You're an idiot." Her teeth dig into my neck. "You're more than a vigilante. I don't think they have a word for what you are."

My lips meet her ear as I whisper. "Try the slang dictionary. It's somewhere between arrogant and zombie."

I didn't sleep much between Cherry, writing, and do you remember when I said we needed to regroup? I've been brainstorming and have a few things to discuss with Shifter today...as long as Cherry doesn't knock him out.

"Cherry," Shifter calls out. He catches up to us as we walk through the crispy white halls of the Trustinex lab. I'm not sure how someone could call this place homey when it feels cold and sterile. "Can we talk?"

With dead eyes, she glares at him. "I think you did enough talking."

"You sure?" I ask, looking between them. "It might be best if you did a little more talking."

Now I get the grizzly stare. "Or not." We should have stopped for lunch.

Lucky you, I'm implementing another life lesson. Learn from my mistake. Feed the beast. A hangry woman, mortal or monster, will drop a two-hundred-and-fifty-pound man to his knee, and not in any desirable way. When she's in this mindset, feed her or run.

"There is nothing to talk about."

"I'm sorry." He tries to stop her as she walks past me, continuing down the hall on her own. Then, she comes to a stop and laughs, turning back to us.

Oh, fuck.

As I run my hand down my face and over my stubble, it's clear she's about to lose her shit. One foot in front of the other, her slow movement is exactly what I was riding against.

"You're sorry?" The giddy tone in her voice is unsettling. "Of all the years I've known you, very few times have you had to apologize. You never hurt me. Not once. And now I see it was only a matter of time. You're a liar."

"And you're innocent?" His brows draw together, teeth clenching below. *Wrong. Wrong, fucking wrong reaction.*

"You treated me like you're gay best friend or a man who wasn't capable of being more than a venting buddy, but you knew. You fucking knew what you did to me." The corners of her lips fall. "Yeah, yeah, yeah, *you didn't know.*" His head tilts left. "You would cuddle with me and then talk about that asshole, Malondo. Let's say you actually thought I didn't have feelings. You still didn't want to hear it when I tried to tell you he was hooking up with other people. You wanted to believe you finally found a good guy when the good guy was *right here*, hanging out with you every night. I had plenty of reasons to hate him, and maybe I was obsessed with destroying him," he admits.

Cherry bends forward and reaches for her shoe. She pulls out a small pocket knife, darting straight for Shifter.

I wrap my hand around her abdomen, interrupting her vengeance. "Cherry." She presses the jagged edge to Shifter's throat, baring her teeth and pushing it tighter to his skin. He swallows and stiffens throughout his body as he slowly raises his hands.

We all know how this ends. She's going to forgive him, not kill him. I don't see her doing that when he tries to justify his actions instead of apologizing. She's not going to kill him... Shit. She might.

"I can't bring him back on my own, Cherry. Think about that for a minute," I remind her. "You're judging him for the same crime you committed."

"I'm judging him for lying!"

"You lie a lot, too, and if anyone in the place wants to kill Shifter, it's me. Not because he did the same thing we've both done. If he didn't matter to you, I would shove that blade clean across his neck for you, but he does. We're people who tend to do bad things. Sometimes we hurt the people we love in ways we can't take back. We find a way to move on because, like it or not, they're your family. They're the only ones who will ever understand what it's like." The weight of my hand on her arm does nothing.

He swallows again. "Cherry, please. Let me redeem myself. I can fix this. Feather has another theory. I know I can push her." That's closer to an apology. "You're not going to do it, so can we move on?"

Oh, come on. Fucking idiot. Say the right words.

A slow trail of blood begins to run down his neck.

"He's sorry," I blurt out. "Right? You're sorry for lying." This fucking idiot needs to come to his senses and give her the correct words.

"Yeah, yeah. Cherry, I'm sorry for the lies. I'm sorry."

Her breath hitches, angrily staring at him before she backs off, wiping the blood from her knife on the tail of his shirt and tucking it back in her ugly sneakers. She doesn't say a word, walking off.

He calmly pulls his plain, distressed black shirt over his head, flips it around, and holds it to his neck.

"I warned you about the knives." His impassive glance is enough. "What's this theory Feather is working on?"

He wipes his neck down, flips the shirt once more, and holds the clean section back to his wound. "A pill. It would be continuous, a lifetime commitment. A low dosage that would keep the side effects at bay while she works on something that can..."

"What?"

"Something that can revert us to our previous form." He sighs.

"Okay. You don't have to take anything you don't want to, you know."

"If she...Maybe, um, I don't know."

"Don't worry about it right now. You need to do some patchwork with Cherry, and I want to hear more about this from the source's mouth. Lab One?" Although it comes off as a question, I'm already headed in the direction, knowing that's where the doctor is.

"Yeah." He follows, reluctantly dipping his head to the side. "I'm going to give *that* a little longer to wind down before I try to talk to her again."

"Yeah, I'm all out of saves for the day." With a wink, I continue down the hallway.

Feather tucks her ebony hair back as she leans forward. "See, this is the difference." She points to a paper full of words and numbers I don't understand. "The approach Jonathan, um, our team lead, had was a series of injections that would leave a lasting effect. It's too much at one time. It made a drastic impact, altering far more than what was intended. Ideally, there would be a procedure that would eliminate taking medication for the rest of your life—that one treatment fix—but that goal isn't feasible. Not right now anyway. It needs to be slowly administered and continuously taken at the same time every day to control the multiple side effects from the original experiment. There are many medications already developed for this—to manage mental illness. We didn't want to manage it. We wanted to cure it. The theory was wrong," she continues to babble off about what she would do differently, talking about formula and longer rat testing. *For a person without a conscience, animal testing seemed to be a quicker solution than that of volunteers. I would think more along the lines of testing on rapists and murderers, but isn't that calling the kettle black? It's a double-edged sword. It makes sense why they chose us—well, why they chose everyone else. I fell into their hands. Whoever made the choice to poke and prod me fucked up. Did they think they could test their magic solution on a deceased body and see if it rejuvenates cells or some shit? I repeat, I'm not a biology nerd.*

"Is Jonathan the brainiac who thought he could create a one-shot cure-all? Isn't there a slew of mental health obscurities in this building? And his think space ended on this perfect one-and-done magic solution."

"There were many hands in the pot, so to speak. They spent years working on this before bringing any subjects in. The documents that were given to me date back over a decade. It's more complex than it appears. It's quite satisfying to see where they started and how I've been able to pinpoint the flaws. It's almost like I've been supercharged."

"Super mind fucked is more like it," I grumble.

She opens the mini fridge below the counter, pulling out a mold of tiny circles filled with the mixture from her paper, along with a bottle of pills that she already prepped. There are easily a hundred. Has he even allowed her to sleep?

"What's the probability that you'll be able to find a full proof, stop all, at some point?"

"There's a possibility. It could take years, and people are willing to take the risk. These pills will work right now. I can adjust them, modifying each set for all of you individually. I honestly should have tried this from the beginning. I had to give their formula a try."

"Their formula? They had a reversal plan?"

"It was a draft, of sorts. It wasn't in any of the authorized documents. Um—" She pinches a tablet between her pointer and thumb. "But these should suppress the headaches, the dizziness. I believe it will lessen the amount of blackouts—"

"The obsessions and rage?" That's the real test. Cherry could deal with the rest. It's the rage that will break her. She hates the person she becomes when she trips into that headspace.

"I don't know." Her hands shake as she tries to open the cylinder. "I hope. I can't guarantee anything until we test it out. I'll need a minimum of three weeks before I can take a second blood analysis, compare, and measure adjustments. Then we'll have to repeat the process, monitoring symptoms and...It's a lot. I'm sorry."

I lick my lips and pull my hands from my pockets. "These are ready to test right now?"

"I got to work as soon as you left." She stacks her folders, moves them to the side, and taps them from side to side, up and down, until they are even. It's barely been twenty-four hours. After this, Shifter needs to slow her down. At this rate, she'll be dead before we can translate her formula to the next controllable doctor.

"Right now?" Her voice cracks. "You...You're confident this will work? Yesterday's attempt was an immediate failure. I was quite depressed about it until David..." Her lips flex, a smiling tugging her cheeks full.

"He believes in you, and so do I. I thought about this from the beginning, you know. Something that keeps the side effects at bay while allowing me to keep the abilities I survive on." Her eyes wander away. "I know what you're thinking. I don't deserve them, and you might be right. If I changed, would I be deserving? If I went around ruining bad guys' lives and saving kids from fucked up homes, would it make me deserving?" Her lips part. "Don't think too hard about it. I already know the answer. We shouldn't have these abilities. Nothing can justify the modifications that allow me to strip the free will of other humans. Despite it, I'm not giving it up now."

"Why is it that important to you?"

"Have you read everyone's files? Not their medical history, personal interviews." Shifter's questionable gaze meets mine. "Mine is similar. I grew up with a sick sister; my parents favored her, and I made a very wrong decision that ended with my demise. I don't want revenge. I want to feel anything but that way—the way I did for years and years—like an inconvenience."

"Now you have a shield made of weapons."

I cross my arms over my chest. "Why would I want to give that up?"

While Cherry gave Shifter the space she needed, he got hold of Hyderton and had him square up Feather's stuff in Florida for eight weeks. When time is up, she has to decide what she's doing...or we have to decide. I don't know if I believe it's ready, but for her sake, this needs to work. If not, she's going to be losing her apartment and that job. Everything will fall apart for her if we die. The opportunity is knocking if she wants to see this out long-term. She has to understand that if I lose my ability to manipulate minds, it would be a lot harder for her to keep her nice things. It'll get sketchy with Hyderton. We'll flee. She's fucked.

I don't want it to come to that. I'd abandon her in a second and be long gone. I won't be caged and experimented on against my will. I won't let something happen to Cherry. I will choose us over her. I'll stack hatred on top of her fear and make myself another enemy, but for each step they make, we'll be quicker. If there's a way out, I'm going to find it, control it, and watch my name in the center of the big screen as they wish they could reach out and take me down.

I don't want to hurt her if I don't have to.

"Have you slept at all?" I grab her hands, holding them still on the counter.

"Three or four hours. I'm certain about this formula." She deadpans. "It will work the way I intend it to."

"I don't believe her," Charlie scoffs. "This is a mistake." He walks from the far corner of the room, next to me. His dead silence let me forget he was here. "Wes died yesterday. Yesterday!" His arms uncross, shooting up.

I look across the counter at Shifter. "Call everyone in here." As soon as I let go of her, she gets to work, sorting the new layer of pills. "We need to talk."

Slow walks into the lab, chewing on a rope of cherry licorice. "Who's dying today?"

"It's a *really* intelligent choice to eat in here," I mutter.

Seth walks around the corner with Cherry, her smile dropping the moment she looks between me and Shifter. Ronnie and Wes follow, hand in hand.

"Wes had a botched job yesterday, and Bennett wants us to take another experimental drug today," Charlie blurts out before I get a chance to explain.

"I'm out," Slow talks with his mouth full, chomping with each word. "That was scary as fuck. Then, we find out Shifter has these other abilities. I'm passing."

"I'm sorry," Seth replies. He takes Cherry's hand, swinging it playfully. "It's too soon." A sympathetic smile flashes on her face, disappearing in seconds.

"I'm not mad, Seth," she admits. "I understand. Maybe we should take a break. I know, I'm doing a lot of *processing* right now."

As Ronnie pulls away from Wes, she flips her hair over her shoulder. "You?" She starts with Cherry. "You knew about Shifter, but *oh, you're processing*."

"I didn't know everything, okay," Cherry barks back.

"Sure." She wobbles her head and purses her lips smugly, gearing up for another cat fight.

"Fuck off, Ronnie." Cherry turns away.

"What did you just say to me?" She grabs Cherry's shoulder, forcing her to return face-to-face. "The little princess learned some new words and thinks she's tough," she obnoxiously bobs. "You're the same person you were before you ran away."

Cherry can handle herself.

"Look who's crying, *princess*. Last time I checked, you came from money, not me." Cherry steps toward her face, and I instinctively make my move toward them.

"Fuck," Wes yells, pulling everyone's attention to him. "Stop fighting. I'll try it. What's the worst that can happen? They have to revive me again?"

What if I can't? If Shifter and I aren't able to repeat our actions? Fuck. We shouldn't be doing this. Not after yesterday. Everyone is on edge, nobody trusts each other, and we all know the doctor should have had more than three hours of sleep before pushing more drugs on us.

"No," Shifter replies. "You're not ready." He leans a hand on the counter beside Feather, straightens, and casually removes his glasses to clean the lenses.

"Nobody else is goin' to do it." Wes shakes his head. "If we don't try it out, we get nowhere."

"You're right," I agree. "I'll do it."

"What?" Shifter gives me a look as he replaces his marbled frames.

"If it works on me, it'll work on everyone. It makes sense."

Cherry...

She's staring at me with those eyes. They're the only part of her face that shows emotion, and it's all anyone would need. They're full of it all—sorrow, anger, frustration...confusion. She doesn't want me to do it. She doesn't understand why I would. She should.

Charlie shrugs. "It does make sense." Of course, he wouldn't protest.

"I agree." And Ronnie. "He should try it first."

"You would agree, Ronnie." Cherry crosses her arms, a gentle chill shaking her.

"Oh, it's okay for my man to risk his life, but when the tables are turned, Little Miss Sunshine can't handle it."

"Your man? Your man! Since when? Yesterday!" *Round fucking two?* "You didn't notice he had feelings for you until he bluntly spilled them on the floor."

I pinch the bridge of my nose, rubbing my fingers across my eyes.

"You don't know shit!"

"At least I'm—"

"Ya'll...chill." Wes shuts it down.

Seth pulls hair from his mouth, brushing it from his face. "Cherry, I'm with them," he says. "Bennett has the most severe symptoms. If it works on him, it sets all of us up."

"Seth, really? You don't think we should hold off and collect our thoughts on this?"

He slowly shakes his head while rubbing her shoulder, which she stiffly ignores.

"Slow?"

He draws his lips tightly together, dipping his chin.

"Seriously? Shifter?"

Baby, please.

Shifter's hands still take the table with his forward hunch. His eyes roll upward, being taken hostage by hers. "It's up to Bennett, sweets."

"I can't believe this. He came back here with me because he wanted to help *me,* and you all threw him in the fire." She drops her arms, balling her hands in fists.

"Cherry, I volunteered. It's logic. Don't make it personal."

"We're all different. Just because you take it doesn't mean...I can't..." Shivers rip through her body, and she shakes uncontrollably. "I need some air." I reach for her, unable to get a grasp on her arm before she runs out the door.

B, why wouldn't you chase her? Why wouldn't you grab her, pin her to the wall, and tell her everything is going to be okay?

I can't lie to her. This is a gamble. I could be making a stupid fucking mistake, and I need her to talk me down. I need her...to tell me to breathe.

Bennett Is The Sacrifice

After five minutes of foolish hesitation, I track her down. "Cherry..."

"Why doesn't Shifter take it?" Her words smack me the second I open the door in the same take as the blustery wind. It settles as fast as it picks up. She doesn't mean that.

Here's the scene I walked into: Cherry is damn near on her knees, keeled over, holding her abdomen with heavy, unstable breaths. Fuck. Will she get a grip already?

Bennett! You're an asshole!

No fuck, darling. And I can't keep doing this for her. Talking her down every fucking time rewards the anxious cycle. She can do it herself. I've given her what she needs. Now it's up to her to dig deep and be a boss bitch concealed beneath the struggle. I'd do anything for her, and that means making sure she's capable of surviving without me.

I stand next to her with my hands tucked away, letting her process her meltdown. "Cherry, it has to be me."

The breeze takes her hair, wrapping it around her neck and face. Falling to her knees, she struggles to breathe. I stand above her, waiting for her to find her voice.

"I'm not ready," she pants.

"You are. You can handle this. Cut the fucking shit and prove it to me." I squat down to her. "Where's that girl who tied me to a tree? She's in there, and I'm done covering for her."

"Count...I want you to count," she commands.

A smirk tugs at my lips. "One. Two. Three. Four. Five..."

"Six." She sits on her knees, exhaling. Her bloodshot eyes flutter shut. "Again."

"One. Two. Three. Four. Five. Six."

She exhales. "You said you wouldn't leave."

"I'm not leaving. If I thought this was going to kill me... permanently, do you think I would be doing it?" I widen my eyes exaggeratedly and shake my head. "Fuck no...Fuck no, darling." I grasp her chin in my fingers. "You're the reason the rain slows in the middle of a storm and the sunshine peeks out just enough to remind me that this downpour won't last forever. The dark clouds have followed me for too long."

"If you die, I die." A single tear strolls down her cheek to the length of my hand.

"If I live, you live."

I clasp my hand around her upper neck, pulling her mouth into mine. The salt from her tears coats my lips, and she tugs the entirety of my lower flesh with her teeth. Her tongue traces, and mine intertwines.

"God, you make me so fucking horny." My airy chuckle falls and twists until it becomes a deep rumble. "You kissed me like that on purpose."

"If you're going to take your chances at a death sentence, the least you could do is fuck me first."

"I love it when you tell me what you want." The heat of our breath entangles. She shoves me to the ground without losing my hand.

Why did I volunteer for this shit? I should have run away with her weeks ago to somewhere remote where we can fuck and laugh and talk about everything and nothing. I better not fucking die.

"Do you see the house?" I ask.

"I see it. I see all of our pain becoming something of the past that no longer haunts our nightmares. I see notebooks scattered in every room, and I see how I'm going to have to sort them all out with you all because you couldn't carry a table or use your phone."

I trail my hand down her neck, slipping under her shirt. "I'm going to run out of things to write about."

"You can always write about sex. It sells."

"Oh, the pearl clutchers will come for us, darling."

"I'm pretty sure we're already going to hell." Her light-hearted laughter soaks my soul in warmth.

"I'm going to have to pick fights with you for the wild makeup sex. I'll miss the crazy."

"I'm not mad at you now and B—" She whispers. "We're in the grass, two feet from the entrance. I could take you right here, right now, or is that too tame for your liking?" She wraps her hands around my neck, pressing her thumbs under my jaw.

"Maybe that's wild for normal people, but we'll never be normal, baby." I glide my hands down her ribs to the curves of her hips.

"We're going to be normal. Normal and boring, and we'll only screw in the missionary before we fall asleep at night."

"The fuck we will."

Her laugh pulls mine out.

She pulls one hand away and reaches back, grabbing something.

What is...hah. It's the fucking blade from her shoe that she went coo-coo on Shifter with. She flips it open, pushing the tip into the hollow below the bone of my chin.

"Ah, fuck, darling."

"You wanna play? Show me what you got...B." Her eyes ignite over me, and her lips part.

I snatch her wrist, rolling until she's pinned to the ground. She holds the knife steady, never pressing too deep or letting off.

"You have to put that down," I whisper.

"Make me," she mouths.

I stand to one foot, slowly lifting the other and rising as Cherry continues to hold her knife. I take a step backwards. "Get up," I demand. "I want you to run and run and don't look back. If you do, you lose."

"What's losing?"

"You're mine."

She stands up, tucking the knife in her bra. "And if I win?"

"You're mine." A rush of floating lights blurs my vision, and my smile stretches wide in the haze. "You lose, I win. You win, I win."

"It's not much of a game, is it?"

"You can make it more."

"Once, I told myself I'd never let the pierced monster take me again." She brushes the dirt from her ass before wiping her hands on her thighs. "See you on the other side." She slaps me across the face and turns away, taking off through the wooded area behind the lab. *Yep, those woods. The ones where I was dumped once upon a time.*

"Hey." A voice carries from behind me. "Where's Cherry?" As I glance over my shoulder, I find Slow and Seth. "Do you know you're bleeding?" Slow continues. "You're face looks kinda red, too."

I smile, chuckling deviously in the worst manner. "She'll be back in a little while. If you hear screaming...we're okay." I walk off into the woods, leaving them with no other explanation.

"Cherry bomb," I call. "You can run, but you can't hide."

She jumps out from behind the truck of a massive bark-covered beast, tackling me to the ground.

Ugh. Fuck. If I could...damn it. "You're a bad girl, Cherry," I grumble. "Very bad."

Her strength doesn't match mine as I roll over her, pinning her down. She claws into my chest, grunting and moaning. I lean forward and pin her arms in place. Her mouth takes my neck, biting the fuck out of me.

"God, fuck! Who's the vampire now? Do you think that's going to heal overnight? You need your ass beat."

"I fucking dare you to try," she spits.

Her hips call me, telling me to flip her to the dirt and slide down her body. I pull one of her shoes off and chuck it. "I fucking hate these shoes."

I grab the other and give it a good toss.

"We're not playing licorice trauma." She arches her ass into my abdomen. "I'll wear whatever I want."

"You're about to be wearing nothing, darling."

Aggressively pulling at her jeans, the button pops, and I drag them down to her ankles. She kicks at me, nearly connecting with my jaw.

"That's what I'm talking about, baby!"

Her jeans go flying, throwing them over my shoulder, as I hold on to her. With a clawing attempt to crawl away, she's left with nothing besides dirt caked under her pretty painted nails. I climb back on top of her, pressing my hardened cock against her ass. Her moans thicken with several deep inhales.

"Tell me you want me."

"No."

With my body flat to hers, I reach to her chest, squeezing between her and the Earth. A chill covers her body, and I tease her hardened nipple before I slip my hand to the knife that's tucked along the side of her breast.

"Hey!" She scolds me, twisting in every direction.

She settles as I kneel above her, striking her in the ass with an open hand.

"Ouch!" She squeals.

"You dared me."

One swipe of the knife cuts her thong clear off, promptly followed by two more slaps to her ass. She screams out, trying to push to her knees and escape me.

"Fuck you, B. That hurt, asshole!"

"Such words for a nice girl. I think I need to teach you a lesson."

"A lesson? You're the reason I swear in the first place."

"So what you're saying is, I turn good girls bad?"

"Shut up and fuck me. I'm so wet." Her ribs flare with every heavy inhale.

I unzip my jeans, pushing them to my ankles as fast as I can. A grunted moan overtakes me as I hold myself between her legs, hoist her hips at an angle, and slide into her tight pussy. I let go of her hips, pushing into my arms as I continue taking her from behind. I swear she loves the game of making it difficult for me, clenching her legs together.

She screams and cries out, and I control where my think space leads. The guys outside must hear us. They wish they had what we have.

"Louder! Tell me how good I make you feel, darling," I demand. "I love to hear you let go, leaving it all over my dick." I slowly thrust into her, digging into my toes.

"Oh, my god," she pants. "It's..." she exhales. "So," she gasps. "Good."

Our moans blend together, uncontrolled and ragged, the same as the loose dirt and rocks wrecking our bodies—my hands, knees...her skin.

"Come for me."

"Bennett," she hums.

Nothing exists—not the birds chirping or the dead leaves that crunch beneath us. The only tone to resonate is the sweet moans of her orgasm, clenching my dick.

I tug her hips up, working for my own pleasure. She reaches back, scratching at my thigh. "Is that all you got?" I twist her hair around my hand, dragging her chest wide as I thrust deeper.

"More." She gasps.

Her arousal coats me, and I groan. "Fuck."

As I tower over her, my dick pulses. Between our release, her thighs have become soaked, and the liquid drips down her leg as I pull out. I fall to the ground beside her, panting. Her ribs flare over and over as she chases her breath.

"I swear you better not die."

"Who am I?"

"B..."

"No. Who the fuck am I, Cherry?"

"Bennett Larson."

"Who?"

"Bennett Fucking Larson!" She screams. "And I don't care if you were the most famous man in the world, if you die on me, I'll chop your dick off so you can't use it in the afterlife on someone else."

"Oh, the jealousy is interesting." I lean closer, kissing her jaw. "But I don't think I'll work like that."

"It's will." She pushes to her forearms. "And then I'm going to use it to make a mold. The whole rotten flesh thing is kinda a turn off."

"Are you saying you only want to fuck me for the rest of your life? That's a big commitment."

"Until I self-destruct."

"Don't you fucking dare start that shit with me." My fingers clasp around her wrist. "If you die, I die. If I die, you fuck my dick clone, annoy Shifter, and shine like the fucking glamorous star you are." I robe her in my arms. Her soft skin crashes into my solid chest. "Promise me you won't do anything crazy for at least six months."

"Six?"

"If I'm broken, that gives them enough time to fix me, and if I'm dead, that gives you enough time to decide if you're fully committed to this I die, you die tribute."

"You're love isn't a phase, B."

"I wouldn't hold it against you if it was."

"Yes, you would!" She scolds.

"I might." A chuckle escapes my throat. "I have dirt stuck to my ass and I'm about to be quarantined in Lab One for a few days."

She giggles, and I fall deep into her oceanic eyes. "Who couldn't have sex in the grass?"

"It wasn't the grass that was the problem. It was the lack of chase," I insist.

"Here I thought you were being considerate and didn't want to expose anyone to your kinks." She shrugs.

"Yeah, I'm extremely considerate. That's my entire personality." She stops scanning the woods for her layers and stares at me. "Solomon and Seth watched me run after you. I hope they know and they're envious."

"I doubt they care."

"Don't ruin my fantasy."

"Give me your hand." She shakes her head. "I could use your expertise in the real world, as in where are my shoes, B?"

Shifter is my second. I have to be prepared for the worst, right? I don't want to be, and having this conversation with him is the last thing I'd ever expect to be doing.

"If anything happens to me, your job consists of two things...have Cherry's back, and don't you dare fuck her," I tell Shifter. "I'll find a way back and cut your tongue out."

This is it. I'm about to take the first pill. For the next seven days, I won't be leaving this lab. Seven. Have I mentioned I'm not ready for this? That statement was accompanied by a laugh one might call sinister. This sucks.

I'll be hooked up to monitors. It might bring back memories I didn't know I had. I could lose control. I could die. Do I think I'm going to die? No. No, you don't. I'm fucking Bennett Larson, darling. Legends never die. Then again, this could be the dramatic ending to my story.

I need to send this to a self-addressed email with a title that catches Justin's interest when he's sifting through.

"B..."

I hold my finger to her lips and sit down on the bed. "Ay," I stop her.

"I, um, Seth, was nice to move a bed without wheels attached to it into Lab One."

"He should have offered that amenity to the doc first."

"Are you going sweet on her?"

"Shut up. I'm never leaving you; I already told you that. I'll always be with you. I could live a million lifetimes and in every single one of them, I would find a way to you."

"You might not come back this time. Shifter can't..."

"I always find a way back. I'm a stubborn asshole, remember?" She laughs, and I try to memorize every contour, line, and divot that makes up her beauty.

"Arogant asshole, but stubborn is quite close."

"I want you to wait outside. I'll be fine. I'll see you soon. Go get a shower, be with your friends, don't worry."

She holds back tears. "I'm never washing you off."

"Darling, take the shower. You're going to fucking stink."

Her lips tighten with a smile. "I'm not the only one that's going to stink."

"I washed up besides, I'll be able to shower as soon as Feather says I'm stable." I grab her chin, softly kissing her lips. "If Justin or Mel calls, cover for me. Now go. And tell Seth, thanks for the blunt he left under the pillow. I'll see you soon. I love you."

"I love you, B."

She walks toward the door, stopping when she reaches Shifter. "If something happens to him, I'll kill you. I mean it. If you take care of him, really take care of him, and nothing bad happens, I'll forgive you."

It's a hell of an ultimatum, but she's a hell of a woman.

"Are you sure about this?" Shifter asks.

"She can't hate you forever."

"If you die, she will."

"It would be iconic."

His brows flex. "How so?"

"You kill all the bad guys in her life."

A huff of air leaves his lips. "I doubt she'd see it that way."

"Get her to talk to you, and if she refuses, make her listen, make her hear you."

"You would do anything for her, wouldn't you?"

"Sometimes a girl just wants someone to put her first at all costs. That girl found me, and I have no problem destroying everything around us for her well-being." I unlace my shoes, pulling them off one by one. "She loves all of you. You're her family, Shifter. She needs you to be better. Don't fucking lie. She can handle the harsh realities."

"How do we go back now?" He asks. "It's a fucking mess."

I kick my feet up and stretch, getting comfortable in my latest residence. "That guy had his head up his ass."

"That's not what—never mind."

"I don't know why you're wasting time talking to me about this shit. The scary blonde is down that hallway. You should know which one. I lost count."

His eyes close, holding back his amusement. "For what it's worth, we're all hoping this goes well."

"Make sure the door locks behind you this time."

Dear diary, I mean, reader, or do you prefer darling? It's alive! I'm alive. It's been three days since I popped the first pill and got locked away from the general lab rat society. For those of you who said I wouldn't die. Congratulations, you win an invisible trophy. I'm not dead...yet.

I've been on a unicorn ride in the clouds. Psych. This shit sucks. I've tripped balls at least twice on the first day, to the point Feather had to leave and watch from outside. At one point, I smoked the favor Seth left behind, hoping that would help. I finger-painted the ceiling. I'm continuously racking my head around how I managed it.

As I stand in the doorway of Cherry's room, I appreciate the distance disappearing between us.

"Hey, Cherry bomb." She turns around, beaming from ear to ear. "Doc Feather cleared me to shower, but I think I need some supervision. You know, a slip might affect my progress."

"Bennett!" She attacks me, springing from her bed.

It's never felt better to have her skin against mine and the scent of her favorite candle overpower my nostrils. It smells like home within these fabricated cold walls.

"You've been crying." I swipe my thumb over her reddened cheek. She's out of tears, completely dry.

"It's been three days!" She smacks me in the chest. "Why didn't I hear anything?"

"Ow." I hold her arms down. "Not to give you any further reason to hate Shifter, but that was his job."

"He told me everything, but I missed you. I missed your voice." She nuzzles into my chest. I have to stink. It's not like I was working out, yet three days without a shower takes me back to the woods. Over the last three days, I spent a good amount of time writing as the memories flooded my think space. They're still broken and blotchy, which I'm fine with. I had enough material. The flashbacks won't change anything.

"I'm here now."

She tilts her head, looking up at me. "How do you feel? Did it work?"

"Come take a shower with me and then we'll have a family discussion."

"Family?" She pinches her lips together.

No. Shut it. I'm talking to you. Yeah, you. I fucking know. I said family. Cherry heard me say family. I'm acknowledging that I'm involved with these people in a collective way that would be labeled as a family. Do I want them? No. Do I need them? Again, no. Am I okay with the reality of these people being a part of my life for the time being? Yes. I see the benefit in people you can trust, okay.

"Don't make me say it again. Ugh," I groan, letting my head fall back. "Fine." I find her eyes. "I love you and I care about you. And I like the idea of having people I can trust, like your weird family, including Shifter. You probably shouldn't kill him."

"Is that a conscience?" She taunts. "I don't know if these pills are working, so Shifter's life is up for discussion until further notice."

"*Fuck*, okay. Fair." I slip down her body, taking her legs from underneath her, and hoisting her over my shoulder. Searching the room, I find the candle, leaning forward to blow it out and spin back around, careful to not smack her head off the door frame.

"B!" She laughs. I smack her ass, and she yips, hugging my waist. "I love you."

"I freaking love you and you're right...You need a shower." She fake gags. "You're stench is somewhere between sour milk and freshly peeled onions. It's better than a maggot-filled trash can, though."

"I'll take that as a compliment."

"He's safe, right?" Charlie opens his mouth just as his left leg passes through the door of Lab One. It's tighter in here now that the bed is set up. It seemed like the right place to hold this conversation.

"Honestly, I'm thinking about slicing your throat right now, *two-thousand-and-two*." I tilt my head in a taunt, hands tucked, as I lean against the counter. A shrewd smirk pulls from the corner of my mouth, slowly up my face. He tucks his chin, blankly staring with wide eyes.

"He's kidding." Cherry calms his stiff shoulders.

"What's 2002?"

"Your hat is from 2002." I grin.

"Oh, right." An unamused smile draws across his face and then falls.

Feather walks around the counter surface, leaning against it, inches from me.

She's become more comfortable around us and seems motivated on her own to help. If you ask me, she's taken to Shifter, which is hilarious since he wanted to tear her throat open in Florida. I don't know what he did or said, but it had to make the difference.

"Bennett's lab work, including his brain scans, is all showing what I had predicted. He's stable. To my knowledge, he hasn't had any obsessive desires thus far, and I think we should move forward, monitoring for four more days. Then I'll examine him every other day until we get to the fourth week, where I'll run a full circuit of tests again, compare, and move forward. I guess it's up to all of you what happens after that. We can start right away or wait a few more weeks to trial the medication on someone else."

It sounds like she's staying in East Grenton for a while. Better her than me.

"Three days is nothing. Keep monitoring him," Charlie insists.

"He didn't die in twenty seconds like I did," Wes says. "Seems like it's more than nothin'."

"This is good." Seth bobs his head. "I have a question, though. When I'm up...I mean, do natural herbs interfere with it?"

"Like what?" Feather questions.

"Natural herbs."

"I don't know what will give you issues yet, individually and all together. I'm making a list of what I want to test. I can add what you have in mind."

"He's talkin' about the medicinal plant of the world. The good old devil's lettuce. He wants the weed approval," Wes chimes.

"If he wants to find out, I'll run the tests."

Seth nods goofily. "I like you. You're good people."

"I'm not here to restrict any of you. I don't want to be like that. I want to work with you and let each of you be in charge of your choices."

"I'm going next," Shifter calls from the doorway where he's propped up. "As soon as he gets the clear. I'm ready."

"You think that's a good idea?" I ask.

"I'd like to make a trip to France next year." He wants to see his mom? His stuck-up bitch mom...huh. Okay. "Is that doable?" He looks at Feather.

"Um, yeah, you're doable. I mean, we can do it. It's possible to have you in a good, stable place to make that kind of trip."

Shifter's a fucking lady's man. Did you see that one coming? I didn't. Should I have? Wasn't he deeply in love with an angel? Maybe he's not the monogamous type, or he's leading Feather on. I didn't think he'd have that in him either. Then again, he seems like he'd do anything to help Cherry. There's a lot I don't know about this family. There's a lot we don't know about what's happened to us.

With most of those who could give me that information being dead, will I ever know? To the deepest extent? Unlikely. I don't plan on staying here long enough for those worms to crawl out. I hate East Grenton, and Cherry does too. It won't be too difficult to convince her to leave when the time comes. The next few weeks are going to be a pain in the ass. They'll pass, and in the meantime, I'm going to pick Feather's brain, dig through these files, and try to put an end to the wandering. I'm not taking my past with me. I'll keep up with our check-ins, make my copies of her documents, and ensure I get to keep living the way I want. I'll encourage Cherry to stay in contact with her family, both for her mental well-being and to keep tabs on the rats.

After this hiatus, I have an idea for a new book—my first series.

Over four weeks ago, we sat in this very room. We celebrated the small hurdle that was climbed and agreed to continue. Now, it's not only me. Shifter started the stabilizers about a week ago. He made it past the first three days, the same as I have.

"Feeling good?" I ask, walking through the threshold and eyeballing his propped-up feet.

"Yeah, yeah, yeah. I can't complain." His tongue runs across his top teeth.

"You can't complain about the pills or you can't complain about the *Feather*?" I gesture toward her, washing her hands at the sink. "What happened to your *angel*?"

I suggested he was fooling around with the doctor a few weeks ago. Now, I'm sure of it. She has those puppy-love eyes for him, the dopey smiles, and the happy-go-lucky attitude. He's either into her or making it seem like it. Personally, I don't care. My only concern is a falling out. I like her working with us, not for us. It's easier on everyone.

"You can love more than one person," he smirks.

Love. You heard that, right? He said "love."

Wait, he also said "more than one person." Is that the start of a thruple? That seems too deep for him to handle. He must mean that he's in love with other women, whom he can't have while loving this one as well. It sounds complicated. And like a pain in the ass.

"Yeah, let me know how that goes." Cherry walks in smiling ear to ear. "Hey, darling. Tell Shifter about the exciting news you got."

"Ah, fuck. You're pregnant." A grimace takes his mouth. "I'm not that daddy, am I?"

"God, no!" She shrieks, smacking his thigh. He winces, shrinking backward. "I'm getting interviewed by Capital Entertainment next week. Don't ever ask me that again."

"Oh shit," he exhales. "That is the best news. They're huge."

"God, what's wrong with you?" She laughs.

Wes slowly strolls through the door with a cocky limp. "Ya'll, I proposed to Ronnie."

Is it "rats with news" day? I need something to top him. Quick, give me a bullshit line that sounds realistic. I snap my fingers, quickly coming to terms with reality, and glance around to see if anyone noticed.

"Are you serious?" Cherry groans. Her jaw hangs as she fights a smile. "What did she say?" I know she's happy for them despite her and Ronnie's catty tension.

"*That's it?*" He mimics. "We're going back to the jeweler tomorrow."

"That was a yes, then?" She snickers.

"Hell yeah." He pumps his fist in the air.

"Before you know it, you'll have the gym and the house and the, whatever amount of kids, dogs, you wanted," I say.

"And a nanny," Cherry adds. "There's no way Ronnie will be a housewife."

"You might want to hold off on that dream until you get on treatment."

"B," Cherry scolds.

"I'm surprised you didn't say it." Her glare tells me to shut up.

"I've got nothin' but time." He shrugs.

"I heard long engagements are all the rage." Shifter winks. "It'll take you several years to find a bridal party anyway."

"Ya'll are assholes."

"I'm sorry, Wes." Cherry wraps her arms around his neck, hugging the bear. "I'm glad you're happy. I want you to be happy."

"What are your thoughts on destination weddings?" He asks.

"Beautiful and requires a thicker wallet." She whispers as if I wouldn't hear. "Bennett likes to throw money around, especially with my persuasion."

"He can bring me back from the grips of Hell any day, and yet, I'll manage to find the funds for sweet dreams on my own."

"Well, I'm here to help if you need me." She exhales, dropping her hands from her hips. "I can't promise I won't want to throw select fingers at your bride."

"How many plus ones do we get?" I ask. "Shifter may need two."

"And Cherry needs a negative one," he retorts.

"I don't care how many people you bring, as long as each of you puts on a fake-ass happy face, if need be, the entire time, and keep the fighting in your hotel rooms."

"Yeah, yeah, yeah. No bloody lips on the dance floor." Shifter grins.

CHERRY, TAKE TWO WEEKS

I'm two weeks into treatment. Two weeks into an unknown freedom. Bennett Larson had been the reason for my nightmares for so long; it's wild to believe in a few short months he's opened doors that I didn't imagine were possible.

"I'm nervous." I flick my thumb over my ring and glance up at B. He rubs my lower back. "This is what I wanted. I looked a killer in the eyes with a smile. Why is it terrifying?"

"They're here to see you. You're not here to see them," he insists. "You'll knock them dead, darling." He smirks. "Please don't do that in the literal sense."

"That's a you problem, B."

"I think you're right. Such a smart one. You always have an answer. You'll do fine."

B had a blackout a few days ago. It only lasted a few minutes, and he was back. He won't admit it, but I've noticed a personality shift in him, too. He's less of an asshole to other people. I used to feel like we lived in an alternative universe and nothing was real. We were aliens with human pasts that haunted us, and we couldn't move past them. It made us angry and evil and out of control, determined to use every ill part of our brains to lean into the obsession of the week...or year, for m e.

Now, we've become human again. We have to let go of the things that hold us back. B is doing a better job than I am. I don't know who he was when he was a kid. He described himself as a pushover and weak with a broken heart, wishing someone would see him for who he was. He wished that his parents would care enough to see his passions and his artistic ability.

Bennett never shies away from starting flames under people, especially Justin. He does it on purpose to watch him run around like a chicken with its head cut off. I don't think the medication changed those parts of him. It was me.

Some days it's easier to present my best self. Other days, I see myself on the wrong rooftop. The darkness haunts me. I want to control it.

Today is a good day. This is the stage where established actors and up-and-coming stars shine. I refuse to fall short.

"Cherry Kass, everyone," Kelly Holland announces from the stage.

"That's your cue." B smacks me from behind. "Kill it. Not them."

"I love you," I call, glancing back. My heels click against the hard flooring as I strut across the platform. With my shoulders pulled back, authenticity leads me, and my best performance evades my stature.

"I fucking love you."

A metallic silver dress hugs my curves. It stretches down my arms and sparkles as I take a step into the light. The stage is mine. This is what I wanted. Nobody is going to pity me unless I give them a reason to.

I'm on this stage for one reason, and that's because I have fans now. They demanded my presence. They love what I do on the screen. I've climbed the ladder...I cheated. I pushed buttons that other people couldn't. Stop. I deserve this. Samantha was the best breakout role I could have gotten. B told me to control the conversation. I can do this. *I can do this. I deserve this.*

"How are you?" The cheery woman greets me as I sit down on the grey sofa next to her fancy oak desk. I glance around at the live audience with a wave.

God, she's gorgeous. Her hair is edgy—short, spiky, and deep chestnut. It matches her entire aesthetic. A fitted double-layered charcoal dress flatters her height, tattered and chic. Who is her stylist?

"I'm great. Thank you." I flash my biggest Hollywood smile. For once, it isn't fake.

"Let's talk about this movie! First, how was it working with Bennett Larson?" I knew she would ask that. "There had been rumors about you two." She shimmies her shoulders, begging for the details. "Care to set them straight?"

"Bennett is an amazing writer and director."

"Oh, you're on a first-name basis." She winks at the audience.

"Yeah, well, working with him...let's just say we butt heads a lot." As I raise my brows, the audience laughs.

"We've heard he's no Jensen."

"He's not," I agree. "The man is quite brilliant, though."

"Oh, yes? As you can imagine, we're all curious as to what's true in the atmosphere. Can you tell us about the *romantic* rumors?" She digs.

"I could, but then I'd have to kill you." I deadpan.

"Oh no." She laughs nervously. "I guess we'll stick to the other questions then. I like my horror to stay on screen."

"Sounds like a good idea." I smile, looking back at B.

He mouths words to me that I can only interpret as *fuck yes.*

"What was the best part of playing Samantha?" She leans forward on her desk, propping her head on her fist.

"Kissing Ames Heart, duh!" I giggle, stirring up the audience again.

"Oh, tell me more."

"No, I'm joking. Ames was great to work with, but I had more of a crush on my makeup artist, Kayla, than anyone else. Kayla, I love you!" I shout. The crowd applauds, encouraging me. "I loved Samantha. She's such a badass character to play. She has all these little layers that you get to see peel back one by one. She's likable and still, somehow, unhinged."

"I can't wait to see it at the premiere, and guess what?" She looks at the crowd. "Two lucky people here today will also be attending as my guest."

I find B again as the crowd cheers, unable to wipe the stupid grin off my face. We did it. I did it.

With my robe on and a towel covering my wet hair, I return from the shower.

We're staying in yet another hotel near Los Angeles. Bennett's standards are unimaginably higher than those I had been used to. In a few short years, I've seen the most dramatic change. It's both terrifying and exciting in the same bite. I'm not sure I've been allowed the time to inhale it. How could I? The rate at which the world spins is tripled when you're trapped in the space between seeking and hiding.

"Charlie said he's feeling better than he has in years," I tell B. "By his standards, I think that's pretty good."

"You talked to the guys today?" He looks over his shoulder as he sits at the desk, typing away. He's been pushing hard lately to finish the final edits on our book. He's nitpicking. It's already perfect. It's everything...and the best part—everyone will believe it's fiction.

"Yeah, when you were on the phone with Justin." I tease my fingers through wet knots, smoothing my hair to one side.

"Have you checked our pill count lately?"

I fall to the bed, lying on my side as I dry the ends of my hair. "Yep. We're both fine for a few more weeks."

"Good, with the premier coming up, I don't have time to run back to East Grenton."

"I almost *don't* dread going back there, knowing that we get to see the guys."

His eyes no longer settle on mine. They fall, and he stares through me, lost in thought for a moment.

"Any update on Hyderton?"

He had to ask that. I knew it was coming. Luckily for him, I got an update from Shifter today, too.

"He's following your instructions. I'm not worried, but I don't know what we're going to do when Shifter leaves for France. Put Charlie in charge? Wes?"

I hope Shifter finds what he's looking for on his trip—answers or connections, whatever it is. He has some type of open relationship with Feather and Raven. He refuses to give me details. He's been mindful of his space lately, and I can't blame him. I left him—them—again. He needs some time to figure out...everything.

He's not the only one, and I'm hesitant to believe that we'll figure out most of this life, besides B. Bennett knows what he wants. What was the name I'm supposed to use? He can search and replace it later. *His goals are cut and dry. While I can't foresee ever being fully satisfied in one place. Acting gives me an outlet to try on different hats. Short-term relationships and flings were a freedom I didn't know until B built a fantasy of us together until the end. He's willing to entertain my sexual desires, but how am I supposed to give him what he wants when it's emotional security? I'm meant to love him through all curves, lows, and highs. I have to listen, communicate, and be in love with him every day. I won't be in love with him every day. And that's where we deeply differ.*

The blood vessels of Bennett's heart have stemmed out of his body and twisted around my veins. He relates to the broken and ugly. He sees something beautiful in the shadows of my being. He's willing to give me what so many women want—a love that would follow you to Hell. A man who wouldn't sacrifice you or himself. He would climb the bodies of dozens to ensure you're always together. You aren't all he has. You are the one that he'd risk everything else for.

Bennett is poetry.

I am prose.

"Shifter's trip is a while away." He turns to his right, his eyes skating over me. "We'll figure it out."

"Close your laptop and come over here," I insist. "You've done enough work for one day."

"Do I get a massage?" He lifts his brows and then narrows his eyes again.

"Full body, I'm guessing?"

"It's the only way I'm quitting for the night. You're interrupting my flow."

"Oh, am I an inconvenience?"

"Never," he backtracks.

"You can have anything you want as long as you return the favor."

"I always return the favor." He closes it and hops into bed. "You're my favorite part of the day."

"I want breakfast in bed tomorrow." I sit up on my knees and toss my towel to the bathroom door.

He adjusts the pillows and lies back on his arms. "I'll make sure they know how to make that cinnamon toast you like."

"You know the way to a girl's heart." I tower over him, dipping down to softly steal the breath from his lips. "B...Are you okay?"

"Yeah. Why wouldn't I be?" He frowns.

An empty silence settles between us as I reach for the right words. "Have you had any, um, *occurrences* like when that car backfired?"

"I'm fine, darling." The chill of his rings caresses my jaw as he brushes hair behind my ear. "I'll let you know if something happens."

I sigh, not completely pleased with his answer, and reach for his hand, forcing the metal around his finger to spin.

"I'll tell you if something happens, okay? Does that make you feel better?"

"I guess. I don't want any secrets. I can't do it anymore, and especially not with you."

He brushes my hair back again and glances at my mouth, quickly flickering back to my eyes. He sits up straight, shaking his messy hair from his eyes. He palms it back, not far above his temple. Deep waves of blue fixate on me, fitting a sinking sensation beneath my core. "I have a scar right here."

I quickly study the two-inch-long line. Hidden well in his hair, it's the first time I've noticed the curved mark that's slightly lighter than his pale skin.

"I got into a fight outside a bar when I was eighteen. I went to watch a local band play for an eighteen-plus event. How fucking cool was I? I was allowed in the bar. I'm sure there's some cheesy photo one of my friends took in the attic at my parents' house."

"How'd it happen?"

"This drunk dirtbag jumped me when I went out for a piss. His name was Derreck. He thought I was this rich kid named Duncan. The good old case of mistaken identity got me a glass bottle to the fucking cranium."

"Why are you telling me this?"

"Just because I got jumped at a bar once hasn't stopped me from going to them. I have issues with East Grenton and apparently backfiring cars. It's not going to stop me, Cherry. You don't have to worry." He lies back. "What about the scar on your right forearm? And the inch-long one below your right breast?" His gaze travels the length of my tank top.

"You noticed those?"

"When it comes to you, I notice everything."

"Why didn't you ask before?"

"I knew you'd tell me about them when you wanted to."

I lift my top, exposing the bottom of my breast and the scar accompanying it. "This one? Car accident when I was seventeen. It was early in the morning and dewy. I can smell it. At the time, someone I considered a close friend was driving. We came around the bend in the road, and there it was—a big, black bear. It didn't have a care in the world, casually strolling across the pavement. My friend swerved, trying to avoid hitting it. Instead, she hit a pole. She broke her nose, and I got this. We both felt it for a while, but it could have been worse." I shrug, dropping my top. "And this one." I hold up my arm. "A cooking burn. Less exciting. I mean, neither are great stories. This is stuff that happens to hundreds of people a day."

"I wasn't looking for excitement. Those are pieces of your life that made you who you are, and I want to know about them. Anything you want to tell me, I want to hear." He noisily inhales. "I don't want trauma licorice or bubblegum. I want sleepless thoughts, deep dreams, and heavy nightmares. I don't want you to tell me something because you have to, you need to, or you're baiting me."

I straddle his legs, and his hands fit my waist in unison.

"I promise, I'll never bait you again."

"I wouldn't blame you if you did. The reason would be worth listening to."

"You keep my demons at bay, and I'll keep yours? Maybe we'll have a tea party."

"Decaf or you'll regret it."

"I regret a lot of things. Never stopped me before." I taste his soft kiss. "B, forever is a long time."

"Don't think about it." The corner of his mouth tugs up. "Think about today, tomorrow, and the next few months."

"It doesn't feel right," I admit. "Being uncertain when you—"

"Shut the fuck up." My jaw hangs. "Respectfully," he adds. "I love you. You love me. The rest is a fucking shit show, darling."

"For a second, I thought I was going to have to slap you."

"Don't change your mind now."

"Cherry." Bennett's gentle tone slowly wakes me. "Hey, your phone is ringing."

A sleepy rasp vibrates my dry throat. "What time is it?"

"Almost seven."

"AM?" I blindly reach for my buzzing phone. "It's too early." As I tap the answer button without looking, I hold it to my ear. "Hello."

"Good mornin' sunshine."

"Wes."

"Did I wake you? You and Bennett need to stop with the wild sex stuff and get those eight hours in."

"What's he want?" B asks.

I hush him and clear my throat. "Is everything okay?"

"Yeah, I was in the gym, and I started thinking. I need your opinion," he replies.

"What's going on?"

"What?" Bennett groans.

"Nothing," I mutter back. He leans in, listening.

"Would it be a bad idea if Ronnie and I moved?"

"Fuck, no," B complains.

"Um...right now?"

"Not right now, *right now*, but if everything continues the way it's been goin', I don't want to stay here. In a few months."

"He can't," Bennett demands.

"You can move whenever you want, Wes."

"No, he can't," B argues.

"Yes, he can," I mutter. "We already left, Wes. It's not fair if Bennett and I get to travel, work, and live outside the confines of East Grenton."

Bennett tucks his hand behind his head and gets lost in the ceiling.

"I don't plan to go far. I understand what's at stake."

"You know how people get married, have kids, raise them, they grow up, and then they leave home? It's time we all leave home, and Bennett is the mom who's not ready to let go of control."

A hearty chuckle rings from the other side of the phone.

"Alright, Hollywood. I'd better see you more than twice a year and on TV."

"We're not the traditional family."

"Certainly aren't," Bennett affirms, stretching his arms up before planting his feet on the floor.

"Somethin' about that asshole boyfriend of yours that I like, ya know."

"Yeah, I thought the effect would wear off once he took enough of these pills, but apparently he's somehow likable."

"He only likes me because I saved his life, Cherry." Bennett fastens the button on his pants.

"Has Charlie, Seth, or Slow mentioned leaving?" I ask.

"Charlie likes to talk, you know, and Seth and Slow might be lifers."

"You underestimate them. New hope can relight the fire in your soul."

"Has either of them said anythin' to you?" Wes asks.

"I haven't had the time to make it past small talk." As I glance over at B, he's fully dressed. "Where are you going?"

"Me?"

"Not you, Wes."

"I have to meet with Justin."

"Why? You didn't tell me."

"I'll be back in an hour...with breakfast." His kiss remains on my lips after he pulls the door closed.

"Cherry?"

"Yeah, Wes."

"Everythin' okay?"

"I think so. Yeah. It's fine," I convince myself. "How's Shifter doing? Really doing."

"He's focusing his energy. The guy wants to make that trip. He already booked his flight."

"He did?"

"Bennett might not want any of us to move along while there's so much, uh, uncertainty in the air, but we're tired of rottin' in this Hell. Three fuckin' years just...lost. You brought the hope back."

"I wanted to be normal. We shouldn't have the abilities we do."

"Yeah, well, I ain't mad." He chuckles. "I'm dead, girl. I don't have family, a job history, references, or money...It evens the playing field a little."

"A lot of people come from nothing. They make it work."

"Does Bennett know how you feel about this?"

"He knows." I exhale. "He likes his life the way it is."

"Are you going to be okay?"

"I spent a lot of time on my own, especially in the past three years. I wasn't knitting or doing paint-by-numbers. The things we're capable of...Maybe I could channel mine for good."

"I don't question it. You're going to do far more than I ever will."

"Do you think you'll be able to have kids, Wes?"

"I'm goin' to talk to Feather about that. If it's not advised, there's adoption."

"I don't know if I'll ever see Ronnie as the motherly type." My laughter is stifled.

"You might be surprised."

I cringe, shrinking back. "I can't think about that anymore. Bennett went to meet his assistant, but should return soon. Do you need anything else?"

"No. It was good to hear your voice."

"You can call me anytime...but not too much if you want to keep Ronnie."

"Things will change, Cherry."

"I believe you, and as much as I seem ungrateful, I do see the potential...in everything."

"You'll be okay, kid."

"Enough teddy bear pep talk. I need to hop in the shower."

"I'll cya soon."

"Stay smart. Stay safe."

Bennett's Happy Ever A—Wait A Minute

"What's the big surprise, B?" I thread my fingers between Cherry's, keeping the wheel steady as I pass the last house for miles.

"I have to tell you something." She brushes her messy waves behind one shoulder and waits for me to drop another problem in her lap. "I've been keeping something from you."

"We agreed on no more secrets, Bennett. I don't—"

"Don't. Cherry, let me explain."

"Fine. What happened?"

"I spent a large sum of money." Her brows furrow. "I can afford to."

"Did you buy another lab? I get it. East Grenton. But I can't keep...you have to consider everyone else when you make a decision that affects us all," she insists.

"Cherry, don't roll those eyes at me. They're too fucking pretty to always be pissed at me."

"I'm not mad. I'm—"

"Disappointed," I finish her thought. "You're going to feel like an ass when you realize what I actually bought."

"A morgue."

I strain my neck slowly to the side. "Seriously?"

"Right. A wooded lot of land is more likely."

"Are you implying I'm an idiot or I'll eventually kill someone...again?" I pull my hand from her and chew at my nail. "I haven't seen stars in a while. No floating lights, lightheadedness. No blackouts."

"Stop chewing your nails."

"Stop spinning your fucking ring."

"Why are you nervous, B?" She stares, deadpan. "Where are we going? What am I supposed to see?"

Shadowed by lush, rich vine maple leaves, a house rests at the end of the long, shadowed driveway. As my SUV crawls into view, it dawns on her. With more than enough privacy, the single-level, white house is the first non-mobile living quarters I've purchased. It's my first piece of land in general.

Overwhelming pressure heats my back, cutting around my ribs and the ever-pounding organ in my chest. My heart is wired differently these days. When it beats this rapidly, it's because I'm feeling real emotion. It's the kind of emotion that makes you messy. It gets you killed or worse, caught. It's harder to regulate, and I often find myself falling into old habits of nail biting or hyperactivity. I paced the hotel for half an hour before I decided it was time to bring her here.

"What do you think, darling?" I pull the key from the ignition and open the center console. She grabs the dangling ring from my finger and steps out of the car.

"What are you waiting for?" I ask, tucking my hands into my pockets as I meet her side.

I've been loved. I've been lost. I've been broke and burned.

I've hated. I've done despicable things. I've hidden from emotion.

I've put my heart under a gun and hoped she didn't pull the trigger.

I've watched someone I loved hold the gun to their temple, desperate for a way out.

She places the key into the knob, turns it, and lets the door hang wide.

"Justin is working on getting a crew out here to set up the new security system."

"This place is ours?" She shrieks, dancing on her tiptoes. "Why did you scare me like that? I thought—"

"I know what you thought." As I tuck my arm around her lower back, I pull her to my chest. "Do you like it?"

"I do."

"Wait until you see the backyard."

"Are you sure this is ours?"

She looks out the wall of glass surrounded by green. The two-bedroom house sits above an immaculate view of the ocean. As Cherry steps onto the wide patio, the sun glistens against the water. She runs around like a child on Christmas, first spotting the hot tub nestled under the enclosed section of the deck. Then, she happy dances near the fire pit surrounded by cozy, grey outdoor furniture. It's everything we never had and, unimaginably, what I told her I would deliver.

"It's all ours." It means too much to her. I wanted it to be…It's hers. She doesn't owe anyone. It can't be taken. She will never have to worry about losing it.

"How much did this cost?"

"It doesn't matter. It's just paper, and you're worthy of every piece. Burn it to the ground if you'd like."

"I'm not going to burn it, B. It's mine. You're mine." She kisses me before dancing around the patio with her fingers tangling in the breeze. "We finally have a home. A dream home."

"I've always had a home. *It's you.*"

She stops, and her smile fades. "I'm sorry that I've put you through all of this."

"I'm not." As I take her hand, I lead her to my desk. "How's this for an ending to our story?" I point to my laptop, and she takes a seat, waking the screen.

I've been healed in more ways than one after fighting everything I couldn't comprehend.

I've been searching for as long as I can remember, and what I needed was never very far.

Am I wrong to place all of my hope on one person? Everything that keeps me from slicing throats and demanding obedience? I don't think so. I'm not worried about something happening to her that leaves me in a fucked think space. Wherever she goes, I will follow.

That's the story of a dead man with alien abilities. He learns to enjoy invisibility again...where it counts.

Dr. Romberg is a brilliant woman. Mood stabilizers help us manage, and yet, our lives are not guaranteed. We might die tomorrow. The meds might stop working. We could become immune or find there are side effects down the road. Some part of our past might catch back up to us—people we fucked over, Hyderton...Someone more powerful. Fuck, Hollywood could tear us down. At some point, I'm going to be canceled for being a problematic asshole.

"I can't wait for the day you get called out."

My glare beats down on her. Then I smirk. "By someone other than you?"

Her blue eyes roll around, and she picks up reading where she left off.

I've spent my entire life invisible, right? Cherry made me realize that I'm part of the problem. It's going to be a long fucking road to feel comfortable in my skin as Benny crawls out from the rock I've trapped him under. As I build relationships and cherish every moment with her, I'll continue to be reminded that this is why we live. I don't breathe for the fame or the money or the fucking murder—definitely not for the murder. I haven't had any urges to strangle anyone. Well, none that we're of the obsessive psychotic realm. Perhaps the dickhead who cut me off an hour ago.

You know me so well, though. Don't you?

You knew I would come around, right? And you know I'd burn every bridge for her. You know I don't plan to stop using my abilities when I need them and as long as I have them. I'm a complex, weird splatter of colors, not grey. As fucking weird as it sounds, I'm the walking dead version of Shifter's painting.

I stare at the huge masterpiece framed above the desk.

He's okay, I guess.

Cherry's gaze follows mine. "He gave you one of his paintings?"

"I bought it. He needed extra money for his trip."

"I love it," she says softly.

"The painting?"

"The ending. The painting. This house. You."

I hover over her, taking her jaw in my hand. "Are you sure?"

"Yep." She rises, pressing her lips to mine, and just as quickly takes off towards the bedroom.

"What are you doing?"

"Justin assisted in furnishing the house, right?" She glances back while I hang in the doorway.

"Yes."

Her smile widens as she pulls the top drawer of the dresser open and holds up a little red triangle bikini. "Did you think you have the upper hand, Mr. Larson?" She struts over to me, dangling the fabric from her finger. "I had a little chat of my own with Justin. He wouldn't tell me what you were up to. So, I might have told him to deliver the remainder of Samantha's wardrobe to our next hotel."

"You did what?" My jaw becomes tense.

"He made me mad," she whispers.

"I thought the pills were working."

"B, I stole a swimsuit and a few dresses. They're working."

I dip forward with a murmur against her skin. "That doesn't sound like you."

"Would you believe me if I said I didn't think it would work?"

"I would." Her gaze rests on my lips. "Don't underestimate what you're capable of."

"I've learned my lesson."

Her taste sweetens my lips, its depth potent enough to ruin the rest of our day. She steps back, playfully teasing me with flesh of smooth curves and beauty, pulling the red number around her hips and over her shoulders.

"What are you doing?" I ask.

"I'm going to take a dip in the hot tub. Are you coming?"

My teeth cut into my lower lip as I try to bite back a smile. "You know we have an event coming up."

Her hands press to my chest, and she smirks. "I promise I won't hurt you." Her vibrant gaze is short-lived, disappearing as she lazily smacks me across the cheek and takes off running.

"You won't win this game," I yell, slowly turning around to watch her ass bounce as she springs out the sliding door and pulls at the strings dangling at the back of her neck. "Why did you bother putting it on?" I call out, following her.

"Bennett, Bennett! What's next for you? Will you be doing more films with Cherry?"

I've met these hungry reporters before in another five-thousand-dollar tux on another red carpet. I'm back and I've come pretty far from that black sheep living in East Grenton. I may have changed, but the reporters never do. They're looking for the next story.

Camera lights flash and voices spread louder, and I find myself fixated on Cherry. Samantha's wardrobe has always suited her well. She looks fucking insatiable in the long, black silk dress.

As unpredictable as it is, the corner of my mouth tugs into a calm smile. "Actually, if you want the exclusive, listen up. Cherry and I have an announcement." I steadily glance into her eyes and squeeze her hand. "For the first time, I have co-written a story. Cherry and I have been working on this project for some time. With a dual perspective, this story is unlike any that I've told before. It will be on presale tomorrow, and you're not going to want to miss out."

"Trust me when I say limited first editions are gorgeous," she adds before she takes a step forward. "I'm Not The Hero by Bennett and Cherry *Larson* is an incredible journey of healing, love, and deep, dark passion." Her smile twists my black heart in every direction. I'd sell my soul to permanently keep it on her face.

Holding a microphone the full length of her arm, a petite auburn-haired woman squeezes around past the barking men. She's spicy like Cherry and easily catches both of our attention. She demands it. "Mr. Larson!" She calls.

"Bennett."

"Bennett," she copies, and her cheeks flush. "Do you have plans to recreate I'm Not The Hero into a film in the near future?"

I connect with Cherry and offer her the reply.

"Bennett and I tend to butt heads on set." Laughter travels through the crowd. "If we come to the conclusion that I'm Not The Hero should go to film, he will be overseeing it. As of right now, it's not in pre-production, and I will not be taking a role in it. I will, however, be playing Tulip Dean in Bradley Austin's *Seven*. It was announced this morning, if you were too distracted." Once more, cheery noises surround us. The Cherry effect. A phenomenon.

"Does this mean you will not do any more Bennett Larson films?"

I wrap my arm around her waist, posing for more pictures. "Don't start that rumor. Nothing is ever set in stone. Cherry might find herself starring in or behind the scenes of a number of my films. One day, I might take the backseat to her. For now, I will be taking a short hiatus. I'm overdue."

I guide Cherry away from the press by the waist, walking down the carpet.

"Real smooth," she mutters, her smile never faltering.

"Always control the narrative, darling. It doesn't matter how thick your skin is. It's going to hurt when one of those piss ants decides to write a load of bullshit about you. More so now than it used to."

We stop, posing for another set of photos. She hit all the angles and poses. She loves this. The lifestyle of the rich and the famous may not be everything, but it's fucking fun.

"Control the narrative. Don't, you know—" She clicks her tongue twice. "—anyone."

"You know who to call to clean it up."

"Shifter?"

I loop my fingers into hers and yank her back to my chest. "Kiss me." Her lips meet mine, and I relish them. "Justin is watching us," I mutter and lead the way into the stone-walled building. I count exhales as Justin chauffeurs us to the private lounge.

"How is it out there?" Every fucking time.

"A fucking zoo, Justin. It doesn't change."

He glances between Cherry and me with a dumb, half-baked grin. "You were smiling and kissing."

"Why the fuck do you always ask me how it is out there if you've been watching?"

"Small talk?" He nervously shrugs, and that dumb grin reappears.

It smells like…is that lavender? "What's that smell?" *Tell me he's not trying out a new cologne.*

Cherry points to the burning sticks. "I requested it. It's calming."

"Where were you at my last premier?"

Did I do the wrong thing with Cassie? I should have refused her money. It might have saved her life. On second thought, I'm glad I didn't know Cherry then. These conscious feelings are a nightmare to navigate.

"I was working on my master plan to destroy you." She taps her fingers together and plays out her best evil laugh.

"I see you're already getting in character to play Tulip." I glance over at Justin while he pretends to do *important tasks* on his phone.

"Of course." She wraps her arms around my waist, and her heart beats against mine, fucking over every worrisome thought I could have.

"Hold onto my demons for me?"

"I don't need to. You're ready to present the world with the wonderful Samantha."

"No. I think you should do it." I twirl her hair, and she smacks my hand away.

"Do you know how long I had to sit in hair and makeup? Don't touch it." She squeezes my fingers. "This is your project, B. Why do you want me to take all the attention?"

Cocking my head to the side, I raise my brows at her sassy mouth. Justin's wide eyes tell a story opposite hers. "If you want to calm your ass down, I have a surprise."

"No more surprises, B."

"One more." I take a step back. "And removing myself from being the center of attention might be a good thing…for a little while, anyway. Simon," I call.

He opens the door, and in walks Shifter.

"No!" Cherry jumps up and down.

His women walk as Cherry practically springs into his arms.

Southern Whiskey and his witchy bride-to-be, the mophead sporting his 2002 hat, and the happy hippy trail in. Slow stays true to character at the rear of the group. All of the fucking lab rats are in the building…because she wanted them here.

The joy painted across her face is irreplaceable. "Oh my gosh! Everyone!" Her jaw hangs in a smile as she wrinkles her nose, shakes her head at me, and dives into Wes's arms.

"Alright, that's enough of that," I interrupt.

"Who's watching the, uh, who's holding down the home base?"

"Shifter is capable. Trust. We'll catch up later, darling." I stroll across the room to the doorway. "You guys can find your seats. Justin, assist them."

"*Please.*" Cherry trades downcast glares with me.

"*Yeah.*" I rub my jaw and walk back to her. "Are you thirsty? The mini fridge is stocked, and there's water and a few snacks. I'm sure I can arrange anything you want."

"You have no idea how much it means to me that you invited all of them."

"Hah, are you kidding me? I fucking know, darling. That's why they're here. It put that smile on your face." I brush her lower lip with the pad of my thumb.

"Didn't you want to invite anyone else?"

"Baby steps, darling. Opening my life back up to my parents isn't going to happen overnight…If ever."

"You'll decide to one day, and when you're ready, I'll be right here." She softly kisses my lips and vastly draws back. Lipstick. "You're regretting that."

"No, I'm not. It's pretty amusing, to be honest. Although red isn't your color, B." Her giggles fill my head, travel the strings attached to my heart, and devour my fucking soul. She owns me forever.

Hey, you.

How pissed are you that you kept reading all the way until my happy ending? Don't be. It's more of a happy for now. Life is forever changing. If you've learned anything about Cherry and me, we fight passionately for what we want.

Lose ends: Cherry Larson? Did we get married?

Fuck no. Cherry can use my name professionally as long as she wants. Maybe someday we'll legalize it. Who knows? We can do that with or without marriage.

One last time: My name is Bennett Larson.

I was invisible. Now, I'm not.

I'm not going to preach that everything happens for a reason. I don't know if I believe in that or in much these days. Heaven? Hell? Aliens? What I can say is I'm going to have a fucking good time while I'm here, even if it's between bullshit and sorrow.

You shouldn't make one person your everything.

When they're gone, so are you.

In my case, it doesn't fucking matter. I'm not afraid to follow her.

P.S. I'm still a bad guy for the right reason.

Aren't most of us?

Shifter darts around the corner, surprising me with his sudden presence. "Bennett!" He yells. "It's Charlie. He blacked out."

"Ah, fuck."

Afterword

Get all K.R. books, updates, and future releases by signing up for my mailing list at **www.krbrendlinger.com**

Find me on social media **@kr.brendlinger**

About Author

A quirky free spirit, K.R. resides with her family on the east coast of the United States. Her favorite form of caffeine is chocolate, she's unapologetically awkward, and multi-tasking is her way of life. When not writing or reading an alternative reality, K.R. can be found seeking out laughter, music, or something with a motor.

K.R. classifies her writing style as easy to digest and raw between the lines. Her stories are character-driven with the same packed and fast-paced pep as plot-driven stories. K.R.'s undeniable Pisces energy emotionally steers her when the pen hits the paper, writing stories with realistic characters you can relate to and plots that submerge you.

Acknowledgments

To my readers: Thank you for continuing with this series. These characters are more than words on paper. They're infused in my soul and I'm incredibly grateful I get to share them and their stories with you. I appreciate you so much.